Little Man

A Novel

T0150205

Little Man

A Novel

Norris Norman

Parkhurst Brothers Publishers
MARION, MICHIGAN

The e-book edition of this book, a Parkhurst Brothers e-book, is distributed to through the Chicago Distribution Center, and may be ordered through Ingram Book Company, Baker & Taylor, Follett Library Resources and other e-book industry wholesalers. To order from Chicago Distribution Center, phone 1-800-621-2736 or fax to 800-621-8476. Copies of this and other Parkhurst Brothers Publishers titles are available to organizations and corporations for purchase in quantity by contacting Special Sales Department at our home office location, listed on our website. Manuscript submission guidelines for this publishing company are available at our website.

Printed in the United States of America

First Edition, 2017

2017 2018 2019 2020 12 11 10 9 8 7 6 5 4 3 2 1

ISBN: Trade Paperback: 978-1-62491-111-8

Parkhurst Brothers Publishers believes that the free and open exchange of ideas is essential for the maintenance of our freedoms. We support the First Amendment to the United States Constitution and encourage all citizens to study all sides of public policy questions, making up their own minds. Closed minds cost society dearly.

Project direction by: Cheryl Tanney

Cover and interior design by Linda D. Parkhurst, Ph.D.

Acquired for Parkhurst Brothers Publishers by Ted Parkhurst

If you enjoy this work of fiction, we invite you to consider the other books by American storytellers and novelists found online at:

www.parkhurstbrothers.com

072017

This book is gratefully dedicated to my older brother Mitchell, who when we were both young, taught me that I could make up stories myself, without relying upon those of others. Over the years, I have occupied myself many an hour inside my own mind. Hopefully, this book will entertain you as well.

CONTENTS

FOREWORD

THE SEEDS FOR THIS BOOK WERE PLANTED YEARS AGO as I listened to my grandparents talk about their lives. While the things they talked about may have been common experiences of their generation, their stories filled my young imagination with wonder. As I grew older, my fascination with their time grew and I continued to ask my grandparents about their early years.

Our family lived in the small farming community of Beech Grove, Arkansas, located in the northeast corner of the state near Crowley's Ridge. On my mother's side, our ancestors were the first family to settle in Beech Grove, arriving in 1824. Economically, we were an average farm family, but we were rich in relatives. There were three older brothers, my parents, both sets of grandparents, an aunt and uncle on my mothers side, six sets of great uncles and great aunts, and two great-grandmothers. Add to this more cousins that I can count today and lots of family friends. I lost one of my great-grandmothers when I was fifteen, the other about a year later. My memories of them are vivid to this day.

Now they are all gone, and their stories exist only if someone else tells them. Fortunately, I was able to preserve at least some of these stories. Starting in 1984, I interviewed as many old timers as possible, starting with my own family. The interviews about growing up in the rural south cover the period when the nineteenth century gave way to the twentieth. These interviews are preserved on hours and hours of audio tape, and one very precious video. By today's standards they didn't have much, but perhaps we who live today could benefit by appreciating what they did have: family and friends, a house, a school, a church, toys, tools, clothing, struggles, and dreams. Theirs was a simple life in which families were much closer and stronger, reality was not nearly so abstract and neither were values. God was more personal, and in the absence of so many material possessions, they were more people-centered. People felt more responsibility, for themselves, their families, even their neighbors.

R. Norris Norman

CHAPTER ONE
Amos

THE NOON TIME SUN FELT GOOD ON AMOS' BACK as he sat astride the split rail fence and watched the game of dollars being played on the ground below. It amused him that the eagerness of his two oldest brothers could not match the skill of his father and grandfather. Actually, it was Grandpa Sawyer who usually decided the winning team, as his dollars almost always landed closest to the hole, if not in it.

Days like this made Amos feel good about the world. Spring had broken winter's hold on the land, and his grandparents had come for dinner after church. There would be lots of happy talk and a big spread of food. The opportunity for pitching several games of dollars among the men folk excited Amos. Normally, because of the shortage of cash money, large washers were used instead of silver dollars. But today Grandpa Sawyer had brought six shiny silver dollars to be pitched back and forth toward the small holes in the ground. Amos wondered about this, but was quickly caught up in the excitement.

Their revelry was broken by his sister's shout that dinner was ready. The game came to a sudden stop, to be continued after dinner. None of these men had to be called twice to the table. They made a quick stop at the well to wash before filing into the kitchen. Of course, Grandpa Sawyer got the place at the head of the table, with Grandma Janey next to him. James and Lissie had raised their five offspring with good manners, but each of the grandsons tried to position himself next to their Grandpa. What could be better, Sunday dinner sitting next to the smartest and wisest man they knew.

Sunday dinner was always a feast when the Sawyers got together. Today, there was fried chicken, corn bread with fresh butter, beans, potatoes, fresh onions, radishes and poke salad. Later, dessert would be apple pie and a chocolate cake. Much talk and a clattering of plates and bowls spoke of a family who enjoyed each other and fine food.

Late afternoon found the family gathered on the long back porch. The dishes were washed, and everyone had taken a turn at pitching dollars. Today, even the womenfolk had pitched because of the chance to use real silver dollars. The pace of talk slowed, as news had been shared about gardens, spring field work, new livestock and such. Seated here was a family, grown over many years and brought together by the shared hardships of those years. Drought, flood, disease and even death were familiar to the Sawyers. In this day, many people didn't live past forty, and anyone in their thirties might be called "uncle" or "aunt" by the youngsters. John Sawyer sat in a rocker near the edge of the porch so that the shavings from his whittling would fall off on the ground. James sat near but farther back by the house wall in a cane-bottom chair. The boys sat, knelt or stood in that area of the porch because they didn't want to miss a word their Grandpa said. Grandma Janey and Lissie, Amos' momma, sat in the swing at the end of the porch while Amos' sister, Cora, and his two sisters in law sat on a wash bench against the end wall. The babies were inside for a nap. "I bought a piece of land last week, for the drainage taxes. Think it'll turn out to be a right nice farm, once it's cleared and built up," spoke up John.

"Whar's the land at, Poppy?" asked James.

"Way out on the Little Sandy River. It's a ways off, but it has good timber and a long high ridge of soft black dirt. Me and Zeke walked over it last winter when we was duck huntin'. The chance came up to git it, so I took it."

"Won't that be an awful long ways to go to work it, Grandpaw?" interjected Tom, Amos' oldest brother. "Wal, I aim to have someone else stay there to work it and I'll jes' look in on it now and agin," John replied. "I was wonderin' bout one of you boys, if'n one of you'd be interested in livin' on it and a workin' it up. I admit that it's not much of a place now. There's only a box cabin and a small log barn fer buildings, and the only fencin' is a broken down horse lot. An' there ain't any neighbors fer comp'ny or hep, so a feller would be pretty much on his own, 'cept I'd be out from time to time. I believe it'll be a fine farm one day. That is, with a lot of hard work."

Now it was out. Anyone who had wondered at the significance of the grandparents visit today and the added treat of the silver dollars now knew the answer to the mystery. John had bought a new farm as an investment and needed someone to work it. And, not just anyone; he wanted one of the family.

Of course, the idea of James taking it on was obviously not the intention, as he had a fine farm of 80 acres, including the hill land for pasture. John had helped him buy it years ago, and it was not something a family man would leave to start from scratch in the bottoms. So it was James' children who Grandpa John had come to approach. There were five in all. Tom was the oldest, followed at about two-year intervals by Sam and then Cora, the middle child, and only girl. Daniel was next, then Amos, the youngest. The older three were married while Daniel had set his sights on a college education, almost unheard of at the time. Amos had just completed his schooling, that is, what was available at Hickory Ford, and was happy to have that part of his life behind him. It was a weighty matter, for no proposal of Grandpa's was taken lightly. This matter of moving way out to the bottoms on the Little Sandy River to clear a farm would be no Sunday picnic. After a few moments which seemed like hours to everyone, Tom spoke up hesitantly. "Grandpaw, me and Liz'beth figure to live with Aunt Mary another year while I farm with Poppa. And Liz'beth's Poppa has said that I could work fer him at his sawmill when I'm not working the crop here." There was both sadness and relief in his voice as an opportunity to help Grandpa was a privilege and yet he knew that Liz'beth would have pitched a fit at going off down in the bottoms to live away from her family.

Quickly then, Sam spoke up. "Grandpaw, I'd like to help you out, but Hattie's Poppa has promised to get me on in his brother's hardware store in Oak Ridge. It'll be reg'lar cash money fer us to git a start." And everyone knew that his Hattie, though a good wife, was more fit for town living.

Since Cora's husband, Cecil, was farming with his ailing folks and preaching around the country on Sundays, it was understood that it wouldn't be the thing for them. They sat their seats in silence, separated from the sense of expectancy by Cecil's commitments, and yet as a part of the family, galvanized by the emotion of the moment.

Slowly now, Daniel took his turn. "Grandpaw, I've been accepted to attend the State Teachers College this summer and then I hope to get a teaching job for next year. If I was free, I'd be glad to help ya."

The mood was quiet now after John's offer had been turned down by his four adult grandchildren. The family knew that he had wanted not just any hand for the new land, but one of his grandchildren. Again, the seconds went silently by. Amos had sat quietly, but with great anxiety that one of the older brothers would get this chance. He had not spoken yet, for the offer should naturally first fall to one of them. But should he even speak up? This was man's work and maybe Grandpa would think of him as just a boy yet. If that happened, Amos would be embarrassed in front of the family. But Amos was free to take it. James didn't need him as Tom was helping work the farm and trying to get his own start. There certainly wasn't enough farm for two families plus Amos. Then he would speak up!

"Grandpaw," spoke Amos with both excitement and fear in his voice, "I'll go!"

Now it was out. Seconds now seemed like days as he sat on the edge of the porch and awaited the reaction, not just from Grandpa, but from the family as well. Presently, John broke the silence, "Well, Amos, you're young yet, and this is quite an undertakin'. Ya'd be stayin' alone, doin' yore own cookin', with no one else to look after ya'." Turning now to Amos' father, he asked, "James, what do ya' thank?"

James hesitated before speaking and thought it all out in his head. It would take a certain maturity and sense of responsibility to live alone in the bottoms and put in the kind of work to clear and farm the land. Amos was his youngest son, the baby of the family. Could he do it? In this moment, James admitted to himself that he had never required the level of work or responsibility from

Amos that he had from the older children. The two oldest boys had started very early with chores because there had been so much to do then, and so few to do it. Amos, in contrast, had an easier and later start at the heavier farm work. But the boy had settled in this past year. He had always shown a sense of planning, even if the plans were often more like dreams. And, like all his sons, Amos knew hard work and wasn't afraid of it. As for the bottoms, the boy loved to hunt and fish, something he had picked up from his Great Uncle Zeke. And, he was a Sawyer.

Speaking now, James replied, "Poppy, he's yore Grandson, an' jest last week ol' Richard said that of all my boys, Amos favors you more'n all the rest. As for takin' ker' of hisself, he's done a sight of cookin' and warshin' over the last year while his momma's been ailin'. I reckon he'd do fine."

After what seemed an eternal pause, John gave his decision. "All right, then, Amos, it's settled. You'll work the new farm. Now since I'm tied up at the store all this week, I'll come up next Mon'dy mawnin' to take ya' down to the new place. Ya' have yore thangs ready, at least enough to get ya' by fer 'bout a week. I'll furnish yore eats and the tools ya need to git started."

Amos sat there on the edge of the porch, mute and so numbed by the answer that he was afraid that he would fall off. He steadied himself with his hands so as not to embarrass himself before the family. As quickly as he had given the answer, John Sawyer turned the conversation to the price of hogs. Amos thought to himself, "Could this really be true? Could it be that this opportunity would be his, and his alone?" But it had to be, as John Sawyer's word was a dead certainty that no one doubted.

At times it seemed to Amos that the next week would never pass. Now, as he anxiously paced under the big white oak in the front yard, he couldn't believe how fast it had gone by. His eyes kept watching the road for some sign of his Grandpa's wagon. He'd been up since before dawn, making sure that everything was ready. Grandpa was not someone to be kept waiting, and besides, Amos was more excited to get to the new place than if he'd been going to a new fishing hole. The rest of the family, already about their chores, were excited about seeing Amos off to the new place. James and Tom were repairing a gate on one of the hog pens while Lissie and Cora were planting more of the garden. The last week now seemed like a whirlwind. So many things had to be gathered, and people had to be seen that Amos couldn't quite remember what happened which day. His mother and Cora had fussed over him all week to ensure that he had this item of clothing or that cooking utensil. And then they had pumped his head full to overflowing with tips on cooking and what to do in case of a snake bite or a bee sting or a cut from an ax. In desperation his mother sighed that " Ya won't 'member ever'thin,' but ya got good sense and ya'll do all right." Amos wasn't sure that she believed this herself, but at least she let up on all the advice.

Even Great Uncle Zeke Miller had contributed to Amos' store of knowledge. "Amos, ya' be mighty ker'ful down in them bottoms. They's water moccasins down there thet could jest about swaller ya' whole, given the chance. And, the little un's are pizzen too." Digging a small package from the bib of his overalls, Uncle Zeke said, "Here, ya' take this new plug of tobaccie and keep it at the cabin. Iffen ya' git bit, work a chaw of it up in yore mouth and stick it on the bite, after ya' cut the fang holes open and dreen all the pizzen out ye kin. Tie it up real tight with a rag. Thet chawin' tobaccie will draw out the rest of thet pizzen fer ye. Ya'll still likely be sick fer a few days, but ya'll be all right." Amos obediently accepted the tobacco, though unsure of it's curative powers. And, he certainly didn't want to have to find out.

His friends were envious of the opportunity to be off on one's own, with the responsibility of a whole farm. Of course, Amos never made much of the fact that there were only two buildings and about seven cleared acres, now overgrown in weeds and brush. What interested his friend Homer Smith was that Amos would live right by a river, with every day to swim and fish and hunt.

This morning held the magic of spring as the birds were singing their songs and the morning sun was already warming the earth. A rich fragrance was in the air signaling the awakening of the earth after a winter's sleep. It was as if this energy of spring spoke of the beginning of a great endeavor. Amos, though too immature to connect with this thought, was heightened in his excitement by what his senses told him.

Now between fits of pacing back and forth, he surveyed his earthly possessions. Like most fifteen-year-olds, Amos had always been something of a collector. He had things ranging from balls of string to old knife blades to animal skins, but he was only taking what he felt would be essential to his new life. The rest he would leave behind for now. And, at his poppa's suggestion, he would leave behind his sow as well as his Jersey heifer until proper fences and sheds could be built at the new place.

There was a wooden box which contained his fishing gear, a flour sack stuffed with another pair of overalls and a shirt. Amos never saw the sense of wearing socks in the summer time, even if he had promised his mother that he would wear shoes every day because of the snakes. Another wooden box held the cooking and eating utensils he would need along with several bars of lye soap ·

and a towel. It seemed that his mother had intentions toward his cleanliness. There were a couple of quilts, a hand ax, a coil of rope, a half a wagon sheet, three rusty steel traps, an old cane knife, and such other items as a young man setting out on his own might need. And, though grandpa would furnish Amos' food, his mother had put together some flour, beans, salt, side meat, lard, corn meal and some seasonings to help out.

Amos looked over what were undoubtedly the three most important things he was taking with him. His single shot .22 rifle would be essential for keeping fresh meat on his table. His hound dog, Speckle, would be his hunting partner, and hopefully, bring him a rich harvest of coon hides. Little Red, his mule, would provide Amos with the horsepower needed to do the heavier work.

In Amos' mind, these three items set him apart from "just boys" and gave him standing among the men. The rifle was earned last winter after many cold days of trapping and many nights of running coons with Uncle Zeke. It was a proud day for Amos when he finally got to pick it up at Grandpa John's general store.

Speckle had been a gift from great uncle Zeke last spring and Amos had raised him from a pup. It was questionable at times whether he'd make a good hunting dog but Amos loved him all the same. Speckle had come a long way during the last winter. He was bred from good hunting stock, so Amos had high hopes for the hound.

Little Red's mother was a red mare belonging to one of the neighbors who regularly traded in horses and mules. The mare had died shortly after delivery, and the mule colt was sickly. As the trader had no nurse mare for a sick orphan, he offered to give it away. So Amos asked his father to ask for the colt. He was sure that with the care he could give it, the little red mule would live.

James was hesitant at first because Amos was only twelve and he was unsure if the boy would carry out the responsibility. And, if the colt did indeed die, the boy would be heart broken. But he gave in to his youngest and gave him the chance. It took some time before the colt shook off all his sickliness, but he had grown into a stout little mule, somewhat trained now for farm work and riding. So this adventure was not Amos' alone, for his dog and his mule would share it with him.

"Whar' could Grandpaw be," thought Amos. His patience was running thin, though if he were waiting on a fish to take his bait, he would be much more relaxed. As he kept his eye on the bend in their road near the end of the hollow, his ear caught the sound of the hammering at the hog pens and occasionally Cora would come into view as she brought tools and seed from the tool shed to the garden. A crow swooped overhead, sending out its caw-caw message. Aloud, Amos spoke to the crow, "Git on outta here ol' crow, or I'll bust yore feathers good." With the uncanny sense of survival common to crows, it flew on over the ridge top.

Just then a broad grin exploded upon Amos' face as he saw John's team of mules round the curve of the road. Looking at them step up the road, Amos thought of how everyone spoke of them as an exceptional team. Gray Jack had been around for more years than Amos could remember. The second mule, Buster, had been bought last fall. Sometimes it seemed that Gray Jack knew what John wanted him to do even before any signal was given.

Amos was all tingly inside as the wagon stopped in front of the house. "Wal, Amos," spoke John from the wagon seat, "looks like you're ready to start farmin', or at least fishin'." As his eye looked over Amos' things gathered under the white oak, the grandfather seemed as excited as his grandson this morning.

The rest of the family left their chores and gathered around the wagon. James and Tom helped load Amos' things into the wagon, along with the boxes and sacks already there. Meanwhile, Lissie and Cora gave him those last minute instructions which they felt he must have.

The two women spoke almost together and with too much overlap in conversation for Amos to decipher whether his mother or his sister was speaking at any one time. Amos heard, "Amos, don't ya go in swimmin', with no one else ther', you'll drown shore." "An' be shore to warsh yoreself, I put in soap and a towel." "Now, don't git out in the weeds a' barefoot, there's snakes ever'whar in them bottoms." "Reckon ya' kin git up in the mawnin' with no one else thar'?" "If ya git sick, ya git on Little Red and head out for home."

Though seeming to pay some attention, Amos' eyes were searching out where his things were being placed and at the same time wondering about all the things that were already loaded. Altogether, the wagon bed would be about full, stirring Amos all the more.

As soon as everything was loaded, it was the time for hugs and handshakes. Amos had never liked this part of any trip, but it always seemed necessary for the women folks. After his mother and sister had hugged, kissed and cried over him, his father gripped his shoulder and told him to be careful and pay attention to his grandpa's instructions. As Amos pulled his spare frame up from the ground to the wagon seat, he had a small feeling that he was pulling himself from the world as he had known it and stepping into one totally unknown, with no possibility of return.

John clucked to the team, and they stepped out, pulling the wagon around and back onto the road for the journey before them. Amos waved and called back until the road curved and cut off his family from view and then there was just the two of them. Amos was the proudest of his entire life in this moment, with him and John together on this farming venture. Though neither would understand it just now, from this day forward, their lives would be changed because of the other.

CHAPTER TWO

The Little Sandy

AMOS SAT BESIDE HIS GRANDPA ON THE WAGON SEAT that bright spring morning. Gray Jack and Buster stepped lively down the road. These were silent moments for Amos, not only because he was almost too excited to talk, but because it was always hard for him to talk to his Grandpa. Unlike Uncle Zeke, who had a way about him that made talking easy, John was a more serious man, harder for a boy to approach. Besides, Amos revered his Grandpa and that made talking to him even more challenging.

But this morning John made talking easy, as he was also excited about this new venture. He began asking Amos about what he had brought for eats and keeping house, knowing Amos' mother wouldn't let him go off without loading him down. John was a thoughtful man, given to planning things out before they happened. His thinking was that if Amos needed anything else for the first week in the bottoms, they could swing the team by his house and store on Red Gum Ridge.

Satisfied with the provisions already loaded, John held the team straight ahead at the four corners crossing, putting them onto the bottom road. Amos looked back to make sure that Little Red's lead rope was secure and that Speckle noticed, in his wide wanderings, which way the wagon went. So far they were still in their home community, and everything and everyone was familiar. Amos had been born in a little house up in Tatum Hollow, where his folks were farming at the time. His entire life had been spent within the few square miles known as Hickory Ford. His only exposure to other places was the twice a year trip the family made to Hampton, about fifteen miles to the east. Hampton was the county seat and boasted almost fifteen hundred people. Such a large place always proved exciting, but the trips were too infrequent and short to have much influence on Amos.

Hickory Ford took its name from the many hickory trees growing near the only easy crossing on Bates Creek. Most places in that area, it seemed, were named after some kind of tree. Hickory Ford, like so many communities of that era, had a large mercantile, a grist mill, a cotton gin, a blacksmith, several churches, a school, and a few other enterprises. There weren't many folks who actually lived in Hickory Ford, as the community consisted of a multitude of farm families over a radius of about three miles.

The land was still mostly timbered, with families living in cleared pockets up in the hills and along the higher land which separated the hill country from the bottoms. Most families had only one team, and made their living on about forty acres, raising cotton to sell and corn and hay for their livestock. All had gardens and most butchered their own hogs.

Farming was hard work, lots of hard work. Large families helped spread the workload and were normal in that era. Large families meant large meals, so much of their efforts centered around providing food. On most farms, springtime saw the garden planted even before the cash crops. Spring was also the time for gathering wild poke leaves. The young pokeberry plant, which grew wild throughout the area, provided the first fresh greens after the long winter months. Early summer brought plenty of wild blackberries, first for fresh cobblers and then as jams and jellies preserved to be eaten throughout the year. Summer was a time of picking and canning since vegetables from the garden had to last through the entire year. In later summer, wild plums, apples, and peaches would also make fresh cobblers and pies as well as be processed for canning. Pork and wild game were the mainstays of most families' meat supply. Late fall, right after the first good frost, was hog killing time. This killing and curing supplied most of the family's pork for the entire year. The excess fat was rendered into lard for cooking, and mixed with lye from wood ashes to make the family's supply of soap. Fall and winter hunting provided such fresh meats as squirrel, raccoon, deer, and duck. Of course, fishing was done year round. So much of their work was directly tied to food gathering and preparation that there was a strong association between working and eating.

As the wagon rolled along, Amos relaxed and began to notice more about the farms along the road. These farms were much like his father's, with an unpainted wood framed house surrounded by the various outbuildings needed on a farm. There was a smoke house for curing meat, which usually sat near the house. A chicken house and coop were farther out, with possibly a tool shed near the garden, and a horse lot surrounding a barn. Scattered about also would be the hog sheds and other outbuildings needed by that family. Some families had an outhouse for their toilet, but others just went out behind one of the outbuildings.

Spring was a very busy time for these farm people. It seemed this morning that everyone was working the earth, either turning the fields with a team and walking plow or putting out a garden. All who noticed the wagon passing on the road turned to wave.

Most knew John Sawyer's team by sight but would have hailed a greeting anyway because their farm culture was outreaching to others.

Coming abreast of the Simmons' place, John and Amos recognized Junior Simmons plowing last year's cotton ground. Mindful of every opportunity to postpone hard work with a little visit, Junior hurried his team toward the turn row, where he could intercept John Sawyer's wagon. Coming up to the end almost as the wagon rolled by, Junior's team was sweating and blowing much too hard for their own good. Panting for breath himself, Junior shouted, "Goin' fishin', air' ya,' Uncle John?"

Caught a little off guard, John Sawyer replied, "Fishin'? Is that all ya think about, Junior? Better pay more mind to thet team!" As their wagon rolled on by without a pause, Junior stood behind his plow with the downcast expression of lost opportunity.

John's tone was one of disapproval as he spoke to Amos, "Must have seen yore fishin' poles stickin' out over the tailgate. Thet feller would pass up puttin' in a cotton crop jes' to fish." After a moments pause, he added, "I'd hate to be one of his mules. Course, he don't work 'em all thet often." Amos turned in the seat to look back at Junior Simmons and his team. Junior was slowly turning the team at the end, but with far less enthusiasm than when he raced to catch them in passing.

Soon their wagon rolled out of the familiar and into a countryside less cleared and with only an occasional farm. At one point they crossed a main road, where John rested the team and Speckle padded alongside and gave a longing look up at Amos. This was his way of asking for a ride, as he was bored with following the wagon. Of course, if he were after a coon, the miles would mean little to him.

As the distance from Hickory Ford increased, the sides of the road became thicker with trees. They had been in the bottoms for about three hours when Amos saw what he would later learn to be the last house before the new place, a good hour's ride farther on. John told him that the family that lived there was named Potter, and that's about all he knew about them.

For the next hour, Amos sat on the seat in awe of the great trees which reached up and shaded over the narrow logging road, almost blocking out the sunlight in places. In some ways, Amos imagined they were in a long narrow tunnel like those he had read about in one of the books at school. Right now the Hickory Ford schoolhouse and its classes seemed very far away. The feeling of separation from his family and from all that was familiar in Hickory Ford began to overwhelm Amos. To escape, Amos began to question John about the new place, its cabin and barn, the cleared land and the river, even how the fishing might be. To protect himself from this onslaught of questions, John responded, "Amos, we'll be there soon enough an' ya'll see it all then." But sensing the boy's anxiety, John began to point out the different trees and their respective uses. This helped to take Amos' focus off the new place. John could point out white oaks, red oaks, pin oaks, regular hickory and shag bark hickory on the higher ground, with cypress and Tupelo Gum in the sloughs.

It was almost noon when they reached White Creek. Here John gave the team a much-needed rest before crossing and Speckle decided that it was time to be afoot again. Amos had been hungry for over an hour and said as much. To this John grinned a reply, "Why, Amos, didn't ya git breakfast back at home this mawnin?"

Amos thought of the sausage, eggs, and biscuits along with all the fresh butter and canned jelly he had for breakfast and now wished for some more of it. "Yeah, Grandpaw, I got breakfast, but that was hours ago."

John chuckled, faintly remembering what it was like to be a growing boy. "Wal', we'll be at the new place within half an hour, and then we'll eat the dinner yore Grandmaw packed fer us."

Underway once again, the team was crossing the shallow water of the creek. Amos asked, "Grandpaw, why do they call this White Creek? It shore ain't white."

"It's 'cause of Ol' Man White who used to trap up the creek near the Little Sandy. He lived in these bottoms most of his life, so folks got to calling this overflow creek White Creek," answered John.

Satisfied with the answer, Amos began to look intently ahead for the first sign of the new place. He was constantly frustrated when the road would turn and what had appeared to have been "ahead" now was off to one side. So went the next half hour's ride through the tall bottomland woods. Some timber had been taken by tie cutters, but the vast majority stood untouched.

At a point in the road beside a large and dying white oak, John turned the team left onto a faint wagon track, almost overgrown. After some distance, Amos looked back to check on Little Red. Turning back to the front, he saw the place before them and was shocked with both joy and despair. His great excitement in seeing "his own place" was offset by what he saw of its condition. Sure, he knew that it had been deserted for the last three years. However, he had not imagined it could be so run down. Apparently, it had not been well cared for by the last occupant. He was silent as John stopped the wagon between the cabin and barn.

While his Grandpa unhitched the team, Amos began to examine what was to become his place. At any other time leaving his grandpa to do the unhitching alone would not have been tolerated, but John Sawyer understood that his grandson needed to look around by himself.

The box cabin was about fourteen feet by eighteen feet with no porch. The one small window had no glass, just a shutter to close it from the weather. There was a plank floor, but the cracks between the dried-out boards were a quarter of an inch wide in places. Amos thought that the structure appeared much like a box, as it had no studs in the wall, depending on the vertical wall boards to hold up the roof. The whole interior was both dirty and damp, not the kind of place where Amos was used to seeing someone live.

The barn was just slightly larger than the house. Amos examined the hewn cypress log structure closely. Through its front door, a corn crib could be seen off to one side while two crude stalls filled the rest of the area. He noted that one corner had been used for a toilet as there was no separate structure for this purpose. As opposed to the house, the barn had two doors. A large opening with a gate faced the cabin, and a smaller side door led to the horse lot. The loft was small but might hold enough hay for a team and a milk cow over the winter.

After surveying the house and barn, Amos took some time to get a good look at the open areas around the structures. A pitcher pump for fresh water was mounted atop a pipe well on the river side of the cabin. Scanning the fencing, Amos saw that there wasn't a section standing which would hold in a cow, much less a hog. And weeds and tree sprouts had taken over both the yard area and the seven "cleared" acres. Some of the young cottonwoods growing in what had been the field were a good fifteen feet tall. Several large dead trees had floated onto the ridge during a previous flood. The paramount thought in Amos' mind was that it would take a lot of work to get that field planted in corn.

The river was the only bright spot in view, but Amos knew standing there that he couldn't spend all his time on the river. As things appeared, he wouldn't be spending much time there at all until the house-place was cleaned up and the field once again cleared, plowed and planted.

Satisfied that he had seen enough for now, Amos turned to see John setting out their dinner on a large stump near the house. The three of them, as Speckle had invited himself, ate in silence. Each was lost in his own thoughts. As always, food improved Amos' mood. Now, the dinner which his Grandma had packed for them transformed his gloom into excitement over what the place might look like at the end of summer.

With dinner eaten, Amos began helping John unload the wagon. In addition to the items Amos had brought, the wagon contained a four cap cook stove, a bed, a table and two cane-bottomed chairs, an assortment of old cookware which Janey had cast off, boxes of foodstuffs, a one horse breaking plow, a single stock cultivating plow, and various hand tools necessary to clearing land and building up a place. In the very bottom of the wagon, John had placed a dozen new planks of varying dimensions.

When the unloading was done, John turned his attention to the cabin. With the swiftness and sureness that comes from a lifetime of hard work, he set about cleaning the cabin from top to bottom. He placed the cook stove under the existing stove pipe which stuck through the roof and set up the bed. Then he built a fire in the stove to drive the dampness from the cabin, making it more livable.

While John cleaned up the inside of the cabin, Amos took

an eye hoe and cleared the weeds and sprouts from the ground between the cabin and barn. So went the entire afternoon. They cleared dirt from the cabin and weeds from the lot and repaired items like the door and the window that needed immediate attention. Also, John quickly turned some of the new planks into shelves on which Amos could stack his foodstuffs and cooking utensils. Some new nails about the walls provided organization for certain kitchen items as well as clothing.

Darkness found them gathered for supper in a warm cabin set in the deep woods of the river bottoms. They were tired and hungry but felt good about their accomplishments of the afternoon. The only light for their supper came from a single mantle oil lamp. Supper tonight consisted of a pot of beans which John had cooked during the afternoon, fresh-baked cornbread, a few strips of fried hog jowl and a mess of fresh-boiled poke greens Amos had collected from along the river bank. No scene could have brought Amos more happiness than sharing this time with his Grandpa. In Amos' mind, there was no one as intelligent or as diligent about his work as John Sawyer. Being the youngest of James' children and thereby getting a late start at farm responsibilities, Amos had always feared that John didn't respect him as much as he did the older boys. His grandpa's respect was very important as to how he thought about himself. Today the two of them had shared this trip and the afternoon's work, culminating in an ordinary supper. The most important opportunity Amos could ever imagine had not gone to one of the older boys, but to him, the youngest. Nothing could have seemed more wonderful than this.

After the dishes had been done, they took the chairs outside and sat in the cool night air. Tonight John Sawyer seemed transformed from the slightly reserved serious workman into a man fired with a burning passion. Sitting there with his grandson he became quite animated in telling all he knew about the bottoms. There were stories about plowing around stumps, draining flood water, shooting ducks in the dawning light, catching catfish by hand from hollow logs, hewing out ties for the railroad, feeding hogs on acorns and so many other things that Amos became afraid that he couldn't remember them all. Amos had never seen his Grandpa talk so much, or with so much excitement, so he was careful not to break the spell. Even Speckle seemed to catch significance in these moments as he lay at their feet and watched. From time to time John would pause to listen to the night sounds and identify those which might be uncommon to Amos. Amos had no idea of the time but was sure that his Grandpa never stayed up this late at home, as he was known to go to sleep even before the chickens some nights.

When his excitement finally settled, John announced that they had better hit the hay, for daylight would come early. And they would literally hit the hay, as the mattress brought from home was a tick, or large flat sack, filled last summer with wheat straw. This particular one had not been used very much and still had some bulk to it. It probably was active with "cheeches" or bed bugs, but a tired man paid little attention to such nuisances. Once stretched out together on the bed, John went to sleep almost instantly, the mark of a man who knew how to work hard and then relax into sleep. Amos lay there thoughtful for a few more minutes while soaking in the good feeling of the day. He knew full well that John would pull out for home in the morning, but for now everything was wonderful as he passed into a deep and contented sleep.

It was still early morning when Amos watched John head his team out the wagon track toward the main logging road. Speckle stood nearby and looked questioningly, as if to ask, "Aren't we going, too?" Paying little attention to his dog, Amos thought over all the advice and instruction his grandpa had given him toward the coming week and realized that now came the time for him to act it out alone. Already the isolation had begun to touch him, but he had no idea how lonely he would become before his scheduled journey to his grandpa's store on Red Gum Ridge on Saturday.

With John out of sight, Amos turned to look again at all that surrounded him. Somehow, while John was there it didn't seem nearly as overwhelming as it did now that Amos was alone. But before the foreboding overtook him, he shook it off by remembering something his grandpa had said, "When faced with more chores than ya kin count, jes' pick one an' when finished with thet one, pick another 'un. Before ya' know it, thar' won't be so many as there was at first."

Directed by that thought, Amos approached the horse lot and began pulling away the rotten poles and posts, piling them away from the buildings so that they might be burned later. After only the solid fencing was left, he walked to the edge of the clearing and cut fresh hickory poles from the new growth. These he trimmed with the axe and peeled with a draw knife until he thought that he had enough to rebuild the lot. Little Red made easy work of dragging the finished poles to the barn. There Amos struggled to set the new posts and hang the rails with the spike nails John had left. Working alone was new to him, and he had to try new techniques in handling the material. Speckle was of no help, and often became a hindrance, getting in the way.

Amos found that every sound resulted in his head turning for a look. Silently he accused himself of being a "fraidy cat" and mentally tried to keep his mind on the work. What had seemed like plenty of poles failed to be enough and twice more he had to cut and peel before the lot was finally finished.

As Amos stood back to look at his handiwork, he became suddenly aware that darkness was setting in here in the woods. True, it would come some earlier here than out in open ground, but he still was surprised that the day was over so soon. He remembered now that the dinner hour had been the same way, almost passing before he realized it. He was so intent on his work that time had passed without his noticing. So what if it had taken a whole day to rebuild the horse lot. It had been a big project, and he hadn't had any help at all. Pride almost overrode his body's signals of hunger and fatigue as he looked at the freshly peeled posts and rails. Turning to look at Little Red, he said, "Boy, ain't you special, gettin' a brand new lot to spend your nights?" With that, he took his tired body to the pump to wash up for supper.

This was one night Amos was surely glad that there were leftovers for supper. He was doubtful that he had the energy to cook anything. Intentionally, John had cooked a large pot of beans the afternoon before, so for dinner and supper today all Amos had to do was to heat them up with the also leftover cornbread. Refreshed by his supper, Amos cleaned up the few dishes and stepped outside to rest in the night air.

As he sat there and relaxed to the night music of the crickets and frogs, Amos experienced both isolation from other people and yet companionship from the animal life which seemed to envelope him. Little Red looked to him from the lot and Speckle laid his head in Amos' lap. He now was reminded of how the woods were always darker when a person was alone. Looking out through the narrow clearing, all Amos could see was a dull semi-darkness with darker shapes and shadows along the edges. As the moon wasn't up yet, the few stars in the sky provided little light. Regardless of his animal companions, Amos felt lonely, and fear began to creep over him.

Amos began to realize that living alone was very unlike hunting alone. Here at the cabin in the bottoms, the isolation would last for days and even weeks at a time. He thought of his home back at Hickory Ford and wondered what the family would be doing right now. His thoughts even went to the Potters and wished very much that he didn't live all of three miles from them.

In an instant of willpower, he decided not to be afraid. He reminded himself that Little Red was secure out in the horse lot. The little mule would bray if anything or anyone strange approached during the night. And of course, there was Speckle, with a hound's nose to smell whatever came close and enough grit to fight a boar coon if the need arose. Feeling somewhat relieved now, he rose from the chair and went toward his bed. Pausing at the door, he called Speckle inside, though it went against his upbringing. "Well," he thought, "the cabin ain't like a real house, it's more like a camp. Anyway, the dog might get lonely out there without any other dogs 'round." With these thoughts, he let the hound into the cabin and closed the door. And just to be sure, Amos set a chair against the door.

Later as he lay on his straw tick, Amos remembered Uncle Zeke saying one night while coon hunting that there was nothing out in the woods at night that wasn't there during the day. With that thought, Amos slowly drifted off to sleep. Dawn found Amos stirring about the cabin, anxious for a new day. It seemed that his loneliness and fears from the night before had fled with the approach of daylight. While preparing his breakfast of eggs, side meat, and biscuits, he began to think about the beans he would cook later in the morning, enough to last him two days. Since he was alone here in the bottoms, Amos would have to do all the chores, the field work, and the cooking as well as housekeeping.

Stepping into a sparkling morning, Amos decided to begin removing the weeds and sprouts from the clearing. Selecting a patch near the house that appeared to have been a garden at one time, he began the laborious task of swinging the heavy eye hoe at the sprouts and weeds, while using the axe on the small trees. Within half an hour the legs of his overalls were soaking wet from the dew, but Amos persisted knowing that they would dry as the day progressed. And so went the morning and the afternoon, with only short breaks to rest except for dinner. Both the axe and eye hoe required a lot of strength and Amos found that he ran out of it quickly. It was a tough day with seemingly little to show for his effort at nightfall except aching muscles and fatigue.

Amos' mood was one of depression as he dragged himself to the cabin toward dusk. True, the garden patch was cleaned up some, but in reflection, it looked like so little accomplishment for so much hard work. Driven by his hunger, he walked slowly first to the pump to wash and then to the cabin to warm up some leftovers for his supper.

Sitting outside the cabin after supper, Amos couldn't keep some doubts from creeping into his mind. Little questions kept coming to his mind about the wisdom of asking for this opportunity. The work was hard and slow. There was never anyone here to talk to or laugh with. Amos thought back to the talk that always seemed to be present back on his family's farm. He thought of all the fun times he once had with his friends. Now Amos wondered if Homer Smith would like such a life after all. Sure there was a river for fishing and swimming, but there was no one to fish or swim with, and Amos realized now that had been half the fun of such times.

But in spite of the doubts, it was certain that he couldn't quit now, or it would be the ruination of him forever. To have quit and failed would never be accepted by anyone, except maybe Junior Simmons. The very idea appalled Amos, to be grouped with such as Junior Simmons. No, he'd go at it again tomorrow. It would have to get better.

While getting ready for bed, Amos thought more about the long hard and lonely days, and he realized that there was no reason why he couldn't fish a little now and then. Why, with the river less than a hundred yards away, he could set out some hooks and just check them occasionally. The prospect brightened his spirits, and he knew now that he had found the diversion which would keep the work from being so monotonous. So he went off to bed with higher hopes for the days ahead.

The next morning he made another decision which would make the clearing go faster. In the garden patch, he had chopped down everything, but the plow would surely turn over much of the smaller weeds and grasses. In the main field, he would just cut the saplings and the larger weeds. That way he could cover much more ground in a day.

The new approach proved to be much faster, but it remained to be seen how badly the remaining vegetation would hang up on the plow. Also, the work became less laborious after he began setting out some fishing lines about mid morning. Not only did Amos have something else to think about besides the drudgery of the clearing, but fresh fish for supper would provide a welcome addition to the beans.

By Thursday evening Amos realized that at the rate he was

working he might have the larger vegetation cut down by Saturday noon when he was supposed to ride back home. This became a goal for him, and his pace picked up. Also, he was learning easier ways of getting to the roots of the tall young trees. Off and on he would turn and survey the brush piles and the open earth from his clearing efforts. Feeling good about himself, he would plunge into the work with abandon, going so fast at times that he exhausted himself. Amos found clearing these young trees and brush to be very hard work that would raise a good sweat even in the cool of spring.

Amos worked hard from early morning until the sun was setting. At night he thought back to life at Hickory Ford. Certainly, the work had been hard, but there were always others to share it. Here in the bottoms, he was by himself. Little Red was no help clearing the brush, and Speckle was always off after some kind of wild animal. Some of the young trees in the clearing were fifteen feet tall and the grasses and weeds covered the earth like a thick carpet. Once again, Amos thought back to Homer Smith and wondered what he would think now of this new life.

Persistence and hard work began to pay off as the undergrowth yielded to the ax, eye hoe and Amos' sweat. Gradually, and steadily, Amos worked down the brush, step by step. When the original seven acres were almost cleared, Amos felt the exhilaration that comes when you can see the end of a great task and continued on with renewed zeal.

So went Amos' first week on his own place. He had experienced isolation and loneliness, exhaustion and frustration, but also pride and self esteem. As he jumped onto Little Red's back and rode out the wagon track, he cast a long look back at "his" cabin and "his" field cleared of the new growth. Though he was anxious to get home to see his family, he knew that he looked forward to getting back and getting another start at the place.

CHAPTER THREE

The First Trip Home

THE AFTERNOON SHADOWS WERE LONG, AND THE AIR WAS COOL when Amos rode up to his Grandparents place on Red Gum Ridge. The tow sack doubled up under him for a riding pad had been pressed pretty thin for several miles. Amos' backside had never before been that sore. As much as he loved riding his little mule, riding him bareback for twelve miles was not the most pleasant experience.

The pain eased some now as his mind went to all the things he would report to his grandpa about his week. Having turned Little Red into the horse lot with a rub down, some hay, and some water, Amos now rubbed his own legs and backside. Glancing around his grandparents' farm, it seemed a far cry from the new place in the bottoms. Grandpa John's store, though small compared to the mercantile in Hickory Ford, was a well-built and well-maintained structure, as were all the other buildings on the place. Amos knew some folks considered John and Janey Sawyer well to do, but he never thought of them as rich. They lived pretty much like all the other farm folks here about, except they always had plenty and their place was always neat and tidy.

Amos' presence was announced as he entered the store by the tinkling of the little bell over the door. Upon seeing him, Janey came with a rush. Like so many grandmothers, she could act like the one grandchild present was her only one. "Why, Amos," she exclaimed, "I didn't think you'd ever git here. Ya must be hungry after yore long ride." Without waiting for him to reply, she went on. "That's good 'cause I've got a big supper cooked over't house. A chocolate cake, I know how ya' love thet."

Returning attention to the customer she had been waiting on, Janey began to tell at some length about Amos' week in the bottoms. She was quite proud that her little grandson had taken on a man's job. Amos was proud himself, but he became embarrassed standing there while his Grandma bragged about him. Seeking a way out, he asked the whereabouts of his Grandpa, and getting his answer, slipped out the back door to find him. As Janey had said, John was making some repairs on the chicken coop.

"Howdy, Grandpaw." spoke up Amos as he approached the hammering.

"Well, howdy yoreself, Amos. I was 'bout to give ya out. Thought ya'd maybe start out this mawnin' 'stead of waiting till dinner." It was clear that John was pleased that Amos had worked until noon instead of starting for home right after breakfast.

Changing the subject, Amos asked, "What happened to yore chicken coop, Grandpaw?" Amos could observe that a hole had been dug under one end and that a larger hole had been torn through the wire at one corner. There were chicken feathers all over the inside of the pen.

With some frustration in his voice, John replied, "Seems some varmint, likely a mink, dug under the fence las' night hoping to get himself a chicken supper. That hound dog of mine tore the wire apart to git at him. Quite a chase followed thet. I don't think ol' Blue ever got his teeth into the varmint, but he scared him some. I doubt thet he'll be back this way fer quite a spell, seeing the reception he got. Now them hens prob'bly won't lay fer several days. Good thang we take eggs in trade at the store, else we might be without an egg for cornbread." Picking up his tools, he added, "Well, Amos, let's head for th' house and warsh up fer supper. I want t' hear 'bout yore week."

Not able to wait until supper, Amos eagerly began. "I got the field pretty much all cleared, Grandpaw. Did ya know that some of them saplings wuz almost fifteen feet tall? I left a lot of the little stuff, hopin' the plow will git it. Hope so, anyways. An', I got the horse lot rebuilt right after ya left. Thet shore is fine dirt down thar. Reckon thet garden'll grow taters as big as two of my fists." Amos' report went on steadily as they put away the tools and washed up until they stepped through Grandma's kitchen door. Here Amos' report suddenly stopped as he took a look at his dirty, sweaty overalls and dirty bare feet. Everybody knew that Janey kept a spotless house and now Amos was suddenly aware of how dirty he was. But Grandma's direction to "Set on down, Amos" brought him relief and he dropped into a chair next to John.

As they began to eat, Amos returned to his report. John smiled and nodded at the account of his progress. Of course, there was much work ahead before the new farm would become productive, but this past week was a good start.

As Amos climbed upon Little Red after supper, John said, "You've done a good week's work, Amos. Now, I'll bring ya some supplies down on Wednesday. Ya head on up t' yore folks, now."

With those parting words, Amos pointed Little Red out of the yard and into the road toward his parents home. Both Little Red and Speckle showed their excitement now as this was familiar ground to them.

This short trip took less than an hour, and his backside had recovered somewhat, so Amos took pleasure in the ride home. Just as he had done so many nights before, he put Little Red in the barn, giving him some hay and corn. The family was watching for him, and his father came out to the barn. "Son, I didn't think ya were a comin' by now. I'd 'bout given ya out."

"Poppa, you know what Grandmaw's suppers are like. It takes a long while for a feller to eat one. And Grandpaw wanted to hear about the week at the new place," replied Amos.

"I figured as much. Well, come on in th' house. Yore momma will expect ya' to eat agin, of course. Think ya' kin manage it?" asked James with a smile.

With a quick grin, Amos said, "Reckon I kin give it a try, Poppa."

Fortunately for Amos, Lissie had only set out some left-over cake, which he ate with abandon, and not just to please his mother. His parents, like his grandparents, wanted to know all about the past week. Particularly, they were interested in how he had fared cooking and being alone. Amos assured them that all was well without mentioning the fears of his first night. After what seemed like hours of talking, James stood and said, "Past bedtime now, and light will come the same time in the mawnin', even if it is Sun'dy." With that, his parents went on to bed, for tomorrow indeed would be a busy day. Amos heated a kettle of water and took it to the porch for a much-needed bath, then headed for bed himself.

Next morning found Lissie packing foodstuffs for Amos to take. Every item had to be packed for the rough ride on Little Red's back. That meant no breakables like eggs. After the sacks had begun to get full, Amos said, "Likely thet's all Little Red should carry on thet long ride back to th' bottoms, Momma. Reckon I kin git along w'th this. 'Sides, Grandpaw's comin' down to th' bottoms on Wednesday. He'll bring all manner of eats and sech. You and Poppa could always send somethin' down by him."

Church this morning seemed much like all the other sermons Amos could remember. Yet, today something was different. He was still a boy in his home church, but somehow folks looked at him differently. His friends, as well as the grown folks, didn't quite look at him the same way. Amos pondered this during the preacher's sermon and decided that right now folks didn't know whether to look at him as a boy or as a man. Figuring that it would work its own self out, Amos made up his mind to just let things happen and watch the changes. He wasn't at all sure which he was himself. As the sermon drew to a close, he knew that he liked life. Passing out of the church house, he gave the preacher the customary smile and handshake. Brother Smith's face showed that he was aware that Amos' thoughts had been far away from the text this morning. Quickly, Amos moved on out, acting as if to allow someone behind him to step forward.

Later that afternoon Little Red stepped smartly along while carrying Amos and several sacks of food. Even though Amos had told his mother that John would be coming down on Wednesday, she had insisted on loading him down with food and supplies.

As he rode back to his new place in the bottoms, Amos' thoughts went back to the short time at home and how good it had felt. He decided it was even worth the pain of the long bareback mule ride. He would have to get used to the long ride because the familiar faces and voices were a welcome change after a week alone. One reason why folks speculated on his getting on by himself was his propensity to talk. Some said that he must be blood-related to

Zeke Miller, who was known to be about the biggest windjammer around. Amos didn't mind the comparison with Uncle Zeke, who had married John's sister Agnes. As a matter of fact, he relished Uncle Zeke's tall tales about hunting and fishing. Amos reckoned that those stories of Uncle Zeke's were better than a lot of books, though he reminded himself that when it came to books, he had only read a few.

Amos was so preoccupied with his thoughts that he was startled to hear a soft voice from the side of the road. "I said 'howdy,' Amos. Ya gone deef, or som'thin'?"

Amos turned quickly as he pulled up Little Red. It was then that he saw Marie Johnson picking wild flowers from the fence row. Her warm and natural smile unsettled him, as girls do to boys of that age. His best reply was, "Uh, howdy, ...Marie."

Breaking the silence, Marie said, "I saw ya over t' the Baptist Church this mawnin'. My fam'ly goes to the Methodist. Hear ya're livin' way off down on Little Sandy River now. Don't ya' get lonesome fer comp'ney, down there all by ya'self?"

Wanting to appear mature, Amos responded, "Naw, there's plenty of work to be done, don't have time t' be lonely."

Reflecting her admiration, Marie replied, "Reckon you're old 'nough then t' take a wife."

Flushing with embarrassment, Amos stuttered out, "Wal', uh, uh, hadn't thought 'bout it. Uh, 'sides, got too much work t' do." As if working would keep a man from marrying, he kneed Little Red into a quick start, calling back, "Be seeing ya, Marie. I mean, uh, sometimes at church or somethin'." Now embarrassed more than ever, he looked straight ahead as he heard Marie's soft giggle behind him.

In the next mile, he thought of nothing but the conversation with Marie Johnson. Not that he was so preoccupied with that particular girl, but that he never knew how to talk to girls. With grown folks or children or boys his own age, he could talk a blue streak. But with girls, he flustered and stammered. Why was this? Amos realized he knew little about things outside fishing or hunting or farming. Girls he certainly didn't understand. And why did Marie Johnson's smile and twinkling eyes bother him so? One thing was for sure, in the bottoms, there wouldn't be any soft smiles from girls to upset him. There it was just hard work and fishing. There, his sole companionship would come from Speckle and Little Red. Right now a hound dog and a mule were enough companions for a young boy soon to be a man.

Enough thoughts were whirling around in the boy's mind to keep the long ride from being boring, and it seemed only a short while before he passed the Potter's house, the last house before his cabin. At church this morning, someone had said that Mr. Potter worked at a saw mill in Willow Point. Amos waved to the children playing in the yard and gave the place another look. All the buildings were made of cypress logs, except for the chicken house and the outhouse. He could see several pieces of farm equipment, and a lone cow occupied a small pasture fenced with split rails.

Riding the last three miles through the tall timber of the bottoms, Amos became quite anxious to see his own cabin. He began to pay close attention to the individual trees along the road and to the lay of the land. The bottoms were fairly flat, but yet the land had a certain unevenness. Most of this was caused when flood waters scooped out here and deposited there. Sloughs, or long shallow depressions cut out by previous rivers or a strong overflow current, were common and usually held water most of the year. Ridges, like the one at his cabin, were also found throughout the bottoms. These were not high, just a few feet higher than the surrounding land. The ridge land was important, though, since it would dry much quicker in the spring and would protect crops from small floods.

Trees in the bottoms seemed uncommonly tall. The fertile soil and ample water made strong plants that raced skyward, each competing for its share of sunlight. All trees look pretty much alike to a city person, but to someone raised in the country, each tree is distinctive. They know whether it's oak, hickory, or a cypress, even know the different types of oaks. Some trees become landmarks, by virtue of an odd shaped trunk, odd limb configurations, or exposed roots along a wash, or growing at an angle. Amos looked for these details as he rode the last three miles. He gave particular interest to trees which held squirrel nests or showed holes suitable for a coon. Fall would bring hunting and trapping for extra money from the sale of hides.

Arriving at his own cabin, Amos looked with a particular pride and joy at the place. He eyed his home, with his cabin and barn, a field, and, of course, the river. It wasn't fancy like some of the farms back in Hickory Ford, but it was his, and for now, that was enough. He knew that time, and hard work would make the place show much more of its promise. He knew that there was good timber and that clearing it would reveal fine rich soil for farming.

In the two days before Grandpa John would come, Amos worked with abandon. He so wanted to make a favorable impression upon his grandpa that he pushed himself both days. The scrap poles that were pulled from the old horse lot were seasoned wood, so he sawed them into firewood. He cleared more yard area, cleaned the cabin and then the barn stall, went over much of the clearing again for thick weeds or sprouts which he might have missed the past week, and somehow thought to wash his overalls and shirt in the river Tuesday after supper. John was known as a hard worker. He also one of the cleaner men in Hickory Ford.

Wednesday morning found Amos feeling quite good about himself and what he had accomplished in a week and a half. The place had a clean look to it with the weeds cut back and the rough stuff in the clearing chopped down. To busy himself while waiting for Grandpa John's arrival, he set about installing large pegs in the barn. Here he would hang the different leather tack needed to farm with a mule and the tools that needed to be protected from the damp morning dew. He had almost finished when he heard the squeak and rattle of a wagon. Looking out the barn door, Amos could see John enter the clearing with the morning sun only halfway up in the sky.

"Mawnin', Grandpaw. Ya' must have left home 'fore the rooster crowed," said Amos.

"The mawnin' is the best time of the day, Amos. Ever'thin' is fresh. Makes a feller feel ready fer whatever." responded his grandpa.

Scanning the changes in the place, Grandpa Sawyer said, "Looks mighty good, Amos. Ya've got a good start here. In another month it'll look better still."

Amos felt good on the inside, but could only say, "Yes, sir."

The two of them began to unload and put away the equipment and supplies John had brought. There were nails, files, lumber, wire, and assorted carpentry hand tools. There was seed corn and a variety of vegetable seeds for the garden. He had a mosquito bar to go over the bed, something that would be almost essential as the summer approached. There were more food staples, plus roofing shingles and other supplies that John felt Amos would need in the days ahead. Amos had noticed a tow sack in the front of the wagon. Before he could ask about it, John had started handing things out of the wagon, and Amos forgot about the sack. Now it was the last thing left on the wagon. Grandpa hoisted it onto the side of the wagon, and with a big grin, slipped back the sack to reveal a saddle. "This is fer you, Amos. Nobody should have t' make thet trip to Hickory Ford astraddle the bony back of a mule."

For a moment Amos was actually speechless. Sure, he had ridden many times with a saddle, but he had never owned one. As he accepted the saddle from his grandfather, Amos saw that it was used but in excellent shape. It was made of full-grain leather and had been kept oiled. The stitching was strong and tight. "Uh, thanks, Grandpaw. Ah, I don't know what to say," Amos finally said.

"Well, Amos, it's all right fer a boy to ride around bareback, but a man needs a saddle under him!"

Amos took the saddle off the side board and with great pleasure carried it over to the horse lot, carefully setting it upon the top rail. "Hey, Little Red, see whut Grandpaw brought me, uh, and for you too, little feller," spoke Amos to the curious mule.

Over the next few hours, John instructed Amos on the work ahead and answered his many questions. Together they walked around the entire farm, looking and talking about what needed to be done next and how to do it. Then with the beans, Amos had started to cook, the two of them put dinner together and ate their noon meal.

Shortly after noon John clucked to his team and headed back for Red Gum Ridge. Again, Amos was alone, but this time the work and the isolation didn't bother him. Instead, he felt challenged in a way which he had never known before in his young life. The excitement was pleasant, but Amos could not know how this opportunity would change his life.

Chapter Four

Plowin' and Plantin'

Amos spent the first hour after John left organizing the new tools and supplies, swelled by a sense of importance at having been put in charge of so many things. Amos had never been entrusted with so much responsibility before. After some thought, he determined that he liked his new life, in spite of its isolation.

Growing up as the youngest child, Amos had lots of attention, but little responsibility. His older brothers and even his sister Cora had been given responsibilities at an earlier age than he. Not only did this affect the way Amos felt about himself, but he thought it affected the way others viewed him as well. It seemed that his image had always been one of a youngster, not someone to be taken seriously. But his Grandpa now took him seriously. And that respect could not have meant more from any other person. What had Grandpa said? "It's all right for a boy to ride bareback, but a man needs a saddle under him." At that moment, Amos no longer felt just fifteen.

With the tools and supplies put away, Amos stood in the yard and made a mental survey of "his" place. Looking from cabin to garden to field, he knew it was time. For over a week he had looked to the plow sitting by the barn and wondered about the day he would actually use it. Though he had plowed many times

before on his father's farm, he believed that there would be something special about his first day of plowing on the new place. He
understood from his father's talks that to cultivate the fresh earth
was to open it up to new growth and to a harvest that would
support not only the family but all the farm stock as well.

True, the field had been cleared and farmed before, but the
soil had lain fallow now for three years. Today would be Amos'
first time plowing in his own field, and it would forever hold
special significance to him. "Yep," he thought out loud, "the time
has come t' begin the plowin'."

Little Red usually stood quietly for harnessing up, but this
afternoon he reflected Amos' excitement. The mule needed some
soothing and reassurance before leaving the horse lot. He backed
the animal up to the small turning plow and connected the trace
chains to the hooks on the single tree. Amos laid the plow on
its side as Little Red pulled it to the edge of the old garden spot.
There he stood, sensing the moist earth beneath his bare feet, the
gentle curve of the handles in his rough hands, and the eagerness
of his mule.

Amos clucked and Little Red stepped out across the garden.
Amos pointed the plow down to bite into the soil, then held it
straight as the dark, damp earth—filled with decaying leaves and
roots—turned over, As the furrow rose to the right, it formed a
long oval row of exposed soil. Reaching the far end, Little Red
instinctively stopped and turned to the right as Amos shifted the
plow around and pointed the mule back down the row they had
just plowed. Again and again Amos and Little Red made trips
back and forth in the garden until all the soil was upside down,
soft and yielding. The air was rich with the smell of freshly turned
earth.

Stopping to catch their breath, both mule and man sensed satisfaction for having done a great thing. Amos admitted to himself that other mules such as Grandpa's Gray Jack would have plowed straighter furrows, but he also knew that his little mule had done well in pulling and guiding a plow by himself. Little Red did not have the advantage of one mule walking the furrow as a guide, as would have been the case with a team. Little Red had to walk just to the left of the furrow and along the edge. One horse plows were seldom used, but there was not another mule available for Amos' use. John had said one mule would have to do. Besides, there were only seven acres to plow, not the forty most men farmed.

With the afternoon now almost gone, Amos decided that the garden had been a good start on the plowing. Tomorrow he would begin plowing the field. After scraping dirt and vegetation from the blade, he unhitched his mule and led the animal to rest. Small chores occupied his time until supper.

Meals always took a lot of time, as he had to stop his work early to cook. Most of the time, meals were plain; beans and fried potatoes. He would have fish when he could work his set lines. Occasionally, he would fry some hog jowl or side meat, salt cured last fall. As long as the pokeberry plants were still small, the dark greens provided some variety. When the wagon came down, he got fresh eggs to go with his pork. Usually, he drank pump water, which wasn't too bad fresh, but if it set a while, it turned a rusty color and took on a strong taste. Amos surely missed the cool spring water from the hills. And, without a cow, there was no milk to drink, and no fresh butter for his biscuits or cornbread. But he did have some of last year's jelly and sorghum molasses. Both added a sweet taste to the meal. Tonight he was fortunate to catch a good sized drum on one of his set hooks. Fish always made meals taste better.

Sitting out after supper in the cool of the evening, Amos had time to relax and think. The bracing night air relieved his sunburn and the night music provided by the crickets, frogs, and birds soothed his spirit. A light breeze brought the odor of the fresh earth and took his thinking back to plowing the garden. He felt satisfaction having opened the ground for new seeds. He thought ahead to the vegetables he would plant, anticipating the rewards that a person could enjoy from the freshness of the earth. Amos felt abiding thankfulness to God for providing his needs.

At this point, Amos' life was uncomplicated. He liked that. There were no soft giggles and sparkling eyes here in the bottoms to disturb him. But all the while he knew that one day he would probably take a wife and have his own family. Uneasy with this thought, he pushed himself up from the cane-bottomed chair and stepped into his cabin. "Well, enough thinkin' for one night," he said to himself, and went to his bed.

The next morning's light was not quite full as Little Red eased the plow out to the edge of the clearing. Stopping him there, Amos checked the fit of the harness and the condition of the plow. Today would be a hard day's work. Amos wanted nothing to work against him and the mule. Finally satisfied, Amos stood behind the handles and looked out over the seven-acre clearing. Though it looked much different than when he first arrived, it was still a rough piece of ground. Most of the cut saplings were piled on the three dead trees left on the ridge by some past flood, but the rest were in piles throughout the field. And until these could be burned in the fall, Amos would have to work around them."Well, Little Red, standin' here burnin' up daylight ain't a gittin' it done.

So, let's go," spoke Amos. With that and a cluck, the little mule leaned into the harness, and the earth began to turn. Both pulling the plow and guiding it were harder here as the field had not been cleared of roots and stumps as thoroughly as in the garden. Both he and Little Red grunted and strained as they plowed furrow after furrow, working outward from the center of the clearing. The air around them filled with the smell of damp fresh earth, mixed with the smell of sweat from the man and the mule. The air was filled with the sounds of creaking leather and the intermittent popping of small roots being cut by the plow.

Here Amos wore his shoes because the remaining vegetation was more likely to conceal snakes. He had killed a rattler and a Water Moccasin so far, knowing they would be more active in the warmer weeks ahead. By wearing shoes, Amos was cautious. The ride for help would be a long one. As the day ended, Amos took a tired look back to the fresh earth in the clearing. It looked good, but he was discouraged because so little area was plowed, probably not quite an acre. And if he was tired, Little Red seemed even more so as they walked together to the horse lot. Tonight the little mule got eight ears of corn with his hay and a rub down as well.

Amos took a quick swim in the river to rinse off the day's sweat and dirt before heating up some leftovers for his supper. Later, with his meal and cleanup over, he wandered out to the clearing to look again at his day's work. The moon wasn't up yet so he couldn't make out the exact boundaries of the plowing, but somehow it was important for him to come back to it. He didn't understand how but sensed that his work was a part of him. Amos knew he had a need to be close to his land, to sort of say goodnight before going to bed. Now walking back to the house, his tired muscles looked forward to the wheat straw mattress.

Each day Amos and Little Red continued plowing. He not only had to work around the growing number of brush piles he had made but also around the many stumps still in the rich bottom soil. Much too often for either Amos or Little Red, the plow would jam itself into the soft outer surface of a stump or under one of the large spreading roots and jerk the mule rearward, slamming Amos forward onto the crossbar of the plow. Then would come the laborious task of releasing the plow point before continuing forward.

During all this hard labor, Speckle did his part, as dogs do when there are chores to be done. He followed at Amos' heels down the furrow until he was tired of that, then he would wander to the edge of the clearing and rest in the warm sunshine. With his rest completed, the faithful dog would check out every bush or hole in the clearing, as if he hadn't already done it several times before. Assured that everything was secure in the clearing, Speckle would go off for a romp through the woods, sometimes treeing a squirrel or other game and bawling for Amos to come. This only made Amos' hard labor more of a drudgery. At times like that, Amos would say out loud, "Danged fool hound, don't he know I'm a workin' and cain't go off t' hunt ever time he trees something!" Then Amos would think ahead to the winter and how good the coon hunting should be here in the bottoms. That thought would cause Amos to set about his work with a renewed vigor. With only occasional breaks for a few other chores, Amos worked at plowing the clearing until Saturday at dusk. After putting up Little Red, he stood between the barn and cabin to survey his progress. All the hard work so far had turned over just less than half the clearing. Sore and tired, Amos ached all over, and his clothes were totally stained with dirt and sweat. Turning now to the cabin, he thanked God that tomorrow was a Sunday, for he and Little Red sorely needed a day of rest.

Sunday morning brought a freshness in body and spirit, though Amos was very sore and stiff from all the plowing. This was to be his first Sunday on the new place. He had told his family that, until the seed was in the ground, he wouldn't take the time to ride all the way back to Hickory Ford.

After breakfast and his few chores had been done, loneliness began to plague him. Amos had never been alone much in his life and this isolation from other people, particularly his family, could sometimes overwhelm him. His busy days were not bad, as his mind was occupied all during the day and his body was too tired at night for much loneliness, but when things were slow and quiet, he thought back to his family's farm with all its pleasant familiarities.

In the years of his growing up, he had come to know every foot of the home place, with all its sounds and smells. His mother's kitchen was a favorite spot. Not only was it a place to fill up on tasty food, but also the place to go for a kind word. The voices of his father, mother, brothers, and sister came clear to him this morning in the far-off bottoms. In his mind, he walked through the barn lot, past its animals and out through the large oaks which overhung the rock-bottomed creek with its clear, cool water.

"Caw, caw," called a lone crow from across the clearing, awakening Amos from his daydream. Shocked back to reality, Amos realized that this new place could also become special to him and that he would have to make a new life for himself here in the bottoms far from what had been familiar and pleasant. As for people, he would just have to ride out to where there were folks. Besides, this was Sunday morning Amos had been raised to gather with God's people for worship. The closest community was Willow

Point, located about five miles west, at the junction of the Little Sandy River and the larger Big Sandy River. "Well," he thought aloud, "if I'm a goin' to make preachin', I'd better git a move on."

Riding out the wagon track, Little Red was as bouncy under the new saddle as he'd been in harness all week. Quickly though, Amos settled him into a lope down the familiar logging road and held him to it until White Creek. Here he walked his mount west along the creek's north bank and on through the woods. John had told him that there was an old logging camp and a shallow crossing where White Creek joined the Little Sandy. Walking his mule into the abandoned logging camp, Amos looked over the old sawmill. Here logs were once sawed into boards for houses and barns. Now the buildings slowly softened under the frequent rains. A few run down buildings remained, and Amos marked their condition in his mind for when winter coon hunting came. He might need a dry place to wait out a rainstorm.

Just up from where White Creek flowed into the river, the Little Sandy showed to be wider and shallower. But not wanting to take any chances with his clean overalls and shirt, Amos stripped off all his clothes and shoes and held them in a tight bundle while remounting. At Amos' signal, Little Red eased his way across the belly-deep current and up the far bank.

Following the Little Sandy, Amos rode into what he figured must be Willow Point within an hour and a half of leaving his cabin. Not ever having been here before, everything was new and seemed larger than Hickory Ford, though he would later realize that they were about the same size. Following the main road, Amos noticed the various businesses common to every farm community. Just past the Methodist church house, he saw the Baptist church house, farther back off the road. Both churchyards were full of wagons with teams and more than a few dogs. Now he was glad that he had left Speckle tied at the cabin. A strange dog usually meant a fight, and that wasn't the kind of attention Amos wanted on his first Sunday at this new church. He tied Little Red to a spreading willow at the edge of the yard and walked into the church house among other folks arriving at the same time.

Everyone welcomed him to the service. He was the only stranger that day, but was so like the others that neither he nor they were uncomfortable. Amos couldn't recall ever before visiting a church by himself, that is, when he didn't know a single soul there. Back in Hickory Ford, he had visited the other churches many times with his friends and relatives, but he was always with someone. Besides, he knew everyone there anyway. Here he was by himself. And, yet he wasn't. The hymns were familiar, and the preacher's text was one that he had studied in Sunday School sometime in the last year. Beyond that, he sensed but did not fully understand a kinship with these people whom he had never met before today.

Of course, after the preaching, they asked him where he was from. Most were more than a little startled to learn that he was living back in the bottoms by himself. The older boys and girls were somewhat awed, which caused him to feel a sense of pride. Maybe he was becoming a man. If so, he liked it. He left these church folks and Willow Point with a good feeling about coming back. Besides coming to the church on Sundays, he would need to come back during the week when the mercantile here was open. It was his closest source for sugar, coffee, flour, and hardware.

After returning home and having his dinner, Amos spent the afternoon exploring the river bank to the north. Speckle, after having been left behind in the morning, was anxious for the outing. Also, Amos had spent so much time clearing the place that he and the dog had not had time for exploring the hunting and fishing possibilities.

The two of them strolled along for about two hours before circling back toward the cabin. Several trees were sighted that contained dens, likely nests for coons. Amos found the lay of the land to be fairly flat, with one round pond about an acre in size. The pond still held water this late in the spring, so it was likely much larger during the winter. During their walk, Speckle tried several different scents, but each time Amos signaled to the hound to come along. After a time, Speckle sensed that this was not a serious hunt and began to play along with Amos. They returned tired but excited about future days and nights of fishing and hunting along the river.

At supper, Amos thought of the differences between the hill country and the bottoms. It certainly was easier to keep one's sense of direction in the hills, as a hunter could guide himself by the lay of the ridges and hollows. The flatness of the bottoms could be more than confusing on a dark night. Also, some of the timber was different. Poplar didn't grow down here, and cypress didn't grow in the hills, except sometimes by a spring. And, of course, there were more snakes, mosquitoes, and turtles in the bottoms because there was more water. The land was much richer, from all the annual overflows which deposited silt and organic matter. Certainly, there was plenty of game and fish here in the bottoms. Amos looked forward to getting the crop laid by so that he might do some serious exploring beyond the clearing.

CHAPTER FIVE

The River

AMOS AWOKE MONDAY MORNING to the sound of rain and was instantly hopeful that it would be too wet to plow. In spite of yesterday's rest, all the muscles in his body ached. He was so sore it hurt to move. Slipping from the bed, Amos opened the door and saw that plowing would indeed be impossible. As he glanced to the river, he remembered something strange from last night. Speckle's barking at something down on the river had roused him from his sleep. That had happened before, but this time he was positive he heard the sound of voices and paddling. He now wondered who could have been on the river in the middle of the night. Maybe it was someone from a logging camp farther up river. He knew that logging camps sort of came and went on the river. However, in the two weeks he had lived in the cabin, he had not seen any river traffic. Amos thought that he would ask Grandpa about it when he came down later in the week.

With the rain giving his sore muscles another day to recover, Amos took more time than usual with his breakfast. "One thing for shore," said Amos aloud, "soon's th' rain stops, I need to git up on the roof and fix them leaks that keep makin' me move my bed around th' cabin. It's a good thing Grandpaw brought some shingles on his last load."

After breakfast, Amos found busywork he could do in the barn, out of the rain. He sharpened the eye hoe and the ax, and cleaned and organized the other hand tools. Late in the morning, the rain stopped, and the clouds began to clear. Since it was still too muddy to plow, Amos grabbed his fishing pole and headed for the river bank. He loved fishing, and this was the first real break when he could just fish and relax. He found a large white oak tree right on the river's edge, with roots exposed where the river was slowly eroding the bank. Here he baited his hook with a grubworm and eased his line down between two logs in the water. With no immediate bite, Amos leaned back against the trunk and looked up at the fresh blue sky. Overhead, the treetops swayed in a light breeze. Sunshine was replacing the clouds. The day was beginning to warm. The air had that fresh washed smell that a rain so often brings. The river level was up slightly because of the storm, but not enough to muddy the water. The Little Sandy still flowed slow and easy.

Startled by a hard pull on his pole, Amos saw that his cork had been taken down into the depths of the river. Jerking back and up on the pole, he saw the water churn as his catch neared the surface. With a final lift, a thrashing, splashing fish followed his lineup and out of the water and onto the bank beside him. Quickly, he put his hands on it to keep the fish from flopping back into the river. After removing the hook, Amos admired the beauty of the bream, with its golden breast and reddish brown body. This was a keeper, fully as large as his hand. A scrappy little fish, bream gave a good fight once hooked. Hooking his first catch on a forked stick and lowering it into the water to ensure that it remained fresh, Amos quickly rebaited his hook and dropped his line into the same spot. He didn't wait long for the next bite, as the fish began to feed after the rain. In the next half hour, Amos caught enough fish for his dinner and supper, slipping his catch onto the forked stick.

Amos looked at the roof as he walked back to the house. The roof was still wet, and it would be dangerous to work on it until it was dry. To make use of the time before dinner, Amos decided to build a live box for his fresh fish. With a live box, he could keep his catch alive in the river until he was ready to cook them, safe from the turtles and snakes that would get them if they were left on a stick or string.

Taking a 1 x 12 poplar board from the stack, he first sawed off two pieces about 24 inches long. Then he used the hand axe to split off some strips for slats. With the slats and the 1 x 12 boards, he fashioned a live box, complete with a hinged door at the top. He carried his handiwork to the river and emptied his morning's catch from the forked stick into the new live box. Keeping out enough fish for dinner, he lowered the live box into the water and tied the rope securely to a large root.

Amos, by now rested and not pressed to hurry back to the plowing for a change, fixed an elegant dinner of fried fish, fried potatoes, and fresh cornbread. He celebrated with some of his mother's canned pickles. These were delicious, but he ate sparingly since this was the last jar until summer. For something different to drink other than pump water, he boiled some coffee. Though he could remember much better dinners back home, this would be about as good as it could get until the garden began to produce fresh vegetables.

After washing his dishes Amos stood in the doorway and thought out loud, "I'm still fuller than a tick, so I reckon the roof 'll wait a little longer." Instead of getting to the roof, he started work on a new hammer handle. Working for an hour with a knife and a rasp, he worked a piece of ash into the shape he wanted. Though still not finished, he set the handle aside until later. Farm life was full of these little projects to work on when there wasn't something bigger to do. Right now the roof just wouldn't wait any longer. It was now dry enough to walk on, and his belly had worked down that big bait of fish and taters.

Replacing the bad shingles was a slow job and one that really required more skill than Amos possessed as a carpenter. John Sawyer was a skilled carpenter, and Amos tried to remember all the lessons his Grandpa had taught him. Roofing is slow and frustrating, as the shingle that needs replacing is nailed up under two others. Finally by supper time he thought that all the leaks were fixed. After putting away his tools, Amos retrieved the rest of the fish from the crate and fixed his supper. With his supper finished and the dishes washed, Amos worked on the hammer handle by lamp light until it had the right shape, then he took a piece of broken glass to dress it smooth. As he finished the handle, Amos thought to the next day and decided that a good night's sleep would make the hard day easier, so he went to bed earlier than usual.

Morning light found Amos and Little Red turning the earth in the clearing. As both of them were rested, they kept up a steady pace throughout the morning. For their effort, a half acre of freshly plowed earth lay drying in the midday sun.

After his noon break, Amos decided to take the time to build the drag he would need to smooth the soil before planting. Though it would be several days before the field he was now plowing would be ready for the drag, the garden was ready now. Anxious to get the garden planted, Amos searched the timber for the right tree for the drag. He selected a red oak about six inches in diameter and dropped it with the ax. He trimmed the small tree, cut an eight-foot length, and carried it on one shoulder back to the barn. There, Amos used a broad hatchet to cut two grooves around the log, each about eighteen inches from the end. Then he tied the ends of a chain in these grooves so the chain wouldn't slip to the middle as it was being pulled. The chain was long enough to tie into a loop at its middle, where a clevis would secure it to the single tree.

After hooking up Little Red to the drag, Amos smoothed off the garden, opening up the surface so it would dry out more quickly, and leveling it at the same time. For good measure, he went over the garden three times before looking back over the still-rough soil. It certainly didn't look like one of the gardens back in Hickory Ford, which would be disked to break up the clods and to cut up and bury any remaining vegetation. At least here he didn't have a clod problem. Here, the humus rich soil fell apart when worked.

Amos spent the remainder of the afternoon plowing the clearing. It was slow work, but work which, once done, did not have to be repeated. Planting would go quickly when the clearing was finally turned over. Amos doggedly worked on through that afternoon and returned to the plowing at first light Wednesday morning.

He and Little Red were beginning to tire at mid-morning when John drove his wagon into the clearing. Amos knew his grandpa was coming today, but had been so busy plowing he had forgotten about it. John's arrival brought a welcome break. Not only could they rest from the plowing, but here was company for both Amos and Little Red.

"Howdy, Grandpaw," called Amos as he led Little Red to the barn. "I've been so busy I plum forgot you were a comin' today."

"I'd say thet you've been busy. Big change here since last Wednesday," replied John. From the wagon-seat, he scanned first the garden and then the clearing. Grandpa was pleased with all the plowing.

"Guess you and thet mule of yourn's bout tuckered out," John added as he stepped down, first to the wheel hub and then to the ground. "Let's go take a closer look at yore plowing, Amos."

Walking out across the rough-turned soil, John talked first of the rich soil here in the bottoms. "Made dirt" he called it because of the steadily decaying vegetation and yearly deposits of silt from upriver. "This here dirt has been in the makin' fer thousands of years, Amos. An' now ya' git to open it up fer crops. Be excitin' to see how tall it'll grow corn. An' I lay that it'll make taters as big as yore head, yes sir."

Coming upon one of the remaining stumps, John said, "Ya know, Amos, come late summer, we just might dig around a few of these ol' stumps and see if they'll burn down into the ground."

Turning back to the house, John added, "Brought ya some more seed fer ya' garden. Prob'bly 'bout time t' plant it."

"Good, Grandpaw," replied Amos, "I know I'm ready to eat out of it."

At this, John chuckled and said, "What ya mean, Amos, is that yore always ready to eat."

John laughed in an easy way down here in the bottoms, a laughter that made Amos feel very close to him. Each of them by now was aware that their relationship was changing and growing, but neither put words to it. They spent the remainder of the morning unloading the wagon and walking about the place.

Grandpa John spoke highly of the work Amos had done thus far and talked with him about plans for improving the place. When the crop was laid by, that time between the last cultivating and the harvest, they could clear more good cropland along the ridge. In the process, rails would be cut for fencing, and ties cut and sold to the railroad. Amos became excited at the mention of tie cutting as the work had always interested him. It seemed to Amos that everyone in Hickory Ford said that there wasn't a better tie cutter anywhere than his Grandpa John Sawyer. Now he would be learning tie cutting from his Grandpa.

Their dinner that day was not the standard plain fare Amos endured, but a box of special fixings sent by Grandma Janey. Besides fried chicken, there were stewed potatoes, fresh onions, black eyed peas, fresh bread and most unusual of all, chocolate cake! Amos ate like he hadn't eaten in several days. At last, he exclaimed, "Boy, Grandpaw, thet shore was delicious!"

"Yore Grandma figured ya were 'bout tired of your own cookin'," replied John. "Ya'd best be careful 'bout any hard work this afternoon, Amos, after eatin' thet much dinner, ya' could work ya'self sick."

"Yeah, but what a way to git sick," said Amos, with a big smile and a swollen belly.

With dinner over, both of them set to washing up and putting Grandma's dishes back in the box for the return trip. As they talked, Amos remembered the strange occurrence from last Sunday night. "Grandpaw, Speckle woke me up in the middle of the night Sunday with a fit of barkin', then I heard someone talkin' out on the river and also someone paddlin'. What do you reckon anybody was a doin' out there on the river in the middle of the night?" he asked.

Thinking a full minute before responding, John finally said, "Prob'bly no good, too far from anywhere fer fishermen or froggers, and this ain't the right time of the year fer trappers as the fur's too short. Don't want to skear ya any, but best keep a good ear out for any other night trav'lers. Let me know iffen ya' see or hear anythin' else that don't seem right."

Throughout the afternoon Amos thought back on what John had said about the sounds on the river. They had let the matter drop as Grandpa needed to get back home before supper. But now that Amos was again alone, the question of the night travelers on the river wouldn't leave him. He had expected John to say they were just fishermen or such and not consider the matter of any consequence. But he didn't, and that left Amos with a nervous feeling about the river at night.

After awhile, Amos shrugged and decided that whoever it was hadn't bothered him yet, and so, probably wouldn't. With that thought, he got out the garden seeds John had brought down and began to plant his garden. Garden planting was always slow work, but by dusk he had everything planted except the potatoes.

Amos enjoyed Grandma's cooking a second time that day as there had been enough left over from dinner for his supper. He particularly savored the chocolate cake. While doing his dishes that night, Amos wondered if he could someday bake a cake. The next time he got to Red Gum Ridge, he'd ask Grandma to show him how.

That night as he sat out and listened to the sounds, he cut the potatoes that would be planted in the morning. Working by lamp light, he made sure that each chunk of potato had an eye. Otherwise, nothing would sprout from that piece. After they had been cut up, Amos filled the tub with water so that the seed pieces would have plenty of moisture to sprout.

By mid-morning the next day, the potatoes were in the ground. Little Red had pulled the single stock and opened up rows about three feet apart. Then with the potatoes dropped about a foot apart with the eye up, he had Little Red pull the pole drag over the rows to pull the soil in over the seed potatoes.

Having finished the garden, Amos stood at the end and imagined all the vegetables that would soon be growing there. There would be onions, potatoes, black-eyed peas, okra, melons, tomatoes, and radishes. "Yes," he thought, "the eatin' from this garden will be fine."

For the rest of that day, then for the rest of the week, Amos stuck with the plowing. It was noon on Saturday when he finished the first plowing. Both Amos and his mule dripped with sweat as they headed back to the barn. Fatigue almost robbed Amos of the joy of the moment as he tied Little Red to the horse lot fence. Amos walked to the pump and drew a fresh pan of water to wash the sweat from his face and arms. Only when he was somewhat cleaned of dirt and sweat did he turn to look upon the fully plowed clearing. A good feeling went all through him as he viewed the completion of such a large task. Yes, it was his field, and that made this plowing mean more to him than any he had done for his father back at Hickory Ford.

Dinner that day was as plain and quick as any other. Soon afterward Amos finished his meal, he took a bucket of water to Little Red. The mule needed to cool off before being given water. Amos then found a soft spot in the shade of the pin oak near the horse lot and stretched out for a noon rest. Amos was careful about Little Red getting an hour and a half rest at noon.

He wasn't sure if he was asleep or not when the shrill yelp

came from across the clearing. Sitting up in an instant, he saw Speckle running around one of the stumps in the clearing and barking angrily at something at its base. "Oh, Speckle, what have you gotten yoreself into now," said Amos as he raced to the barn to get the eye hoe.

Arriving at the stump, Amos found Speckle barking at a coiled cottonmouth water moccasin. Amos struck the snake's head solidly with the heavy eye hoe, killing it instantly, though its body continued to twist. Turning to his hound, Amos noticed a little blood on Speckle's face, just forward of the left eye. Holding the dog for a closer look, Amos could see that the dog had been bitten and that the area was already beginning to swell. Acting quickly, he used his pocket knife to cut open the fang marks and then held the dog's head down to speed the bleeding. With fear gripping his insides, Amos hastily carried Speckle to the cabin where he got out the plug of tobacco given him by Uncle Zeke. Cutting off a bite size piece as he had seen the men do many times, Amos put the tobacco into his mouth and began to chew it, all the while careful not to swallow any of the juice as he knew it would make him sick to his stomach. When the tobacco was thoroughly wet, he stuck it to the wound on the dog's face and tied it securely with a rag. Speckle couldn't open his mouth with this arrangement, but the poison had to be drawn out of the flesh.

Sitting there in front of the cabin on what had been such a wonderful day, Amos now knew real fear. His dog could die from the snake bite. He felt anger toward the snake and wished he could make it suffer like his dog, but the snake was dead now. It couldn't be hurt anymore.

Sensing fear within the hound as well, Amos held Speckle as he had done when the dog was a small pup. Amos thought back now to his getting the speckled pup from Uncle Zeke just last year. Uncle Zeke's hounds were well known far beyond Hickory Ford as great coon dogs, and he got top dollar for all his pups. But Speckle was the runt of the litter, and no one offered to buy him. Uncle Zeke knew how much Amos wanted a coon dog of his own. One Sunday after preaching he had called Amos out to his wagon. Lifting out a basket covered with a tow sack, Uncle Zeke said, "Here ye go, Amos, this is fer you." The glint of mischievous surprise in Uncle Zeke's eye assured Amos that the puppy was his, for real.

Speechless, Amos had managed to collect himself enough to pick up the puppy and hold him close. The dog and the boy had bonded almost immediately. Now, in the face of this threat, they drew together for comfort.

After an hour Amos figured that the tobacco poultice had done all it would do and also that Speckle would work the rag off as soon as he was released. Taking off the poultice, Amos led Speckle to a small pin oak near the cabin and tied him there in the shade. Standing there above the poison sick dog, the young man felt helpless. He asked himself repeatedly if there was some-thing that could be done, but knew of nothing. "Only if Grandpaw were here," he thought, "Grandpaw would know jest what to do."

Looking to the clearing where the snake was killed, Amos realized that he should go back to work. There was nothing more he could do for the dog now. Only time and the strength of the dog would tell the tale. So he slowly walked to the horse lot and untied the mule, all the while feeling guilty for leaving his dog.

Hitching now to the pole drag instead of the plow, Amos drove Little Red into the clearing and began to drag off the open and uneven soil. As opposed to the plowing which had taken about eight days, the dragging was completed that very afternoon. The plow had worked eight inches of soil with each pass and was slow work, often interrupted by the plow lodging itself under a root or stump. By contrast, the pole drag was eight feet wide and was fairly easy for the mule to pull. Also, it bounced over most obstacles instead of jamming underneath them.

With the excuse of resting the mule, Amos stopped often and walked back to the pin oak to check on Speckle's condition. The dog seemed to be very sick, and Amos hoped he just needed the time to recover.

That night while washing his dishes, Amos remembered that once on a fishing trip, Uncle Zeke had told him of another home remedy for snake bite. It was bacon grease and baking soda, mixed together and rubbed on the bite. Quickly he mixed up the paste and went to the dog, rubbing the remedy on that portion of the face which was swollen. By this time the swelling filled the entire left side of the hound's jaw and had closed the left eye. Amos looked with pity upon his hound dog and wished Speckle had left that old snake alone. There were just so many cotton-mouths in the bottoms that it was probably certain that either he or the dog would be bitten sooner or later. For certain, they would both be more careful after this.

First thing Sunday morning, Amos checked on his hound and found him still swollen and sick, but seemingly no worse than the afternoon before. All during his breakfast, Amos debated in his mind whether or not to go to church, with a sick dog to leave at home. On the one hand, he thought God would understand if he stayed, and besides, wasn't this like an ox being in a ditch?

But, on the other hand, there was nothing he could do for Speckle but what had been done. Besides, God might look upon the poor hound with more favor if Amos went to church. In situations like this at home, Amos remembered that his father would do what he could for the sick critter and then go on to church, trusting God to do the rest. "All right," said Amos aloud, "I'd better be gittin' on them clean overalls if I intend to make preachin' and not be late. Momma would throw a fit if she knew I ever showed up late for church."

The ride to Willow Point that Sunday morning would prove over time to be the longest Amos would remember. The sermon seemed to cover the entire Bible. During the closing prayer, Amos slipped in a few words on Speckle's behalf. Unsure whether God heard prayers for animals, Amos figured God knew how he felt about the dog. Afterward, one of the ladies asked Amos to come home with her family for dinner, assuring him that there would be lots of eats for a young man. Surprised by the invitation, Amos stammered while he was deciding between sitting at a table of delicious food and getting back to his sick hound. His affection for the dog won out, and he did his best to explain to the lady about having a snakebit dog back at home. She seemed to understand and said that perhaps he could make it another Sunday. Amos thanked her again and hurried off to the willow where Little Red was tied. Sensing Amos' excitement, Little Red eagerly loped out of Willow Point.

To Amos' relief, Speckle seemed to feel some better. The swelling was less than it had been that morning. Before his own dinner preparations, Amos recoated the jaw with bacon grease and baking soda paste. While cooking his dinner of hog jowl, beans, and corn bread, Amos cooked some extra just for Speckle, since the dog couldn't forage for himself.

Amos ate his dinner that Sunday thinking about all the

cottonmouths up and down the river. He couldn't help but think that there would be another snakebite since Speckle loved to roam. To tie up the hound all the time was unthinkable. His dinner hour was consumed by an emotional mixture of fear and anger.

After dinner, Amos lifted the single shot .22 from the nails on the wall and with a handful of shells, walked to the river. Having thought this over during dinner, he came to the conclusion that though bitterness wasn't Christian, it would be only wise for him to eliminate as much of the threat from snakes as possible.

During the plowing, he had killed several without going out of his way to look for any. Now he walked the river bank with intent. Over the next weeks, he intended to kill every cottonmouth that he could find near the cabin. Amos knew that snakes moved about and that he could never eliminate all the snakes, but he felt sure that he could reduce their number.

He spent all Sunday afternoon searching the river bank as well as the river itself. The anger which raged within him didn't help his aim any, and he became angry at himself for such sloppy shooting. It had taken him twenty shots to kill thirteen cottonmouths and that frustrated Amos because .22 shells were expensive and hard to come by in the local stores. But as he walked back to the cabin late in the afternoon, Amos felt that the cost was worth it. From now on he would be on the look out for any snake which might come near the clearing.

On Monday morning, Speckle still had a swollen mouth, though the left eye was opening some. Now more relieved than the day before Amos turned his attention to the garden to check for any seeds that might be popping through the surface. Some were through already, encouraging him. Amos began the day by dragging the clearing twice more. Though still not satisfied with its condition for planting, he decided to call it good enough. He accepted that only a team and disk would improve it. At the end of the day, Amos checked his stock of seed for the next day's planting.

About mid-morning on Tuesday Amos put a small plow point on the single stock, a simple cultivating plow. Without a drill, the seed corn would have to be dropped two by two from the hand into furrows made by the plow blade. Hand-dropping would be slow, but at least he wouldn't have to dig every hole. The single stock would open up the soil to the right depth. But where he had been able to cover the potatoes with the pole drag, the corn would have to be covered by rake.

It took until Thursday afternoon to plant the corn. When surveying the planting from the end of the clearing, Amos couldn't help but squint at the crooked rows. It was sure that Little Red wasn't an experienced mule, but then neither was he an experienced hand at driving. "Well," he said aloud, "I guess the seed will come up as well anyway, Little Red. But you and me both will have fun plowin' it, thet's fer sure."

Late Thursday afternoon, Amos planted half an acre of whippoorwill peas. He chose a spot at the far end of the clearing, planted by broadcasting the seed by hand, and then covering them with the pole drag. The shadows were long when he led Little Red back to the horse lot and unhitched him. The planting was finally done, after 25 days of straining and sweating. Both Amos and Little Red were leaner and stronger than the month before. Also, both of them were more seasoned workers at what was to become their life.

Amos gave Little Red extra ears of corn and brushed him down before going to the cabin to fix his own supper. He looked about him as he walked from the barn and made mental notes of those things that needed doing tomorrow before he left for Hickory Ford. It would be good to be home with family again, even if this clearing in the bottoms was fast becoming a part of him.

CHAPTER SIX

Summer

AS THE SUN SET THURSDAY EVENING, Amos perched on the horse lot fence and looked over the seven acres, plowed and planted. There it was, the first field he had worked alone. It was planted mostly in corn, with the far corner in whippoorwill peas. It certainly wasn't the smoothest looking planting job Amos had ever seen. In fact, it was probably the roughest. Amos had the uncomfortable thought that even Junior Simmons' fields would look neater. In spite of all his hard work, there were still clumps of weeds and grass, as well as the tops of old stumps which as yet had not been removed. The rows were so crooked that they could have been laid out by a snake.

His frustration was interrupted by Little Red's soft muzzle against his arm. Broken from his depression by the warm gesture of his mule, Amos said aloud, "What am I thinkin' of, Little Red? We did a right fine job of clearin' and plowin' that ol' rough clearin'. You especially worked up quite a few good sweats. I doubt if anybody could have done any better, 'specially with just a single mule, a plow, and a pole drag. Sure 'nuf, ol' Junior Simmons wouldn't have done near as good. Pro'bly hev' quit right off and jes' fished."

Reaching back and rubbing the high bony area between

the mule's ears, Amos remarked, "You're a right fine mule, Little Red, and gonna' be even better when this crop is picked come fall. Wal, I'd better git to puttin' thangs away, so we kin ride back to Hickory Ford in the mawnin' and git some of momma's good eats."The next morning the miles faded away quickly on the trip to Hickory Ford. It seemed that soon after he turned Little Red into the wagon track back in the bottoms, they were beginning to see the familiar farms of their home community. Neighbors called out to him as he rode down the dusty roads. Speckle, still weak after having been snakebitten, rode in a tow sack hanging from the saddle horn.

In the several weeks, they had been in the bottoms, there didn't seem to be much change in Hickory Ford. Amos, on the other hand, had changed dramatically. He was no longer a young boy, unsure of himself and living deep in the shadow of his family. Because of events of the past few weeks, he now had confidence in himself and the beginnings of his identity as a man.

Amos himself was not sure about all of this, and most of the time acted and thought much the same as any other boy his age. Though he was willing to work hard and long, thoughts of play and cheerful fun frequently came to mind. The new place had given some opportunities for fishing and swimming, but right now Amos was looking forward to Sunday afternoon and the crowd which would gather in the pasture by John Sawyer's store for a game of baseball. Amos himself was no great player, but probably enjoyed the fun of the game more than any other person there. For Amos, the game was secondary to the fun of the neighborhood gathering.

Soon they arrived in the area called Red Gum Ridge. It was actually a long stretch of high ground about a mile out from the edge of the hills. Its name came from the large stands of red gum trees that had originally covered the ridge. Most of these trees had been cleared to make way for the crops which now grew in large, open fields along either side of the road. There was a house about every half mile along the road, home to one of the many farm families which barely sweated out a living from the soil.

Before Amos knew it, Little Red was turning into his grandparent's place. Their store and house were well kept and tidy. Amos looked out over the fields behind the barn, fields that were well worked, with straight and even drill tracks from end to end. There appeared to be a good stand of cotton and corn. "That's good," Amos thought out loud, "no one likes to plant over." As Amos turned Little Red into the store yard, he wondered how good a stand of corn he would get back in the clearing.

"Wal, howdy, Amos," called John as he loaded sacks of groceries into the back of a customer's buggy. "Guess this means that you've got yore plantin' all done."

"Thet's right, Grandpaw, and I'm shore glad. Figured I'd come on home fer a few days and fatten back up at momma's table," answered Amos.

"Your momma's a fine cook. But come on in ta' the house and let your Grandmaw get a head start on yore eatin' before ya git home," said John.

Over dinner, they talked about the new place and the work to be done next. Grandpa planned to clear the timber from more land, increasing the acreage available to farm. Some of the timber to be cut would be hewn into ties for the railroad, some would be split into rails for fencing. Amos said he sorely needed some fencing so he could bring down his heifer and sow. John said that every tree either too big or too small for ties or rails would just be killed to stand and die. There was too much timber available to make it worthwhile to haul it to a mill for board lumber.

Before mid afternoon Amos arrived at his parents' farm. Disappointed to find everyone gone, he wondered where they could be. They seldom went anywhere during the week, so Amos made a quick ride around the fields. Puzzled at finding no one home, Amos turned Little Red into the horse lot with a few ears of corn and went on into the house. Seeing some leftover fried pies on the sideboard made Amos forget that he had just eaten dinner at his grandma's. After taking two of them for himself, he knew just what he wanted to drink with them. He walked outside to the cistern and drew up the bucket. Sure enough, he was in luck. In the bucket was a jar of sweet milk, chilled in the depths of the cistern. Amos could remember back to the previous winter when he and his father had filled the cistern with snow, chilling the brick-lined cavity even more than the natural deep-earth frigidity. Sitting down on the edge of the porch with the fried pies and a large glass of sweet milk, Amos said out loud, "Boy, this is what I call good eatin'."

Finishing the pies and milk, Amos decided to check on his heifer and sow. First, he walked to the hog pens to see how his sow was doing. Watching her sleep under the shade of a small tree, Amos thought back to his getting her from his poppa. She had been the runt of the litter and had not grown as large as the other gilts. James gave her to him as she wouldn't bring much at a sale. She was still small for a grown sow, and had never had more than seven pigs at a time. But she was easy to work with and had always been a good mother. Her last piglets were now fattening out, about ready to sell. Amos figured that from the looks of her, she should have another litter within the next few weeks. He noted that those pigs would be just about the right size for butchering come fall.

Next, he walked out into the pasture where his father kept the milk cows. It didn't take long to find his Jersey heifer feeding with the other cows. Amos didn't think she knew that she belonged to him, as she had lived her whole life right here on the farm. He figured that in the next few months she would be ready to breed and next spring there would be a calf.

Walking back to the house, he decided to look for something to occupy himself until his folks returned. Noticing that grass and weeds had gotten a foothold in the garden, he spent the next hour or so hoeing the garden. He was on his way to put the hoe away when he heard a team approaching. Looking out to the road he saw his parents coming into the yard in their wagon.

"Howdy, ya'll, good t' finally see someone t' home," called out Amos. "Whar' ya been?"

"Down t' the Benson's," responded his mother in a flat voice, "Mr. Benson took sick las' night. Doc Miller cain't do nothin' fer 'im. He's just so old. Likely won't last the night."

"Thet's a shame," answered Amos, "Mr. Benson was always so nice to us kids."

"Yore poppa's goin' to go back after supper to sit up with the fam'ly, likely be a long night," said Amos' mother before she walked on into the house to fix supper. Amos followed his father toward the barn to help unhitch the team and feed the stock.

"Wal', son, hev ya got yore crop planted?" asked James.

"Yeah, Poppa, it's all in the ground, but ya should see them rows, crookeder than a hound's hind leg," said Amos.

"I recall thet my first rows weren't any too straight either, it takes practice," said James. "You'll get the hang of it in time."

"I hope so," said Amos.

"How's it goin' down thar', all by yourself," asked James.

"All right, I reckon. Kinda tough at times, though. Nobody to ask questions of, like when I'm workin' with you, " said Amos. "Like when Speckle got snakebite this past Saturday. I shore wished you or Grandpaw were there. I was scared he'd die, though I done all I knowed. First I bled it, then I put a chaw on it, and then I doped it with a poultice of bacon grease and baking soda. It took till yester'dy for all the swelling to go down."

James heard the isolation in his son's voice and replied, "Sounds like ya did all any man could 'a done. In situations like thet, just remember what ya've been taught and think things through. Yore momma and me worry 'bout ya, but at the same time, we have faith in ya. I guess ya do get awful lonely though."

"Yeah," replied Amos, "at times it bothers me t' be alone. I've gone to church twice at Willow Point, and that has hep'ed, gettin' out with other folks."

"Good, Amos," said James, "a body away from his family needs other people, and 'specially the Lord. I'm proud of ya for goin' to church on yore own, instead of fishin', or even jest keepin' on workin'. The good Lord knew that six days was enough fer a man ta work. Thet's why he made Sunday. An', there's been many a Satur'dy night when I was shore glad, too."

"Yeah," laughed Amos, "my Satur'dy nights have been that way."

Supper caught them up on all the news, both from the new place in the bottoms and from Hickory Ford. After supper Amos helped his momma with the dishes and his poppa walked the mile down the road to the Bensons to wait with the family for whatever happened.

The dishes gave Amos and his momma some time together,

something that they hadn't had since he had gone to the bottoms. The two of them were close for several reasons. Beyond being mother and son, he was her last child, her baby, and would always be special. And during the years of illness which had plagued her, as the youngest he had been given the task of staying at the house to cook and clean while the older ones in the family were in the field. So his lateness in maturing as a farm hand had positioned him to become very close to his mother.

"How's yore cookin' comin' along?" asked his mother.

"Fair, I reckon. Mostly purty plain, though. An' it's tough to work in the field and cook too," replied Amos.

"Yeah, I know all about that. I raised you kids and cooked the meals and warshed the clothes and put in long days in the field besides. An' it seemed like thar' was always one of you kids on a pallet under a shade tree. It's a wonder a snake didn't bite one of ya. Many a hard day, that's for sho'."

Amos sensed a bitterness about the hardness of those days and intentionally turned the conversation to her teaching him to bake a cake. She brightened, finding a paper to write down a few recipes for sweets such as cobblers and cakes. They enjoyed their time that evening, and each felt good upon retiring.

Walking out into the kitchen the next morning Amos remembered about his father's business of the night before and asked, "What time did poppa come home, momma?"

"Jest a few minutes ago. He's out feedin' now. Mr. Benson died about daylight," replied his momma. There was a choke in her voice now. "Shore goin' to miss 'im. He was a mighty fine neighbor, an a good father fer them young 'uns too. You know they's Myrtle's kids from her first husband who died several years back. He always treated them kids like they's his own."

His father came in with the haggard look of sleeplessness and deep sorrow. The breakfast was unusually quiet. Over coffee, talk of the day's needs began.

"I'll go on down ta hep warsh and dress the body. Myrtle shouldn't have to do that. An' I'll stop and git Clara and Reba to hep too," said Amos' momma. "Has anyone told the neighbors so's the men will know to come and dig the grave?" she added.

"Jack's takin' care of getting some men together. I said that I'd meet 'em at the graveyard about mid mawnin'," responded James.

Amos spoke now, "I'll go hep dig, poppa. Ya need to git yoreself some sleep."

James turned now to his youngest son and nodded both out of agreement and pride that Amos was now taking the responsibilities of a man.

While his father slept, Amos drove the team to the graveyard to help with his first grave-digging. The red clay was stubborn dirt. Even so, in a close-knit community like Hickory Ford, there were several men and older boys to share the effort. They talked mostly of crops and weather, trying to avoid talking about the death. The time for tears and sadness would come with the funeral.

Death seemed to come often but people really never got used to it. The country folk were strong from hard work and fresh air, but death was a common occurrence. The very young and the very old were the most frequent to die, but accidents and illnesses took the otherwise active and healthy also. Pneumonia was a big killer, with virtually no cure. When a doctor was needed, half a day was a fast response.

After the grave digging, Amos drove back home, where he

washed off the sweat and dirt before putting on his best overalls and shirt. Meanwhile, his mother had returned to cook several dishes for the Benson family. Before the sun was straight up, his family loaded the food dishes into their wagon and drove a mile to the Benson's. Helping carry the food into the Benson kitchen, Amos noticed that other women had also brought food. The table and sideboard were heaped with dishes of freshly prepared food to help the family through their initial grief. Amos' family and several others who had come to help before the burying shared in the dinner also, the companionship encouraging Myrtle and the children to get some food into them.

The mood was somber in the house. To escape it, Amos stepped out to the woodshed. There, he was startled by Mr. Benson's body, lying on some boards and covered by a sheet. He had forgotten about the body and scolded himself that it made sense that Mr. Benson had to be kept somewhere until the funeral.

Amos walked away from the woodshed and was even with the front of the house when he noticed Willie Taylor drive into the yard with a coffin in the wagon bed. On short notice, Willie had turned some rough boards into a final resting place for Mr. Benson. Now, at James Sawyer's direction, the wagon was positioned near the wood shed. Amos felt it most unfortunate that he had to help place the body into the long box. He thought that he was glad Mr. Benson was dressed so the coldness of the body couldn't really be felt.

Most of the neighbors turned out for the funeral at the graveyard, probably a hundred people altogether. Several ladies from the Methodist church sang hymns, but, of course, there was no music to accompany them. It was a somber time for each and all as Mr. Benson had been well-liked. Death has a way of reminding every one of their own mortality, particularly the elderly.

Sunday afternoon finally came. With the crops planted and farm work slackened a little, there was a holiday spirit among the many who gathered around the large oaks at the near end of John Sawyer's pasture. The field was kept particularly clean and was a favorite gathering place for a Sunday afternoon baseball game.

By mid-afternoon the store yard was filled with wagons, horses and mules. Teams were picked as soon as there were enough players to justify hitting the string ball. Before long, there were more than enough men and boys to have field teams. The women and girls sat on pallets under the oaks, chatting and occasionally cheering a hit or a run.

After the past month of isolation, Amos became animated with the excitement and used his usual position of shortstop as a stage before a crowd. He would taunt the batters and runners of the other team while cheering on his own teammates. In the last inning of the game, Amos had singled to first base, then stolen second just before Avery Dacus slammed a ball over the pasture fence for an easy home run. Amos took the opportunity to show off by doing a handstand and working his way around third base to home plate in this inverted position, a feat no one else there could have performed.

The ball game left a happy and exhausted group around the pump for a cold swallow and wash-up late that Sunday afternoon—a joyous time after a week of farm labor followed by a funeral. Now the next week would not seem quite so bad, and everyone would be looking forward to another game next Sunday. After the washing and goodbyes, Amos turned to go into Grandpa and Grandma Sawyer's house for a piece of pie or cake. But there before him stood Marie Johnson and Myrtle Jackson, all flashing eyes and smiles. "Wal, howdy, Amos. Ya shore air a good ball player. Whar'd ya larn to walk upside down that-a-way?" Marie's eyes could have cleaned his face, if they's had a cloth, Amos though.

"Uh, ... jus somers, ... I guess," responded Amos, caught entirely off guard.

"Will ya do it agin fer us next Sund'y, Amos?" asked Myrtle.

Something in Amos caught emphasis upon the "fer us" part and shied around it. "Wal," said Amos, "I don't know iffen I'll be back next week. May jes stay in the bottoms."

With the change of subject, the girls showed no less interest in Amos. "Amos, don't ya git skeared, I mean, down in them bottoms all by yore own self?" asked Myrtle.

"Naw, of course not. There's nothing down there I cain't handle," said Amos. Even through his swollen pride, Amos still noticed the admiration of the two girls. He wondered if he had just stepped into trouble. Too late now, he thought, as he said goodbye and walked toward the waiting dessert. As he walked into his grandma's kitchen, Amos couldn't help but wonder why he said such foolish things around girls.

The next few days Amos busied himself by helping his father with general farm chores. To learn more about farming, Amos now pried his father with questions about everything from protecting stock from flies to holding a plow straight. By having his own place to work, Amos now felt a great need to know more about farming. It seemed only natural for him to follow in the life of his father, grandfather, and generations before.

Thursday noon found Amos riding Little Red down the wagon track to his cabin. It had been a long time since he was here at his new home—it seemed—yet it was in reality only a week. Riding into the clearing, he gazed in awe. His corn rows had emerged now, long green stripes running from one end to the other. The peas at the other end of the clearing were up and gave the ground a greenish cast because they were so thick. Stepping into the cabin, Amos looked out to the garden, pleased to see all the vegetables taking form there in the dark soil.

Turning Little Red into the lot and giving him a few ears of corn, Amos began to carry his parcels to the cabin. Halfway, he stopped stock still as his eyes were fixed upon footprints in the yard. They certainly weren't his. It had rained while he was away and these tracks were made just as the ground was beginning to set again.

Setting down his bags, Amos followed the tracks into the cabin and looked around at his belongings. Everything had been gone through, but nothing seemed to have been taken. Reaching up above one of the few attic planks, he pulled down his .22 rifle and let out a great sigh of relief. Now he was glad that he took the precaution of hiding it. But in the future, he would have to do a better job of hiding his things, or see about putting a lock on the cabin door.

Walking back outside now he followed the tracks down to the river where the mark of a dugout canoe was obvious in the mud along the water's edge. So this man had come from the river and probably knowing that Amos was gone, had investigated his place. Who could it have been and why? Certainly, it was only neighborly to come visiting, but somehow Amos believed that this barefooted man had not come to visit, but to spy. And that was another thing, not many men went barefooted, especially down in these bottoms with all the cottonmouths about.

With his supplies stowed and his dinner eaten, Amos put an edge on the eye hoe and began hoeing the garden as the weeds and grass were growing as fast as the vegetables. Once that was finished, he used the hoe and rake to open up the soil for another row of radishes and onions. Now satisfied that his garden would soon produce something for his table, Amos turned his efforts to hoeing the corn field, an effort which took until Saturday night to complete. Riding to Willow Point for church Sunday morning held more pleasure than past trips as now Amos felt some identity with the bottoms and even Willow Point itself. Also, there was no sick dog at home to fret over during the preaching. This Sunday Amos took a dinner offer from one of the church families. He was always happy to eat a woman's cooking again, as his never quite measured up. It was near dinner time on Monday when Grandpa John's team pulled into the clearing. Amos had been anxious for his grandpa's arrival and wondered if something had happened to delay him. This was to be a longer trip as John intended to spend several days to help with clear some more land.

"Howdy, Grandpaw," shouted Amos, 'bout give ya out."

"One of the sows picked this mawnin' to have her piglets and I jes' couldn't leave Grandma to see to them," Looking first to the corn in the clearing and then to the vegetables in the garden, John spoke with unveiled pride, "Wal, son, ya got a real good start here. This place sure looks a sight better than the day I dropped ya off. You've done real good, Amos.""Thanks, Grandpa," was about all Amos could say in response. Praise was sometimes difficult for a young man and for Amos praise from his grandpa was about the greatest thrill in the world.

As usual, Grandma Janey had sent along a nice dinner for the two of them before they had to rely upon their own cooking. Their conversation slowed as they each ate with an appreciation for the tasty food. After eating their fill, they put up the leftovers for their supper. During their meal, Amos told his grandpa of the unshod visitor who had searched the cabin. Disturbed, Grandpa John hesitated before telling Amos that though there probably wasn't anything to worry about, it wouldn't hurt to keep a sharp eye out. Also, Grandpa John said that he would bring a chain and lock on the next trip to the bottoms.

From the moment they finished their dinner on Monday until noon Wednesday, the two of them worked steadily at enlarging the clearing. Double bit axes were used to cut a groove around the trunk of any tree over eighteen inches in diameter. These "girdled" trees would eventually decay and fall down. All the smaller trees, suitable for rails or ties, were cut down. From these, Amos would also get his firewood. He would burn the small limbs with the rest of the brush.

Amos knew clearing out the remaining small trees and sprouts would be hard work. Any roots that might catch the plow had to be dug up. Among next year's corn, the standing dead trees would appear as great gray ghosts around the clearing. Amos thought it a shame to waste so much good timber. As John had explained, there wasn't much market for lumber since there was so much available. But the land, once cleared, would produce crops which could be converted into cash. With Grandpa John gone back to Red Gum Ridge, Amos faced several weeks of hard work cutting and piling the small trees and brush. Of course, Speckle helped by investigating each turn of the earth or new pile of brush. Both he and Amos were especially careful of cottonmouths and for their vigil escaped being bitten.

For several weeks he would alternate clearing and other chores. One task which he had been thinking of but putting off all summer was the cleaning of the cabin floor. Until now it had only been swept. What it really needed was a good scrubbing. A hot summer day would be the time to do it so that the heat of the day would dry the floor quickly.

One morning when he would rather do anything than go back to clearing, Amos decided to scrub the floor. Taking some ashes from the ash bucket and mixing them with hot water to make lye, he poured the solution over the floor. As he had no brush, he used corn shucks from the barn and twisted them into a makeshift brush. Thus outfitted, he got on his hands and knees and scrubbed the planks until only the wood showed. He then rinsed the floor with hot water, but as he had no mop, he just let the water run through the cracks between the boards. He had watched women and girls scrub floors just this way many times, remembering that it looked like hard work. Now he knew it was.

Some of these cracks, those over a quarter of an inch wide, could admit cold drafts during winter months. Amos had no rug of any kind and thought that he would just have to live with the cracks. Actually, such cracks weren't all that uncommon in houses. Some people even believed that the fresh air helped people stay healthier. The weeks sped by. Amos found that he enjoyed building up a place in the bottoms all by himself. Never before had he borne a responsibility such as this. Before, Amos had worked in the shadow of his family. In large families like his, it was common for big jobs to be given to older children while only basic chores were assigned to the younger.

Life in the bottoms was not so hard as he had imagined in the first few days. True, the bottoms had swarming mosquitoes whereas the hills back home had few. The mosquito bar supplied by Grandpa John helped. Besides, after a few weeks, Amos didn't even seem to notice the flying pests.

The garden was now providing fresh vegetables as a welcome variety to Amos' plain diet of corn bread and beans. Still, he was dependent upon John's trips for eggs and butter, and he had no fresh milk. Wild blackberry thickets grew throughout the bottoms. As they ripened, the juicy berries provided a big treat for Amos at meal time. Not only did he have fresh blackberries every day for several weeks, but he had picked a large tub full and sent them back to his Grandma Janey for jelly and jam. Amos looked forward to eating those throughout the coming year. As the vegetables and the corn began to get some height and strength, Amos and Little Red cultivated the crops with the single stock. This was a slow procedure as the plow only had a single iron point which displaced the soil to either side as it was pulled by a single mule or horse. Three passes were required to work the middle area between two rows, and even then some weeds would be left by the small plow. But it was faster than hoeing the middles by hand.

Though there was much work to be done during the summer, it was not accompanied with the same pressure that attended spring plowing and planting. Amos was able to take many explorations in the bottoms away from the clearing. His mental notes of trees with hollow pockets up high that could be used as dens for coons or squirrels would serve him well come winter. He memorized unusual features, such as odd-shaped trees or sloughs for those dark nights when a hunter struggled to find his way home.

It was during one of these trips away from the clearing when Amos came found the sign of wild hogs. The sign was in a cane thicket where the hogs had upon occasion bedded down. These were pigs which had escaped some farm and had become wild. It was natural for hogs to go wild once away from the domestic life of barns and daily feedings. Here in the bottoms, they found their own feed and sought out other hogs for company. Amos knew wild hogs could be extremely dangerous, so he was wary whenever he came upon their sign. As the weeks came and went, Amos kept an eye to the river, but there was no sign of the night people, as he had named them. There were nights when Speckle set to barking out by the river, but whenever Amos got up to check it out, he found nothing. Either a boat had passed before Amos could get up, or perhaps it was just a raccoon feeding along the river bank.

The Little Sandy was only about twenty-five feet wide and averaged about four to five feet deep in the middle. As rivers go, it was small and short, adding its water into the Big Sandy River at Willow Point. The river channel had, over the centuries, cut such a meandering course that the locals said it was "crooked as a snake." The river was of great significance in Amos' life. The tall timber surrounding its banks was a haven for wild game. It gave Amos his two favorite recreations: fishing and swimming. The very land Amos farmed came from the river. Silt deposited over thousands of years provided a fertile soil that was easy to work. Also, it could be a route of travel, as the night people used it to get wherever they were going.

The river fascinated Amos. It provided the very elements of life itself, from the crops growing in the rich soil it had left in the bottoms to the fish that were a mainstay in Amos' diet. Not only that, it offered something equally important in the life of a boy becoming a man - challenge and adventure. Early in the summer, Amos asked John to show him how to build a dugout canoe. After some coaxing, John assured Amos that later in the summer they would build one together. It was difficult for Amos to think of anything besides the promised dugout canoe as he plowed the corn for the last time. This time Amos used the largest plow point for the single stock because he wanted to throw as much dirt to the rows as possible to cover any remaining weeds and to bank the roots to hold moisture. This last plowing was called "laying by" the crop as it was now too big to work without damaging it.

The very next day after Amos had laid by his corn, he heard a team approaching. It was not only John but Uncle Zeke as well. Amos exuded excitement as he ran to the wagon.

"Howdy, Grandpaw. Howdy Uncle Zeke," shouted Amos, "I can see by yore fishin' poles that yore on serious business here."

"Thet's right, Amos," replied Zeke, "John made the mistake of comin' by my place this mawnin', and I jes invited myself along. I aim to ketch me one of them big cats ye got down here in this river."

"Uncle Zeke, sometimes I catch 'em so big that it takes me several days to eat 'em," responded Amos. At this Zeke's eyes bulged and he stepped down from the wagon so fast that he almost fell. "Hold on thar, Zeke," shouted John, "thet river's been thar since before ya were born and it'll still be thar when we leave. Ya fall and break a leg, and there'll be no fishin' fer any of us."

It turned out that the two older men had come down for a few days of fishing and taking it easy. And, of course, they would help Amos with cutting out a canoe. It was this task that Amos insisted they start that very afternoon. John agreed, but Zeke complained that he hadn't even gotten his fishing line wet. He relented when Amos reminded him of the big dew in the early morning that would soak them if they waited until tomorrow morning. "Besides, Uncle Zeke," said Amos, "the fishin' is better early in the mawnin'." Somewhat satisfied, Zeke agreed, and the canoe cutting effort was under way.

Leading John's mule Gray Jack and carrying the crosscut

saw, ax, sledgehammer, and wedges, the three of them set out for some fallen cypress trees which Zeke recalled from their duck hunting last winter. Speckle fairly bounced with the excitement, but Little Red bawled out a loud protest at being left behind. After some searching, John selected a solid but dry fallen cypress about 30 inches in diameter. By using the long cross cut saw, a fourteen-foot length was cut from the trunk. This log was then split lengthways into two pieces with the wedges and sledgehammer. The thicker slab was then chained for Gray Jack to drag back to the cabin where it would be shaped into a dugout.

Once back at the cabin, the log was positioned over two smaller logs which would bring it to a working height. At this point, Uncle Zeke abandoned the dugout project to pick up his fishing gear and walk to the river. In spite of the hard, physical labor of the afternoon, Zeke headed for the river with a spring in his step. John stayed behind to show Amos how to use the axe to shape the ends. The insides would later be taken out with an adze, and the final shaping would be done with drawknives.

Amos let the older men fish during their trip while he steadily worked on his canoe. From time to time his grandpa or great uncle gave advice and more than once this served to keep him from ruining the craft. This was a high time for Amos because not only did he enjoy his grandfather's and great uncle's company more than about anyone's, but to be here in the bottoms with them and all the while cutting out a dugout canoe for himself was an exhilarating experience.

On the afternoon before John and Zeke had to leave for Hickory Ford, the three men sought relief from the heat. Down in the timbered bottoms, it was rare to feel a breeze unless one blew along the river channel. Amos usually took a swim to escape the heat, but he was surprised to see the older men join him so quickly. Though he was used to swimming without his clothes, he was embarrassed to see his grandpa and great uncle shuck theirs. But it wasn't a problem for these men who had swum naked since early boyhood.

After the river water had cooled all of them, Zeke asked, "Amos, air thar' any good logs in the river here bouts?"

"Ya mean fer hoggin', Uncle?" asked Amos.

"Yep, I aim to git me one of them big cats one way or t' other," answered Uncle Zeke.

Amos knew what his uncle wanted, though he had never hogged fish. Hogging was what folks around Hickory Ford called it when a person waded into the river and used their hands to search the sunken hollow logs for fish. Catfish particularly liked the security and shade of a hollow log. Always in the person's mind was the hope of not catching hold of a cottonmouth water moccasin.

After Amos had pointed out the location of some nearby logs, the three of them worked together to locate all the openings and block them off so Uncle Zeke could feel his way along inside to locate the fish. His initial efforts produced two catfish that would weigh five or six pounds each, and though he was quite pleased, he still wanted a "big un" to take home.

Uncle Zeke's persistence paid off when he felt the head of a large fish. Usually, he slipped the thumb of either hand into the sides of the fish's mouth and got a good grip before hauling the fish out of the log, but this fish was so large he ran a small rope through the fish's gills before he set to pull out the large catfish. Getting the fish out of the log was one thing, but holding onto it once it was in open water was quite another. After a long hard struggle the fish tired out, and Zeke pulled his prize out of the river and onto the bank.

Shaken with the excitement, he shouted, "John, would ya lookie here, sech a fish as I've never hogged 'afore. Why, John, it'll go at least thirty pounds."

Though caught up in the excitement as well, John ventured his opinion that the weight would be closer to twenty pounds. The fish was so big that it would barely fit in the wash tub the men had brought to take their fish home in. As the big catfish curled around the edge of the tub, his tail was almost back in his mouth. Amos was sure that John and Zeke would have several hours of friendly argument until they reached Red Gum Ridge. There the scales at the Sawyer's store would settle once and for all just how big the fish really was.

As the summer progressed, Amos' days were full of hard work and good fishing. The canoe enabled him to explored up and down the river for several miles. On all of his exploration trips, thoughts of the night people often came to him. He looked everywhere for signs of other men but never saw anything. Upriver he did find more sign of the wild hogs and hoped that they didn't get close to his clearing. Hogs could do a lot of damage to crops and gardens.

By early September the corn was so tall that Amos couldn't reach the tops. He anticipated a large yield, which he would need for feed. It would take a lot of corn to get his mule through the winter and then in condition for the hard work of next spring. And, he did feel some guilt that his father was still looking after animals that were indeed his responsibility. He wanted a good crop to prove that the place would produce enough corn to feed all of his livestock. While he knew that he couldn't bring his livestock down to the bottoms this year, that was his ultimate goal. Over the last several weeks he had, with John's direction, split enough rails for a hog pen and small pasture so that he would be ready when the time came to bring down the stock. The only thing left to do on this year's crop was harvesting the corn, but that would have to wait until October. However, there were weeks when Amos doubted that there would be any corn to pick. The local raccoon population, which up till now Amos had so treasured, had quickly found the corn as it ripened to the milk stage. Morning after morning he would walk the middles and survey the damaged ears from the coons having feasted the night before. Many nights he slept out in the corn with Speckle and the single shot .22, but only managed to kill three of the night marauders. Speckle though did keep enough of the raccoons away to allow most of the corn to mature past the sweet stage. Amos controlled his fury by reminding himself that this winter he would get his turn at a fur harvest and hoped that his fur sales would make up for the corn losses.

The late weeks of summer had been the time for cutting and shocking of the pea hay. The hay had been cut by hand with a scythe, as the effort to bring a mowing machine from Hickory Ford was too much trouble. Amos and John had cut the hay on one of the grandfather's trips as a wagon was needed to move the dried hay to the barn.

The haying had proven to be some of the most difficult work of Amos' summer. Every stroke of the scythe through the thick pea vines had been strenuous. And, even with the vines laid to dry, they still were heavy burdens to fork into the barn loft for winter storage. During these days of late summer, little air stirred and the high heat and equally high humidity made hard work almost unbearable. By noon their clothes were as wet from sweat as if they had been swimming in the river. But the two of them persevered. They knew that this hay was rich and would serve as good feed for Little Red throughout the winter. Amos was amazed at his grandpa's strength and endurance during the hay work. He had always known that his Grandpa was one of the stronger men around Hickory Ford, though he was smaller than most. Amos wondered at how a man of his age could still work as hard and as long. All this was part of the mystery Amos found in his Grandpa.

Several trips had been made to Hickory Ford during the late summer as his chores at the cabin would not require his constant presence again until the corn needed to be picked. Also, late fall and winter would be the beginning of some serious timber cutting as the sap would have gone down from the trees to the roots, making for better timber.

It was during one of these trips that Amos' momma surprised him with a birthday cake. The occasion was a Sunday dinner, and all the family was gathered at his folk's place. It seemed that everyone wanted to celebrate Amos' birthday as much as he did, or at least, they were as interested in eating some of the chocolate cake. Amos enjoyed the cake and the time with his family, but within himself sensed something changing which was more important than cake. Amos realized that he was now considering things more important than chocolate cake.

Sixteen was a special birthday, for it marked a turning point. Many girls were married before the end of their sixteenth year. Boys usually waited a little longer. It was a time when the community expected the young person to "make a hand" in the field or around the house. Word seemed to have gotten around the community for during the next week several people congratulated

Amos on his birthday.

Much to his frustration, Marie Johnson was one of them. It happened while Amos was getting some items for his mother at the store in Hickory Ford. "Happy birthday, Amos," Marie called out from the other side of the store, "herd ya've turned sixteen now. I'll be sixteen next summer, an I'll shore be glad. My Poppa says I can git hitched when I'm sixteen."

Embarrassed that Marie would say such a thing in front of the people in the store, Amos went outside and made conversation with some of the men until Marie and her momma left the store. Though he refused to look at her, Amos could tell from the corner of his eye that Marie was casting glances his way as they walked away. Amos was wise enough to know that Marie was hinting for him to court her for marriage, but he was not to be caught up in such a trap. Amos just hoped that word didn't spread all over Hickory Ford that they were sweet on each other.

CHAPTER SEVEN

First Harvest

IN LATE SEPTEMBER AMOS DECIDED to spend a few weeks with his folks back at Hickory Ford. The work was caught up on his place, and his corn wouldn't be ready to pick until late October. Amos knew that his parents could use some help in picking their cotton and he was willing to help even if cotton picking was one of his least favorite jobs.

After stopping for a short visit with John, Amos rode on to his parents', arriving in the early afternoon. He found the family in the cotton patch where they were heavy into their first picking. The family was pleased but surprised to see him as he was unexpected. After the greetings were over, Amos offered to take his mother's sack and finish the afternoon for her, since there wasn't a spare cotton sack for him in the field.

"Wal', Amos," responded his mother, "I don't know what to do with an afternoon off."

"I do, Momma," answered Amos, "take the extra time to fix me somethin' special for supper."

Walking away laughing, Amos' mother began to talk to herself about what she might fix for their supper. Amos bent his back over the stalks and began the steady picking which would fill the sack with cotton. He knew that he could never keep up with his mother at picking, but did feel good about taking her place, even for just half an afternoon. For the rest of the afternoon, Amos joined the family in the picking, all the time sharing news of the weeks since he'd been home.

The cotton had begun to open in mid-September. The picking had started when about half the bolls were open. Later pickings would follow as the rest of the bolls opened. It would take three pickings to get all the cotton from the plants, with the last picking being rough and yielding little. It took about 1500 pounds in the field to make a bale, with an average adult picking about 250 pounds a day. Whenever the pickers' sacks were full, they lifted in concert, carrying the load to the wagon. Each sack would be weighed and then emptied into the wagon. An adult sack would be six feet in length while children's sacks would be smaller in proportion to their size. A six-foot sack packed with cotton would weigh around 60 pounds, and a good picker would weigh in around 300 pounds per day, with pay being given per hundred pounds.

A wagon full of trampled down cotton would hold about one bale. When the wagon was full, they would hitch up a team and pull it to the gin at Hickory Ford. There a suction pipe would pull the cotton up from the wagon a little at a time. The gin would clean the trash from the cotton and remove the seed. Each processed bale would weigh about 500 pounds and would be sold through the gin for the cash money needed by the family to buy those items which could not be made or grown at home.

But more than helping his folks with the cotton picking, the fall was a time for Amos to enjoy his home community. Families who had little or no cotton crop of their own would hire out to help their neighbors, and the picking became a great social

event. There would be a steady run of talk in the field and sometimes even singing to pass away the hard hours. And the dinners
would be large meals at the home of whoever owned the crop.
This required that one of the women or older girls remain at the
house all morning to cook for the family and field hands. Some
neighbors worked together every fall. Though unrelated by blood,
neighbors in this way became close over the years.

Cotton picking was symbolic of their way of life: long hours
of hard work out in the elements, shared by a family and its neighbors. In the mornings the green cotton leaves would be laden with
the heavy fall dew. Everyone's pant legs and shoes would become
soaked before the sun dried everything off. The cotton was soft,
but the ends of the open bolls were sharp. After several weeks
of steady, rapid picking, the ends of the pickers' fingers would
become scratched raw. And, the long hours bent over the rows of
stalks made for very sore backs.

Usually, only the steady talk relieved the harshness of the
days. But one afternoon the pickers in James Sawyer's field were
treated to a surprise and mystery. Oscar Jackson rode his old mule
to the field and called to his daughter, Myrtle, to come out of
the field. Quickly, there began a heated discussion about which
the father was markedly upset, and the daughter was short on
words. After just a few minutes of this, he remounted the mule
and pulled her up behind him and rode off toward their place.
This drama gave the pickers something to take their attention off
sore fingers and backs. James expressed a few moderating words
about the Jackson's having a family matter which was of no one
else's concern. That put a stop to the chatter, but not the mental
speculation.

The situation somewhat resolved itself the next morning

when Myrtle returned with Homer Beasley and announced that they had just gotten married the night before. They both seemed elated about their situation, except that Homer did not appear pleased at living with Myrtle's folks. Congratulations were in order from all hands. Much thought was given to the suddenness of the event, but such matters would not be spoken of in public.

Amos stayed with his folks for almost six weeks until most of their crops were out of the field. During this time he had taken three quick trips back to his place in the bottoms to check on everything, though there wasn't much to go wrong. Still, he felt better knowing that everything was all right, though the fifteen-mile trip took him up to four hours, with Little Red trotting part of the way. Because of the distance, he always rode down in the afternoon and spent the night before returning early the next morning. On each trip, he looked carefully about for any signs of the night people, but there was no evidence of anyone having been around the place. Amos was glad that he had taken the precaution of hiding the dugout in a nearby slough and had carried the .22 rifle to his folks. Also, he had left the cabin door chained and locked to deny entrance to any would-be thieves. With summer now past the nights had a sharp coolness to them which was a relief from the hot nights of the summer. It was common for folks to sleep fitfully in the heat and humidity of summer, but this was not so in the fall when the cool nights made a quilt feel good. Also, the cool weather and nearness of frost considerably slowed down the flies and other insects that could in the summer make farm life miserable for the people and stock alike. The coming of the first hard frost would signal a time of great change. Leaves fell from the trees and small plants, increasing visibility in the woods. The frost also set the stage for corn picking as now the ears could be snapped from the stalk easily. And, the lower temperatures allowed for the killing of hogs as the meat would not spoil while it was being preserved by salt during the cool weather.

Hog killing, like so many events in farm life, was shared by the entire family and some of the neighbors. When the chosen day arrived, much preparation would have been made for the process. A large kettle of water would be heated over a hot fire until the water came to a boil. Then the hog in question would be shot with a .22 rifle or knocked between the eyes with a large hammer. In either case, a long-bladed knife would be stuck into the hog's neck to let it bleed out to drain the meat of blood. The hog then would be dragged to the kettle and the hot water applied to its skin to break loose the hair which would be scraped away. If the family possessed a large enough kettle, the hog would be immersed in the scalding water. Sometimes the hair was caught and later cleaned for various uses. Once the hide was scraped clean, the hog would be cut open and the entrails removed. The carcass would be cut in half, sawn down the middle through the spine.

Most of this work was accomplished by the men while the women were in the kitchen getting ready to put up the meat. The larger pieces like the shoulders, hams, and sides of bacon were cut apart and laid in the smoke house to be heavily salted. The scraps were ground up for sausage and seasoned according to that family's taste before being fried and packed into glass jars for storage. The whole process took a full day but yielded enough meat to last the family for months.

With the Sawyer's cotton picked and two hogs killed and salted down, Amos' father turned his attention to the corn field, where another series of long days at hard work for the whole family awaited. It took four workers to make it go smoothly, with

James and Amos on opposite sides of the wagon and picking two rows each. Tom walked behind the wagon to pick the row which was pushed down by the wagon, called the "down row," as well as a row on each side. Tom's wife, Lizbeth, rode in the wagon seat and drove the team.

In this manner, the family could pick seven rows on each pass through the field. The ears of corn, complete with their shuck, would be snapped off the stalk and tossed into the wagon bed. When it was filled, everyone would get a break of sorts as the wagon had to be taken to the barn for unloading. Here it was driven alongside the corn crib so that the ears could be shoveled out of the wagon and through the crib window. And so it went until the entire field was gathered. Though the crop had been picked, the ears too small to gather and the stalks would provide forage for the livestock throughout the winter. Once in the crib, the corn would serve as feed for the livestock throughout the next year. The mules could get through the winter, when there was really not much heavy work on a farm, eating hay and just a little corn. Next spring would be a different story. Plowing took lots of energy, more than a mule could get from just hay or grazing. Several ears of corn had to be fed to each mule every morning, noon, and night during this critical period of heavy work. Corn was important to the family's cows, also. The cows provided milk and butter, two essential elements of farm life. Cream, the source of butter, was important in another way. Separated from the milk, it was taken to town once a week and sold, one of the few sources of cash for many farm families. Excess milk would be given to the hogs to supplement their diet. The primary winter feed for the chickens was corn, either fed whole or ground. Chickens were kept mainly for eggs, The occasional fried chicken dinner was a real treat. Corn was also the primary feed for the hogs, although at certain times of the year the hogs could live pretty well by foraging in the woods. It was a common saying that corn in the crib was like money in the bank.

The corn picking, like all other hard tasks, was not without its amusements. Family members competed and joked among themselves. Those overthrown ears kept everyone wary of the others' throwing ability, as an ear of corn thrown against one's head was a painful experience on a cold day. Lizbeth, perched on the wagon seat, was particularly wary of ears which might catch her in the back.

The fall was a favorite time for hunting as game animals born in the spring were large enough to be hunted in the autumn. Plus, the weather was much more pleasant. The relative lack of biting insects to distract the hunter helped improve a rifleman's aim. Many evenings after the field work was ended Amos took his rifle up the hollow above the barn and shot a few squirrels for the next day's breakfast. Also, without leaves on the trees, game was much easier to locate.

Toward the middle of November, Amos loaded up Little Red with what loose supplies he could carry and, with Speckle following along, headed back to his cabin on the Little Sandy. This trip seemed to take longer than most as Amos paid attention to the changes in the farms along the way. These farms were also progressing with the seasons, and Amos noted the yields of the crops as well as the growing stacks of firewood in preparation for winter.

In the past few months, he had grown to see the world larger than Hickory Ford. Though these farms and the people working them were so very similar to his own surroundings back in Hickory Ford, it expanded any person to see beyond his own beginnings. Amos slowly realized that he was beginning to break away from Hickory Ford and identify with this bottom country. As Amos passed the Potter place, he saw Mr. Potter working in the woodlot, splitting firewood for winter. He had talked to the Potters several times on Sundays in Willow Point, but he had never stopped and visited their home. As Amos passed, Mr. Potter motioned for him to stop. The Potters were genuinely pleased to see Amos on a weekday. Mrs. Potter insisted that he have a piece of apple pie. Amos quickly accepted. During his pie, the children hung around Amos like he was a novelty and Mr. Potter expressed interest in his crop and volunteered information about hunting, floods, timber and anything else he could think of at the moment. As he rode out, Mr. and Mrs. Potter called out that he should call upon them if any need for assistance should arise.

As he rode into his clearing, Amos sat on Little Red for a few moments and admired the autumn on his place. The rich bottom soil had produced corn taller than a man. The soil and the buildings looked even neater in appearance than when he and Grandpa John had ridden in here in the early summer. Amos reflected that though he had enjoyed his time with his folks, he felt a decided joy to be back on his own place once again. Over the next few days, Amos set about collecting his winter firewood. He thought at times that splitting up oak and hickory for the cabin stove was a test of wills that he might lose, but he persisted, and the work progressed. On the Monday after his return, Grandpa John brought down a wagon load of supplies, consisting of grocery items, extra quilts for the cold winter nights, and various tools.

Working together for two days, Amos and Grandpa John cut selected white oak trees suitable for railroad ties. Under his grandpa's tutelage, Amos learned the art of shaping ties with a broadax. His first ties looked as if they had been cut green and then had dried crooked under a hot sun. But he improved as Grandpa John demonstrated again and again the techniques which had earned him a reputation as a top tie-maker. These ties would later be hauled by wagon to Willow Point and sold to the railroad. A man talented with an axe could make real cash money for his family at seventy-five cents a tie. If he stayed with it.

After two days of tie cutting, Amos realized why not just any man could make extra money cutting ties. The work was hard and shaping a tie to the railroad's satisfaction was an art that not just any man could master. As for Amos' crooked ties, they could be used as fence posts on his place. The railroad wouldn't have accepted them. In jest, Grandpa John instructed Amos to "set those back against the woods somewhere. Otherwise, the crows will laugh at you if they see them when they fly by."

With a stack of fresh ties near the cabin, the two of them set about getting the corn picked. Amos had no wagon for bringing it to the barn. The crop was so good that three days were required for the two of them to pick the whole field. As the small crib in the barn wouldn't hold all the ears, it was decided to add a small shed to the back of the barn. This shed could hold the remainder of the corn as well as serve as a tool shed. In the meantime, the excess ears were piled near the proposed shed and covered with a tarp. Saturday morning Grandpa John left for Red Gum Ridge. He could only be away from Grandma and the store for so long. Immediately, Amos gathered the tools he needed for making shakes and walked downriver to the cypress blocks he and John had sawn earlier in the week. The cypress they had chosen had been uprooted by a storm some years ago. Now it was cured dry.

Amos set about the work as his grandpa had shown him yesterday. First, he used a sledgehammer and iron wedges to split the round blocks into rectangular ones which he could lift. Next, he used the froe and maul to split off the shakes which would cover the shed roof. After each one had been split, Amos had to lift and upend the block before splitting the next shake. It was a slow process, but as with so many others, persistence brought results.

From time to time, Amos took a break from the shake-splitting to cut and trim poles for the shed frame. Little Red could pull these back to the barn, but the shakes had to be carried on his shoulder, a stack at a time. Luckily, Grandpa John had brought several pounds of small nails on an earlier trip. The whole project of the shed took four days: framing, covering walls with small poles which would hold in the corn while allowing it to air- cure, and roofing with the shakes. Standing back to inspect it after its completion, Amos wondered what John would say about his carpenter work. "Wal," he addressed himself aloud, "I guess it's good enough for who it's fer, as I've heard Grandpaw say so many times." With a smile, Amos put up his tools, satisfied that his work was good enough for now, but would improve with each effort.

The next several weeks were bliss for him as he continued to work his own place. The bottoms were majestic in the fall with the colors in the dropping leaves and the coolness in the air. The cool nights and occasional frost had gotten rid of most of the flies and mosquitoes. In these days Amos enjoyed the bottoms as he never had in the preceding months. He hunted and fished every day, though he accomplished lots of work as well. Speckle, though, liked the hunting and fishing much better than the work.

Amos' most pressing project was the cutting of the corn stalks. They would become a great hindrance to the spring plowing if they were not removed beforehand. This hard work required cutting the stalks off at their base with a cane knife. Oftentimes, farmers just cut and piled them for burning, but John had encouraged Amos to haul them to the barn as fodder for Little Red through the winter.

Tired of not having any way of moving things around the place, Amos took a day to build himself a sled. It consisted of two poles for runners and boards overlaid for a floor. Stakes were secured to the sides to hold a load, and a short length of chain could be connected to a single tree for towing.

The sled allowed Amos to haul the stalks to the barn where they would be placed in the new shed on top of the extra ears of corn. Amos was quite proud of his handiwork on the sled, maybe more so than anything he had built on the place so far. He had visions of Little Red pulling the sled out into the bottoms to retrieve shakes, firewood or anything else Amos wanted to haul home.

It was during these days that Amos took the opportunity to burn the large brush piles throughout the clearing. Once started, they burned on their own while he tended to other chores. When they had burned down to almost going out, Amos would pick up brush around the edges which had not burned initially. This brush was used to build the fires back up until everything was completely burned.

The days began to turn cold, and Amos realized that winter was upon them. Looking out the door in the cabin, he surveyed all the work of the summer and fall. As opposed to when they had arrived, the place had a lived-in look about it now. The clearing had not only yielded a crop of corn and hay but was now enlarged by two more acres. The new horse lot and pasture fence gave an image of expansion to the structures. From this viewpoint at the front of the cabin, Amos couldn't see the new shed on the back of the barn, but in his mind's eye, he could visualize it clearly. Even the dugout down at the river showed the progress of the past months.

These past months had changed Amos. Instead of his mind focusing mainly upon play, his thoughts now were purposeful toward the work which would make this "cabin place on the river" into a farm.

Pulling the window's door closed, he longed for the day when he could have a glass window from which he could look out instead of this one made of planks like a barn window. Not only could he not see out without opening the little door, but also the cabin was dark within when it was shut up. Amos knew that he would have to wait for a glass window as he would for so many other things.

Looking now at the interior of the cabin, he flushed with satisfaction here, also. Certainly, it wasn't womanish with curtains and such, but it was clean and neat. Grandpa John was one for all things to have a place. Shelves and nails covered the walls so that household and kitchen items were arranged in order. The cabin was in a sense divided into two areas, separated by the two stoves which fed into the same stove pipe. A simple four-cap cookstove faced the kitchen table and shelves holding the foodstuffs while a heating stove faced toward the bed. Around the bed were shelves and nails for Amos' clothing and personal items.

This was his home now, and there was a certain pride about it. But he did not fool himself about the loneliness which would accompany the long cold winter ahead. The five-hour trip back to Hickory Ford would be made unpleasant and even dangerous by foul weather most of the time. Amos figured on staying here in the bottoms most of the winter.

He intended to busy himself with further enlarging the clearing as well as doing as much coon hunting as possible. A fat coon would be a tasty treat after a steady diet of squirrels and fish. And if the price of hides was good this winter, Amos could make some cash money for his hunting efforts.

CHAPTER EIGHT

Winter

ONE NIGHT IN LATE NOVEMBER, Speckle again bayed at the river. As always before, by the time Amos pulled on his overalls and shoes, there was nothing to be seen or heard anywhere. He could tell by watching Speckle where the dog's interest lay, and it always seemed to be up or down the river, never around the clearing or across the river. This had led Amos to believe that someone was passing in a boat.

Since Speckle didn't sound an alarm every night or on nights of a pattern, Amos had no idea when the night people might appear next. The night people had become part of life in the bottoms for Amos, though he had no idea who they were or what they were about. Amos determined to find out about them, no matter how long it took.

With the coming of winter, Amos began his seasonal coon hunting. Speckle, of course, had been practicing since the day of their first arrival in the bottoms. Winter was the best time to hunt coon because the fur was the longest then. Also, the work of farming slowed down enough that one could hunt most of the night and not have to put in a full day's work the following day.

After supper one evening, he readied the equipment he would need. There was the axe for chopping open the hollow logs where coon loved to hide, the .22 rifle to shoot a coon when he could get a shot, a tow sack to haul back the coons he got, and the carbide head lamp necessary for walking around the bottoms after dark. He put on warm clothes along with gum knee boots as this night would be cold and the sloughs were full of water. Gathering his equipment, Amos walked out to untie Speckle. He had tied the hound up at supper as he would likely have wandered off from the cabin.

They walked downriver this night, using the river itself for their bearings. Speckle ran out ahead before they had gone two hundred yards. The dog knew the significance of the lamp, rifle, and ax. Content that the hound would continue in the general direction already set, Amos walked on downriver, all the while waiting for the dog to strike a scent and sound off in that deep voice so characteristic of hounds.

It was exhilarating for both of them to spend the night walking and running through the dark woods, wading sloughs and pursuing their quarry. Speckle took several trails, but as many times as not the raccoon outsmarted him by taking to water where there would be no scent. After a short, fruitless search, the hound sought the trail of yet another 'coon. All the while, Amos followed the sound of his hound's voice, guided only by that sound and the dim carbide light.

With only a few hours left before dawn, Amos and Speckle wearily trudged their way back into the clearing. They were wet, muddy, cold, scratched and happy. Amos' shoulder ached from the burden of the three dead coons inside the sack, and his arms were tired from carrying both the axe and rifle. But this was what he and the dog had been longing to do ever since that first day back in late April.

December nights were mostly spent the same way. Amos had made up several hide-boards for stretching the pelts, but now he needed more. Fortunately, Amos' farming activities during the winter time were pretty much limited to tending to his mule, so he had the time to make extra boards. Not only was he getting hides from coon hunting, but his three steel traps set along the river yielded a steady return of coon and mink.

There was no way he could eat all the raccoon meat he was getting. Amos had been raised to not throw away good meat, so he frequently took fresh carcasses to the Potters. He even took some to Willow Point when he went to church on Sundays. Some of the town folks paid him twenty-five cents for a 'coon, and this went a long way to replenish his supply of cash.

It was during one of their night hunts that Amos got his first look at the night people. In the large expanse of the river bottoms, a hunter could go for weeks without seeing another person. Since April, Amos had only seen Grandpa John, Uncle Zeke, and the Potters'. So when he saw these men, he was more than surprised.

The night it happened the weather was terrible for coon hunting. A Light rain had begun to fall shortly after they had left the cabin. Within the hour it was falling heavily. The falling rain in the timber became so noisy that Amos had difficulty hearing Speckle if the hound was any distance away. After Amos reached the thicket where the hound had treed a coon, he decided that they should call it a night and hit it out back for the cabin and a warm bed.

To compound their situation, when Amos looked up to shoot the coon Speckle had treed, the rain doused the carbide flame. No amount of effort on Amos' part could relight the lamp. Standing there in cold desperation without getting the coon and having no light for the return walk to the cabin, Amos resigned himself to a long and hard walk. He tied Speckle to a short length of rope to keep him from striking another trail, and the two of them began to work their way through the dark woods.

Knowing that their surest way back was to find the river and follow it to the cabin, Amos sought the river and walked its edge, keeping the blackness of the water always to his right. After some time the storm passed, and the stars and a partial moon penetrated the woods with a small amount of light. They were still following the river when Speckle stopped and growled deep within his throat. Feeling threatened by some beast out in the darkness of the woods, Amos eased his finger onto the trigger of the little rifle and looked hard around them. He could not hold back his fear. Without a light, he couldn't see ten feet, except for out on the river, where the water's surface reflected some light from above.

Then the sound came to Amos' keen ear, the sound of a paddle being worked in water. Instantly, he knelt beside the dog and put a hand to his mouth to prevent him from barking. Something deep within Amos told him that he should not be detected by whoever was out on the river. Quietly, the two of them crouched behind a log twenty feet from the river's edge. Directly, Amos heard voices as a boat approached. He could see two men paddling a flat-bottomed boat upstream. Their conversation was limited, but he could tell that they were very disgruntled at having to be out on the river in such a winter storm.

As the boat came abreast of where he and Speckle crouched, Amos could see a tarp covering what appeared to be sacks of something in the middle of the boat. These sacks were obviously heavy as the boat sat too low in the water for just the weight of the men.

Amos and Speckle watched as the boat slowly passed from

sight upriver. After giving it time to get out of earshot, the two of them resumed their long walk back to the cabin. As wet and cold as Amos was during that walk, he thought of nothing other than those two men and their loaded boat. Again and again, he asked himself what they could possibly be doing out in such weather. They had no dog, so they were not coon hunting. And, no one had heard of trappers working this part of the bottoms since old man White.

Arriving at their cabin about midnight, he stoked the fire and changed out of his wet clothes. Even after he finally warmed up and blew out the lamp, his mind continued to search out the mystery of those men. Certainly, these were the night people. But, who were they, and what were they doing? It was an hour or more before he finally drifted off to sleep.

The weather was bad for the next several days, so Amos and Speckle kept to the cabin at night. During the day Amos busied himself by doing odd chores around the place. When there was a break in the rain, he split more wood for the stove, and when it rained, he worked at fashioning new wooden handles for the various tools used on the place. Also, in the shelter of the lean-to, he split more shakes for either patching the roofs or building new ones. Though as busy as he kept himself, his thoughts were never far from the night people.

Christmas brought a break in his isolation as he risked the weather to ride home to Hickory Ford. Amos had delayed the ride home to Hickory Ford for several days hoping for a break in the weather as it was either very cold or very wet day after day. But with tomorrow being Christmas Eve, he felt that he could wait no longer if he were to share the Christmas season with his family. So before finding his bed that evening, Amos resolved to ride for

Hickory Ford in the morning regardless of the weather.

The morning of Christmas Eve broke gray and cold. Without the resolution of the previous evening, Amos likely would never have set out on a fifteen-mile ride in such weather. As Amos rode out of the clearing, he was wearing most of the clothing he owned to protect himself from the bitter cold. By the time he passed the Potter place an hour later, a light rain had begun, and a cold wind picked up to drive the chilly air through his layers of clothing. Amos thought to himself that he and the animals were fortunate that most of the ride was through uncleared timber where the wind could not blow so hard.

On and on he rode through the cold damp air. For much of the trip, he occupied himself with the many thoughts of the previous eight months. In some ways, it seemed like a lifetime ago when he first came to the clearing. So much had happened and so much had changed in those eight months that Amos felt detached from the life before. Somehow over these eight months, the old Amos had disappeared, and now a new Amos rode toward Hickory Ford.

New or old, it was a happy Amos that rode into the store yard on Red Gum Ridge. And not only Amos, but Little Red and Speckle as well, for this was like home to them. Also, they were able to get out of the weather while Amos ate dinner and dried himself in his grandparents' comfortable home. As usual, he had a great deal to tell. Amos waited until Janey was washing dishes in the kitchen before he told John about actually seeing the night people on the river while coon hunting.

John listened intently and hesitated a moment. "Amos," he replied, "This may scare ya, but I want ya t' start lockin' your door at night, and keep an eye out fer anything out of the ordinary.

Them fellers air up to no good, thet's fer sure."

Later, as Amos rode on up to his folks' place, he thought back on his Grandpa's admonition. For a fact, he was scared, though he tried not to show it. Not knowing who the night people were or what they were about was the anxious part. He could imagine all sorts of terrible activity, even if none of it was plausible. Somewhere within him, Amos found a determination that these people were not going to scare him off his own place. He would remain there in the bottoms and work the land no matter how many night people there were on the river. At least, he hoped there weren't many of them.

Amos stayed with his folks for two weeks. He probably wouldn't be able to get back again until sometime in February when the weather began to warm up. In those two weeks, Amos ate more than he had in the last month and a half. Everywhere he visited there were Christmas dinners with special desserts. Many of his friends and relatives expressed astonishment that he had lasted this long down in the bottoms by himself. At first, this angered Amos. It seemed that they had little confidence in him, but as he thought more on it, he took the meaning to be that what he had accomplished was quite a feat for a young man. Then he felt a strong sense of pride, realizing that his friends saw the new Amos.

But at times this new Amos was someone uncomfortable to him. Like the time he was picking up some items at the store in Hickory Ford. He was so intent on getting just the right things for his mother that he didn't realize that someone had come up very close behind him. All of a sudden there stood Myrtle Johnson. And the look on her face was that of a child who'd just opened a large present.

"Why, Amos, I heard ya was back t' Hickory Ford," spoke Myrtle, "Whar have ya been keepin' ya'self?"

Again taken aback by Myrtle's presence and conversation, Amos stuttered, frozen to the spot. "Wa, wa, wal, up to my folks mostly, Myrtle," replied Amos.

"Ya must be so very brave, to stay down in them ol' bottoms all by yore own self. An' I hear thet ya've made a crop by yoreself too," said Myrtle. "Why, yore pretty near growed up," Myrtle added, with a heavy touch of admiration in her voice.

"Wal, I guess, Myrtle. Uh, I'd better be getting back home now," stuttered Amos. With this last comment, Amos found within himself the strength to step away toward the counter where he could charge his purchases and get away.

On the night before his return to the bottoms, Amos spent the night with his grandparents, as he and his grandfather had much to talk about in regards to the new place. Both of them agreed that more clearing needed to be done before spring, with ties and rails being cut out of any tree which would make them. There wasn't much else to do during the winter months, and the ties would produce some cash money. John had told Amos that he could have any money he made off the place, either from hides or ties. And, the crops were his also for the time being as the yield was not large enough to make a difference to John, and Amos needed all of it for mule feed.

It was a bright but cold morning when Amos rode away from Red Gum Ridge. For the sake of comfort, he had delayed his departure until mid morning when the sun would be up high enough to raise the temperature. It was to be a snug ride for not only was Amos again wearing most of his clothes, but the bundles of food stuffs tied about the saddle didn't leave much room to shift himself.

By the time Amos got to the Potter's place three hours later, he was about frozen stiff into his saddle. Carrying in firewood when he saw Amos' approach, Mr. Potter hailed him to stop. It was a welcome invitation for Amos, as the next hour would be miserable without a chance to warm up.

After a good hour of sitting near the Potter's stove drinking coffee, Amos felt ready to ride that last hour through the bottoms to his clearing. It was good to visit with the Potter family, who once again, seemed to enjoy his visit also as they saw almost as few people as Amos.

Riding into the clearing as the light was beginning to fade, Amos looked around at what had become *his* place. To an outsider, it wouldn't look like much, just two small plain buildings set in a small clearing deep in the bottomland woods. But to Amos, who had cleaned it up and worked a crop, it was a farm with great promise. And, more than that, it was *his* farm. At least, he lived here and worked it, though John Sawyer owned it. Amos then wondered if he would ever own a piece of land. The idea was paramount to him as he could imagine no greater thrill than to farm his own land.

In the days after Amos' return to the clearing, he resumed 'coon hunting and trapping. With some of the cash he had accumulated from coon meat and hide sales, he had bought three more traps. These and the three he had before were now set up and down the river to add to his cache of hides. Selling coon hides and meat was one of only two sources of cash available to him. The other was the cutting of ties for the railroad. Both of these sources would only last through the late winter.

Amos filled his days by continuing to enlarge the clearing.

The original clearing had been done along a ridge that ran southeast from the river. Since it was important to keep the crops as high as possible to reduce the risk of flood damage, he followed the original pattern. It was easy for Amos to know where the ridge lay, as the high water line from the winter rains outlined it perfectly. The clearing then would continue to be oblong as it followed the ridge line.

Winter gave the bottoms something of a gloomy appearance. With all the leaves off the trees, the gray bark cast a pallor on the day. The gray sky of an overcast day just added to the gray pallor. On these days, and there were many of them, Amos had to work extra hard to be cheerful. Mud was everywhere except when the ground was frozen. To facilitate getting back and forth from cabin to barn, Amos laid heavy planks on the ground to form a walkway.

About the third week of January, John arrived with a much-needed load of supplies. This was a great relief. Amos' groceries were running low. The weather hadn't broken as John had hoped it would, but he came down anyway. Besides the grocery supplies, Amos needed some company as there wasn't enough to do to keep his mind occupied during the winter.

Amos was even more glad when John announced that he was going to stay with him several days so the two of them could cut ties. Although Amos had practiced his tie-cutting, he still could only turn out rough work, and the procedure took much longer than it should. This would be an excellent opportunity to become more proficient at one of his few sources of cash money.

The two of them worked hard for three days, and Amos did improve substantially under his grandpa's constant tutelage. The cutting of a tie was a step-by-step process. First, using a crosscut saw the log would be cut to the proper length of eight feet. Then a chopping axe would be used to score the sides of the log every few inches from one end to another. A broadax would next flatten each scored side until the remaining log was squared, seven inches by eight inches. Though trimmed and shaped, the tie was still a heavy beam to move around. Amos had been shocked the first time he watched John lift and shoulder one all by himself and load it into the back of a wagon. Amos himself was a long ways from such a feat, having to be content with working the tie into the wagon one end at a time.

On the third and last day of John's visit, they hauled two loads of ties to the railroad at Willow Point. It was just daylight when they pulled out for the first trip. The weather was in their favor as a cold front had moved in the day before and the ground was hard frozen beneath the heavy wagon. A muddy road would have slowed them down considerably and given Gray Jack and Buster a much more difficult pull.

They returned to the cabin for a quick noon meal after the first load. John wanted to get back from the second load before dark. On the return of their second trip, Amos thought back to their dealings with the railroad men at Willow Point. He was old enough to know that men didn't always act cooperatively or considerate in their dealings. The foreman at the yard had been friendly with Amos, but had acted differently towards John. His attitude had been respectful, as if John was someone of authority. Thinking back to Hickory Ford, the men there acted in the same manner toward him, but they knew him. These men had never met either John or Amos. Reflecting upon this as they rode the last miles back to the clearing before dark, Amos realized that men recognized something in John Sawyer that signaled to them that he was no ordinary man, but someone of knowledge and strength.

As they were pulling up before the barn, Amos wondered if anyone would ever see him in such a light. But before he could give the matter any more consideration, John spoke, "Amos, ya rustle in th' cabin, and git supper started while I unhitch the team. If we want to git us a 'coon by midnight, we'd best git at it."

"All right, Grandpaw," responded Amos before he jumped from the wagon seat.

With their supper eaten and the dishes washed, Amos and his grandpa bundled up for the sharp cold of the night and, amid their cheerful talk, stepped out of the cabin. By now Speckle was used to hunting after supper, so he stayed close by the cabin door in the early evening.

Walking was easy tonight, as the ground was frozen. They set out east from the clearing, a course which would take them across the logging road and toward White Creek. Speckle didn't get a good track until about a half an hour after they had set out. This 'coon seemed to have been trailed before because he set out straight and fast for White Creek, apparently to lose the dog in the water.

Speaking between heavy breaths, John said, "Seems he's already crossed White Creek. I don't think we kin cross at night in these knee boots, Amos."

"Don't worry, Grandpaw," responded Amos, "I know us a place ta cross, on a big red oak thet's fell across the creek. Jes' foller me downstream a ways, and I'll lead us to it."

The fallen tree was just where Amos said that it would be, so the two coon hunters crossed in short order. They had barely crossed when Speckle's barking remained in one place and the tone shifted to something of a bay. Knowing that the young hound had treed his coon, they rushed through the timber.

Arriving there within ten minutes, they both quickly sized up the situation. Speckle stood with his front feet high upon the trunk of a red oak and continued to bay toward its top. Walking around the tree's base and using their carbide lights, they searched for the coon. John spotted it first, calling to Amos that the coon was sitting in a large fork about twenty feet off the ground. The coon had chosen a bad tree for itself as it stood alone in a small clearing with no close limbs from other trees to which he might have jumped to escape from tree to tree.

"Wal, he must have had Speckle right on his tail fer him not to git to a better tree than this un," said John.

"Kin ye see his eyes, Grandpaw?" asked Amos.

"Not now, but you come 'ere and git yore rifle set, and I'll git him to show them eyes to us," replied John before he turned out his light and stepped back from the tree to the edge of the clearing. There he took hold of a large bushy sapling and in one instant gave it a violent shake and chattered like another coon.

Instantly, the coon high above Amos looked out away from the tree. The carbide light barely showed a clear outline of the coon at this distance, but the animal's eyes glinted their reflection of Amos' light. Taking a steady and quick aim, Amos touched off the .22. A thud followed the sharp retort of the rifle, and the coon lost his grip and fell to the ground. Speckle was on the coon almost before he hit the ground, lest the coon—possibly still alive— might try and run off from them.

The 'coon, heavy with winter fat, made a load by itself in the tow sack Amos had brought along. In good spirits now, with their first coon so early in the night, Amos and John set out north along White Creek. Speckle only walked with them a short distance before setting out ahead on his own.

The hound lost the next two trails along the creek, but kept the third and treed the coon in a large pin oak. It wasn't too high, and Amos thought it would be an easy catch. But when the coon dropped, it lodged in a fork a good twelve feet off the ground.

"Amos," said John, "nothin' to do but climb on up thar after it."

"Reckon yore right, Grandpaw," replied Amos as he removed the carbide light from his head and stood the rifle against a nearby tree.

"Come on, now, I'll give ya a boost up," said John.

With his Grandpa's help, Amos scrambled high enough to reach the first limb and then pulled himself up onto it. From there he climbed on up and out to retrieve the coon from its fork. After dropping the coon down to his Grandpa, Amos worked his way back down, dropping from the last limb onto the frozen ground below.

Now with two 'coons to carry in the sack, Amos suggested that they cross back over White Creek and circle their way back to the cabin, hunting all along. The night was a profitable one for them as they got two more coons before reaching the clearing. One had holed up inside the base of a hollow tree and John had used a long slender stick to twist the coon back out of the hole. The other had crawled deep inside a hollow log. John had used the axe to split the log open. Four raccoons made for a heavy load by the time they returned to the cabin, as each coon weighed over fifteen pounds.

At daylight the next morning, John headed Gray Jack and Buster out the wagon track for Red Gum Ridge. As Amos stood watching him drive away, he thought back over all the activity of the past few days. It had been a joy to work alongside his grandpa and learn the art of making railroad ties. Though he was still far from proficient, John had said that he had a good start. For Amos, a compliment from John was memorable.

And, having his grandpa to coon hunt with was a special treat. Actually, just having someone to talk to around the place was a treat for Amos. His grandpa's visit was certainly a welcome break in the isolation of the bottoms.

Winter began to wane about mid-February. But the warmer weather kept him closer to the cabin and barn than the cold, as now the ground was a mire of mud after the winter rains. To get a change of pace, Amos saddled up Little Red one day after dinner and rode out for Hickory Ford. It was a muddy walk for the mule and the dog, probably the most tiring since they had moved to the bottoms the April before. In fact, much of the ride was through flood waters which rose at times above the mule's knees. Speckle had to swim through these deeper areas. Consequently, Amos had to stop often to allow the mule and hound to rest. It was almost dark when they arrived at John's store on Red Gum Ridge, making it their longest ever return trip. Grandma Janey had no difficulty in persuading Amos to spend the night with them before riding on to his folk's place.

CHAPTER NINE

Another Spring, Another Beginning

SPRING CAME EARLY as the clear sunny days dried the winter's mois-ture from the earth. As anxious as Amos was to begin plowing, the soil in the clearing was still much too wet. To busy himself he did more work on the newer parts of the clearing which had been cut over the previous fall and winter.

Working around the girdled trees which would not bud out this spring like the rest of the woods, Amos picked up the remaining brush and chunks of wood. Though he wanted to begin the plowing, Amos contented himself with this additional cleanup. He knew that it would save him time and frustration when he finally did sink the plow below the surface.

Also, he picked up around the large brush piles which he had burned last fall, restacking the unburned pieces. The ground was still muddy in places, and the unburned pieces were blackened with soot, making it dirty work. Once he set himself to these tasks, it was not difficult to spend a solid week in the cleanup efforts.

For reasons unknown to Amos, John had instructed him to return to Red Gum Ridge after the final cleanup and before any plowing. So in early April, Amos set out from the clearing for a home visit before he tackled the long tasks of plowing and planting. It was just as well that he spend some time with his family. The soil here in the bottoms was still too wet to work. Amos stayed with his folks for several weeks to allow his clearing in the bottoms to dry out enough to plow. While there, he helped his father break and disk the land. Amos' work in the fields while at his folks' would put his father several days ahead with getting his crop planted.

These were good days for Amos as he worked alongside his father in the fields and got to put his feet under his mother's table each evening. By now he truly loved his clearing in the bottoms, but at times the isolation was uncomfortable. Being home with his family was a welcome break, both in work and in solitude.

As usual, Amos stopped by Grandpa John's as he left to return to the bottoms. He and his grandpa always had last-minute talks about what should be done about the clearing. This morning would be no different. These talks had become vital to Amos. During the conversation, he felt as if he were like a partner to John, even though his grandpa owned the land and was always the one giving the directions. Maybe it was that neither his own father nor any of his brothers were a part of this venture, allowing Amos to have John solely to himself. Also, it could be that John listened to what Amos thought about things, an entirely different situation from back home, where he was always the youngest.

John had little advice as they sat on the bench in front of the store on this morning. John said spring was early this year and they all should have a good crop. John, like Amos' father, had his ground almost ready to plant. Amos' clearing in the bottoms was probably only just ready to turn over.

"Wal, Amos," said John, "this'll be yore second crop down thar. Ya think it'll be a big 'un?

"Hope so, Grandpaw, least I'll git a lot earlier start this spring," replied Amos.

"Ya've worked mighty hard this past year, Amos, an' I'm proud of ya. But ya've got a sight more work down there yet, an' I got ya' something to make it go a little easier," stated John.

Leading the way back to his horse lot, John pointed to a strange mule tied to one of the lot posts. It appeared to be an older john mule, one having several crops behind him. He was about the size of Grandpa's Grey Jack, though lacking the intelligent eyes of that venerable animal.

With a sly smile, he stated, "Thet's Ned, bought him from an old feller named Luther over at Beech Flat. His teammate had died of the colic, so Mr. Luther decided to give up farming and go live with his daughter at Hampton. Ned'll make you a team, hooked up with Little Red. I know he's a sight bigger, but we can adjust the harness. Besides, that little mule of your'n is quite a puller hisself. An' thet wagon yonder by the barn is fer you to use too. A man needs a team and a wagon if'en he intends to do any serious farming. Thet also was Mr. Luther's, said thet in town he'd have no use fer a wagon and team."

Amos stood there in the barnyard as if his feet were rooted, speechless and immobile. After a long moment, he finally spoke, "Grandpaw, ... a team ... uh, thanks, Grandpaw."

"Come on, now, let's git the two mules hitched together and see how they look. I bought Mr. Luther's harness too, so Ned already has a harness fit for him. We'll have to do some adjustments to fit the other harness fer Little Red."Amos led his little mule around from the front of the store so that he and his new teammate could get acquainted. At first, they stuck their ears straight up stiff, then relaxed and extended their noses to one another to check each other out, communicating in their own way. Amos tied Little Red to a post on the left side of Ned and began helping John bring out the harness. Of course, Ned's harness went right on as he had worked in it for several years, but it took quite a while to rig and adjust Little Red in the tack of a much larger mule. With the harnessing done, John said that they should now let the two mules stand side by side for a while and get a little more used to one another before being hitched together behind the wagon.

The two of them walked to the house for a cup of leftover breakfast coffee and a talk about the future for the farm in the bottoms. It was at times like this that Amos felt something like John's partner, as his grandpa talked *with* him, and not *to* him.

"How big do ya reckon thet clearin' is now, Amos, after what you've cleared over the winter?" asked John.

"I think we've added another four acres, Grandpaw, so there must be eleven now all together," replied Amos.

"Wal, thet'll keep ya busy plowin' for a couple of weeks. And iffen ya think thet new land is clean of brush and such, jest wait till ya sink a plow in it. Why, ya'll turn up a sight of roots thet'll keep ya stopping every other minute to clean the plow. Thet's why I've got ya a special plow, jes' fer new land like that clearing of yours. It's called a Vulcan New Ground Plow, and it'll cut most of them roots for ya as ya pass through. It's quite a deal."

With their coffee and conversation finished, Amos was anxious to see this new plow and wagon. Walking out now to the barnyard, Amos went first to the wagon while John had an errand at the chicken house. It was an old wagon, but in good condition. The original paint was still tight on the wood, as it had always been kept inside out of the weather. Looking below the box at the running gear, he saw in clear lettering the Studebaker name across the front of the bolster. Well, thought Amos, it certainly is a good wagon. They don't come any better than a Studebaker. He knew that to have a Studebaker wagon was something of a status symbol in the farming communities. He couldn't wait until he got a chance to drive it to Hickory Ford.

John returned and called Amos to help him bring the new plow out of the barn. With a quick stride, Amos caught up with his grandpa at the main door of the barn and looking about saw the plow off to the right. There it was, a brand new plow with fresh paint. As John had said, it had a special point of steel coming up from the plow point to cut through roots. To Amos who had seen very few new plows and never one such as this new ground plow, this was an impressive piece of machinery. A special cutter blade had been fitted to the lower front point of the share for the purpose of cutting roots as the plow passed through the soil. The cutter was about six inches high, sweeping back in a slight arch. It was his to take to the bottoms and use for himself. As he lifted the beam in front while John lifted the handles in the rear, he had the sensation of his future picking up.

Within the hour, Amos and Speckle were heading toward the bottoms in a Studebaker wagon behind two mules. In honor of the occasion of the new wagon, Amos put Speckle up in the seat where the dog could look out over Little Red and Big Ned, as he was later to refer to the new mule. Amos felt a great sense of pride as he drove "his team" down the rutty road. He thought back over the last year to the time he and John first drove to the bottoms together. When his grandpa had left him in the bottoms with only a mule and a hound, supplies of any bulk or quantity had to be brought down by wagon on one of John's visits. Now Amos would be able to haul his own supplies.

They were halfway to the clearing before the pride wore off enough for the reality of the rough ride of the wagon to sink in on Amos. Regrettably, he admitted that, pride aside, riding Little Red was a great deal smoother than sitting atop a wagon. The mule's four legs absorbed the unevenness of the rough roads, particularly at a walk. On the other hand, the stiff framed wagon telegraphed every bump up into Amos' backside. But he decided that rough or not, having a wagon was a great feeling.

The ride to the bottoms was uneventful as far as Big Ned and Little Red were concerned. Amos began to think that this new mule would be a good match for Little Red, even if he was much bigger. Though long-legged, Ned moved slowly enough that Little Red had no trouble keeping up with him. The ride down gave Amos an extended opportunity to size up the new mule. He was long-barreled with thick legs and big feet. The muscles of his shoulders and hips were large and well-developed, meaning that he should be quite a puller.

Driving by the Potter's, Amos hoped that they were outside where they could see his new mule and wagon, but there was no sign of anyone on the place as he drove past. Disappointed, he drove on toward his own cabin and clearing. The last hour's drive to the clearing brought a different sensation from the seat of the wagon as opposed to from the saddle. Amos began to feel more permanent to the bottoms on this trip. In the past, he had felt like a hired hand who was just temporary, but now he sensed that he was more a part of the bottoms. He was already grateful to John for getting him the extra mule and wagon.

In the first few days after his return, Amos did chores on the place while giving the soil more time to dry. The weather was warm, but a few spring showers had brought new moisture. Ned took some getting used to about the place. Amos was used to having only Little Red and Speckle about the clearing. Ned proved to change that picture. On the one hand, he was standoffish where Little Red was affectionate. Where Little Red was no trouble to keep, Ned seemed to make one problem after another. If he could reach anything through the poles of the lot fence, it would appear inside the lot. And gates had to be latched *well* or Ned would work them loose.

In late April Amos decided that the soil was dry enough to plow. As he had done last year, he chose to plow the garden first so he could plant the vegetables soon. Though the garden was relatively clean of roots, Amos tried out the Vulcan plow just to learn the way it handled. The implement worked well, sliding beneath the surface and turning the soil over in a neat row.

The real test would be in the freshly-cleared parts of the place. These parts were latticed with tree roots to catch up a plow. When Amos first began to cultivate the clearing, he started in the middle, which meant that he didn't get into the new clearing until later. Still, there were enough old roots to appreciate the special cutter which projected up from the plow point. As they began to turn the new parts of the clearing, the root cutter did its job. Whereas the ordinary plow which Little Red had pulled last year had pulled up the small roots and hung up underneath the larger ones, this plow cut through all but the very largest roots.

As John had predicted, a great many roots came up with the plow. So many that Amos had to hitch the team to the wagon and go about the newly cleared areas to pick up several loads of roots before planting. Otherwise, these pieces of roots would be in the way of all the plowing and hoeing throughout the entire summer.

These were happy days in the clearing. Spring brought with it a freshness, both in routine and in the air. Everything smelled fresh and vibrant as Amos and his team worked the soil. Animal life was abundant. Creatures large and small were getting active again after their winter routine. Birds, in particular, knowing a free meal was to be had behind Amos' new plow, were attracted to the clearing. The overturned earth exposed countless worms and grubs which furnished a feast for the birdlife of the area. The birds swooped in and around the team as they pulled the plow through the rich soil.

Hour after hour, Amos stepped along the open furrow while guiding the Vulcan plow through the thick mat of weeds and grasses which had grown up in the past few weeks. The air was warm and damp and filled with the rich smells of spring. Besides the calls of a myriad of birds, there were the footfalls of the team, their occasional blowing, the creak and jingle of the harness, and the steady popping of roots being cut by the plow's special cutter blade.

With only short breaks, Amos and his team plowed for two weeks to get the eleven acres turned. He had taken the time to drag off and plant the garden so that there might be fresh vege-tables for the table shortly. Amos used the drag in the clearing on the plowed ground as soon as the turned earth had begun to dry out. Timing was important in preparing the soil as it falls apart well when the moisture level is at a certain point, not dry nor wet. And to preserve the moisture in the soil, the drag would seal the surface to lessen moisture loss due to sun and wind. Ned had proven himself in the field as a good work mule, even if he was a problem around the barn. He was very strong and knew what was expected of him in the field. Because of his experience and height, Ned was placed on the right side of the hitch to walk in the furrow. Little Red had worked many times with another mule, so he adjusted well to the change in hitch. Also, he seemed to appreciate the company around the barn, especially when Amos was away from the clearing without him.

Another week of work in the clearing after the plowing and Amos had his corn and hay planted for another crop. As last year, it had been several weeks of hard work. True, he had not had to clear the land of its fresh growth like last year, but field work in new ground with a team was always hard work. He, like his mules, had walked every foot of every eight-inch furrow, then had walked around in the loose dirt to pick up load after load of roots and chunks, then had walked behind the team through the loose dirt as they dragged it off for planting. And, as he had no planter, he had opened up every corn furrow with the single stock and had dropped every seed over all eleven acres by hand. The seed for the pea hay had been broadcast by hand over two acres of the new clearing.

Now it was time to do what every farmer must do with a certain level of anticipation, wait for the seed to sprout and rise through the surface of the soil. Amos chose to do his waiting at Hickory Ford where he could pick up a load of supplies for the summer's work. So on the second day after the planting, Amos hitched Little Red and Ned to the Studebaker wagon and drove out the wagon track toward Hickory Ford.

CHAPTER TEN

The Flood

IT WAS JUST PAST DAYLIGHT WHEN AMOS LEFT FOR HICKORY FORD. Before driving out of the clearing, Amos stopped the team. For several long moments, he surveyed his place. The morning air was cool, with a light fog hanging over the river. A lone crow watched vigilantly from the high branches of a dead tree by the river. At the far end of the clearing, a pair of squirrels raced up and down a shag bark hickory. Even from this distance, he could hear their chatter and the scraping of the bark from their excited movements. A peckerwood beat a steady rhythm on some dead tree in the direction of the track. These were the sounds of his clearing.

He remembered so very well how it had looked just one year ago. When John first brought him here, the effect of three years of neglect was obvious. All seven acres that had once been cleared had become one big thicket, with the new growth reaching fifteen feet high in places. The cabin had been filthy, and the roof leaked badly. The yard and horse lot were covered with weeds, grasses, and sprouts as high as a man's head. The barn was in a terrible state. The whole scene had been shocking to someone from an established farm community like Hickory Ford. Today was a different story. The cabin and barnyards were clean, and both structures were in good repair. There was a new horse lot. A new split rail fence enclosed a small pasture. The original seven acres were joined by four more, and all were freshly planted. Amos felt pride swell up from inside him over what he had accomplished here in one year.

He thought back to the circumstances surrounding his being here. He had always respected his grandpa and enjoyed his company, but now John seemed almost larger than life to Amos. Sharing this new endeavor had strengthened their relationship over the previous year. All seemed right with the world as he clucked to Little Red and Big Ned to start the wagon. Amos certainly felt like a man, though he wasn't quite sure he knew what it was to be a man. He did know that he felt proud of what he had accomplished and felt good about being able to do things on his own. He was now able to do many of the things expected of a man, specifically, to work a farm on his own.

It had been three weeks since he had seen his family, three weeks of plowing and planting. Although Amos had been away for longer periods over the last year, he was most excited about seeing his family this time. For reasons he did not understand, he wanted to be with his family for a few days. He sensed that his family was his emotional touchstone and that he needed to be near them now to check out these new feelings.

But he also knew that he wanted to show off his team and wagon to his friends back in Hickory Ford. He didn't think Homer Smith would really like living down here in the bottoms with all its hard work and isolation, but Homer would be impressed with Amos' team and wagon, even if Little Red was the only part he actually owned. But Ned and the Studebaker wagon were like his own, as they were purchased for the place in the bottoms where no one else would use them.

The ride to Hickory Ford was always exciting to Amos. Most of the trip was through timber. What cleared land there was could mostly be found around small pockets of farming communities, though a few folks had sought a solitary place to clear new fields. Amos knew who lived in the various places along the way, and the landmarks were all comfortably familiar to him. Each landmark told him how much farther he had to travel. The whole trip from his cabin to the Sawyer store on Red Gum Ridge was about twelve miles. It took four hours. He could ride it faster on Little Red if he trotted or loped most of the way, but usually he was carrying too much with him for that to be feasible. His grandparents' place was always his first stop upon arriving in Hickory Ford and his last stop upon leaving it. This was partly because he and his grand-father always had plans to discuss the place in the bottoms. And, Red Gum Ridge was the point of the Hickory Ford area which was closest to the Little Sandy River.

Almost at his grandparents' place, Amos looked about him at the freshly planted fields. The new crops were vibrant green stripes in plowed fields. The early spring had given farmers a head start on their crops, and it already looked like a good year. In Hickory Ford, a good year meant that after harvest there was plenty of corn and hay for the livestock, there were enough preserved fruits and vegetables to feed the family through the winter, there were fat hogs to butcher in the fall, and there were bales of cotton to sell for cash. While most families were able to feed themselves, cash was vital. There were some things, essential things that a family couldn't raise or make themselves, things like shoes, sugar, and iron implements.

When Amos arrived at his grandparents' place, he found them in the garden. Janey was cutting weeds with a hoe. John was plowing the sweet corn with Gray Jack and a single stock. Janey gave her usual cheerful greeting as Amos stepped into the garden."Wal, howdy, Amos. Sure glad to see ye agin ... 'ceptin ye look thin. Like as not yor' a workin' too hard and eatin' too little."

"I guess so, Granny. There are times when I git so busy in the field that I forget it's time to eat. Course, then I've got to cook it my own self. I guarantee ye, Granny, thet my cookin' ain't anythin' compared to yours," responded Amos.

Flattered and pleased by his compliments regarding her cooking, Janey said, "Here then, take this hoe and finish hoeing out this row of onions while I go on to the house to finish up our dinner. I won't let you waste away."

Amos picked up Janey's hoeing where she had left off while John continued plowing the sweet corn. Finishing before his grandpa, Amos used the hoe to cut down any weed he could find, working the ground anywhere that seemed to need a little attention. After Gray Jack had pulled the single stock up the last middle, John unhitched the plow at the end and drove the mule on toward the barn for his own dinner of corn and hay. Amos fell in behind the two of them.

"Fine spring ain't it, Amos," said John as he slipped off Gray Jack's bridle for the mule to eat the hay and ears of corn which would be placed in his feed box.

"Yeah, Grandpaw, it's hard to believe that I've my corn planted already. This should be an excellent crop," responded Amos.

"Ye have to be mighty careful 'bout countin' yer chickens 'fore they've hatched. As good as prospects fer a good crop look now, it's a long ways till pickin' and a whole lot can happen 'tween now and then."John's comment caused Amos to think back over some of the bad crop years in his own memory. There were years of heavy rains and years with almost no rain, not to mention the hail storms and bugs. Farming certainly was a risky venture, mostly dependent upon the weather.

Though Janey hadn't expected Amos for dinner, she set out more than enough food for the three of them. As usual at his grandma's table, Amos ate with abandonment. Today Grandma made the remark, "Slow down, Amos, there's a plenty, an' besides, no one's goin' to git it afore ye." At this Amos slowed down, now self-conscious.

With their dinner over, John and Amos sat outside in the sun on a bench. John was interested in the progress on the new place, particularly he was interested in how the new mule and plow were working for Amos.

Amos' stay at Hickory Ford lasted for about a week. He even had a chance to visit with Homer Smith and a few other of his boyhood friends. With the crops planted, they all had a little spare time to enjoy themselves. One evening at dusk they all gathered at a favorite fishing hole on Bates Creek. This group, friends as boys and now each growing into a man, had no purpose tonight but to have fun together. As well as fishing lines, some of them had brought food from home to share with the group. Homer's folks had a good many laying hens so he brought a bucket of eggs that they could boil over their campfire. They fished and told wild stories until they were all frantic with laughter. They teased and chased one another, climbed the trees around the campsite, and some even shucked their clothes and took a swim in spite of the chilly water.

Their reverie was broken by Homer's cry of anguish when he realized that he had just stepped into his own bucket of eggs.

The whole group changed its tune from unbridled laughter to one of somber misery. The eggs were to be their supper that night, and none of them relished going hungry. Ezra Edwards showed a cool head as he picked up the bucket and began removing its contents. This showed only about half the eggs to be broken. These eggs were taken to the creek and washed clean of the mess created by the broken ones. Then Ezra filled the bucket with fresh water from the creek and added the good eggs. He set the bucket in the fire to boil before a catastrophe befell their remaining supper. Calmed now by the egg incident, everyone set about catching some fish to augment the boiled eggs. When it all came together, there was enough food to go around, though this group would have eaten more had it been available.

Sunday services held a special appeal to Amos this week as he would get the opportunity to show off his new mule and wagon. The pair of mules stepped lively as Amos carried his folks from their hollow out to the main road leading to Hickory Ford. But Amos didn't have to wait until they got to the Baptist church at Hickory Ford to show off the wagon. They stopped numerous times on the way to pick up folks who were walking. Many people walked to church on Sundays, or at least until a wagon came along upon which they could ride.

Once at the church yard, Amos pulled his team and wagon with its load of the faithful alongside the Edwards wagon. This was a time when people came early to church for a time of visiting. The men sat on their heels out under the trees and talked over the crops and such while the women went to the church house to talk of house things. Several of the men commented to Amos on "thet big mule" and upon the value of a Studebaker wagon. Amos swelled with pride so that he lost track of the sermon on more than one occasion. He admonished himself back into reality but didn't think it too awful a sin to appreciate his growing up among the men folk. For his feelings were not about pride of self, but his continued arrival at manhood. These thoughts were still in his head as he drove toward his place on the Little Sandy River. Amos concluded by thinking that he didn't understand what it was to be a man, but he believed that manhood was coming to pass within himself. And, he knew that he liked these feelings.

As he so often did while going back to the bottoms, he thought over the goings on back in Hickory Ford. His mother had informed him that Daniel, his brother next in age, had taken a new school position for next year in Cummings, a small community thirty miles to the south. Also, she had told him that his brother Sam and his wife, Hattie, were doing well in the hardware business in Oak Ridge. In his own mind, Amos figured that the town living was what Hattie liked best, next to the regular pay from a town job. Amos had seen Tom, his oldest brother, while at home. He and Lizbeth had taken to farming the little Spain place just out of Hickory Ford. Tom also helped their poppa some with his own farm. Amos recollected that each of these couples had had another child over the past year. Amos thought that he was in no hurry for a wife and babies, as he had his hands full with his little rough clearing in the bottoms.

Thoughts of marriage and babies reminded Amos of Marie Johnson. Just a few weeks ago, he had learned that she had married Luther Tate, a young man from over on Poplar Ridge. Amos wondered if she had given up on him because he spent so much time off in the bottoms. Amos smiled to himself as he thought that he hadn't been in Hickory Ford enough for Marie to spark him. However little Amos may have known about girls, he did know that the real sparking was most often done by the girls, not the boys.

Amos rode on feeling secure now that Marie was hitched up with another fellow. He knew Marie to be a fine girl, but one who had an itch to get married. And, that just wasn't in Amos' plans yet. Losing the thoughts of Hickory Ford, Amos looked about the road at the seemingly endless timber growing up out of the rich bottom soil. Amos figured that these trees and ones like them had been here since the Lord created the earth and would always be here. The few cleared fields were nothing but dots among the vastness of the timbered bottoms.

In the days after Amos' return, he tended to various chores. First, he hoed the garden, then the corn patch in the clearing. Next, he plowed the middles with the single stock. All of this took most of a week. With the fields cleaned, Amos took an afternoon to catch a mess of fish from the river. It was then that he began to notice the change. While watching his line for bites, Amos realized that the river level was rising and that the usual clarity had been replaced by a dinginess. He was used to the river rising and falling from day to day in accordance with water flowing into the river from upstream, so he took his catch to the cabin and thought no more of it.

A glance to the river the next morning got his attention. The level of the river was at least two feet higher than the afternoon before. Amos knew that this was not the result of a shower of rain upriver, but was instead produced by an overflow from the Big Sandy. "Must have been some rain up above to put thet much water in the Big Sandy all at onct," said Amos out loud.

Amos worked in the barn through the morning, cleaning out the manure and arranging hand tools. He continued to think of how big that rain must have been to back up the Big Sandy so much. Toward noon, he heard the first raindrops on the shingles of the barn roof. By the time he headed for the cabin to fix his dinner, the rain was coming down hard. All the low areas between the two structures were filled with water, forcing Amos to run a circuitous course. As the rain continued to come down hard all afternoon, Amos could do no work outside the barn. He found the cleanup tedious, especially since he was forced to stay inside. By mid-afternoon, he could find nothing else in the barn which needed doing, so he made a dash through the downpour to the cabin. There he washed up and took his time in fixing a more elaborate supper than he normally enjoyed.

With supper over and the dishes washed, the cabin took on a pleasant warmth which comforted Amos. Last year, the roof had leaked at even a little rain. Now it was dry and warm inside, with the new shingles turning back the pelting rain. Thunder and lightning lashed the late afternoon sky as if some kind of war were going on in the dark sky above.

Time and again Amos stepped to the door and opened it to survey the gathering water. It became so dark that only when the lightning flashed could he see beyond a few feet from the cabin door. But then the clearing would sometimes be as light as day. During these brief flashes Amos would quickly look from the corn field to the barn where the two mules sought refuge from the storm, and then on out to the river. Speckle had taken up his customary position near the cookstove where Amos had placed a tow sack for a dog bed. The hound cringed when Amos opened the door as the frequent peals of thunder could more easily come to his sensitive ears.

It was near midnight when Amos finally blew out the lamp

and laid upon his straw tick. He lay there sleepless for yet another hour thinking of the crop which just this morning had looked so good. Amos thought to himself that if the rain stopped right now, which it gave no indication of doing, the garden vegetables, pea hay and corn would still be set back in their growth.

Before giving up the vigil for sleep, Amos had to get up one last time to stand in the doorway and look out over the standing water all around the clearing. At times the lightning flashes were so frequent and close together that for several seconds at a time the clearing was as bright as day. Again and again, he cast unbelieving glances at the rising river, which had overflowed its banks and was beginning to spread out over the woods.

Going to his bed for the last time, Amos marveled at the amount of rain in so short a time. He reminded himself that the river was already swollen from the apparent heavy rains upstream. His last thoughts before sleep were of what he might look out upon come morning.

A tired Amos awoke later than usual and began to recount the memories of last evening. As his mind began to focus, he recalled the torrential rains and realized that the quiet of the morning meant that the rain had stopped. Quickly he leaped from his bed and swung open the cabin door to be startled by seeing water everywhere he looked.

The water of the river stretched up to the cabin and barn, surrounding them both, and reached far out onto the field of corn. Only out there was there any land showing. Taking time to only step into his overalls, Amos walked through the cold water covering his yard out to the barn lot. His mules stood there in ankle deep water, the water covering the inside of the barn as well. He climbed up into the loft to throw some pea hay down into their manger before returning to the cabin. Speckle had come out also, but was disconcerted by all the water over that which he knew as his home.

Back in the cabin, Amos tried to sort out their situation. With water all around them, there seemed to be nothing that they could do outside. And, though the rain was stopped, the sky was still heavily overcast, and the wind overhead was whipping dark clouds across the small clearing. Amos knew that only time would tell if the clouds were breaking up or another storm was moving into the area. He also wondered how much rain had occurred upriver as that would determine if the river would continue to rise before it drained away the water from the immediate area.

Since he was in no hurry, Amos fixed a bigger breakfast than normal, with fresh biscuits, three fried eggs, fried potatoes, and several slices of the little remaining cured ham. But in spite of the extra food, his appetite was dulled by the seriousness of the situation. And when his dishes were washed, he found himself sitting in front of the open doorway, staring out at all the water. On occasion, he could see fish swimming through the shallow water of his yard but could find no interest in trying to catch them. He did wade out to the river bank and pulled his dugout away from the river. After tying it to one of the limbs of the big pin oak, Amos got a small bucket and bailed most of the water from the craft.

Throughout the morning Amos could tell that the water level was rising around the buildings, meaning that more was moving down from upriver. Noon brought the return of the rain, and Amos found no appetite for fixing dinner. Amos spent much of the afternoon moving the remaining ears of corn from the crib up into the loft with the hay. There they would be safe from the water which could quickly ruin them. Also, he moved all his hand tools into the loft to prevent the metal from rusting and the wooden handles from being soaked to the point of splitting. At dusk with the barn taken care of the best he could, he waded his way back to the cabin. Upon entering, he noticed with a certain heaviness that the water level was up on the cabin steps.

All afternoon the rain came heavily, and by dusk Amos couldn't see much of his young corn out in the field. By this time the mules were standing in water almost up to their hocks. Amos felt sorry for them, but had no high land close to the house for them.

Though he hadn't even fixed any dinner, Amos had only a limited interest in supper. He made himself cook some supper as it was something to do and his body needed the food regardless of his interest level. But with the dishes done he had nothing to occupy himself but to reread the newspapers which he had tacked up on the walls last winter. He supposed that the one advantage of his being a slow reader was that one story could keep him busy for a long time.

Speckle though could not read and would only remain on his sack so long before rising to pace the small floor. Amos had allowed him to go out when he wanted, but with the water rising that was not often. In the past twenty-four hours, the cabin had shrunk immeasurably, even more so than in the cold winter months. At least, then he and Speckle were free to get out for chores or to hunt. Now they were both prisoners of the rising water.

It was a long night during which the rain seemed to have never stopped, only slacking occasionally. Amos awoke earlier than usual as something wasn't right about his bed. As he gained his wits, the realization came that Speckle had made a place for himself near Amos' feet, something that he had not done since the cold nights of the past winter.

"Oh, wal'," said Amos aloud, "there's no harm in it, even though mamma wouldn't like it." Lifting his legs from under the covers he made to set his feet on the floor as it was near enough to daylight to get on up. Anyway, he wanted to check on the water outside.

With a sudden start, he jerked his feet back from the cold sensation on the floor. At first, he didn't know what it could have been, and then he knew the sensation to be both cool and wet. This time he reached out a hand and sure enough, his floor was covered by water. And not just a little water, but a good two inches.

Somewhat unsure of what to do, he stepped out into it to reach the table where the lamp sat. With the lamp lit, he gazed at the strange scene around him. His cabin floor and everything on it was covered ankle deep in water. Quickly he began to pick up things and became angry with himself for not being neater. He just couldn't understand why he hadn't foreseen the possibly of this before he went to bed.

As most of the wood box was dry, he had no difficulty in getting a fire started in the cookstove. Amos certainly felt odd standing there in his long underwear and gum boots while he cooked his breakfast over a stove which stood in water. Fortunately, he found some humor in it. Otherwise, the situation might have unnerved him.

Daylight revealed that all but the far end of the field was under water. The full realization of the loss of the corn crop settled upon Amos like a heavyweight. His farming experience told him that without a doubt the young corn plants were drowned and

would never recover from this much exposure to water.

Forcing himself to think of other things, Amos now feared for his animals. The water in the barn was upon the knees of the big mule, and it wouldn't take much more of a rise until Amos and Speckle could find no refuge even on the bed. Knowing that he had to do something before conditions worsened, he determined to paddle the dugout out the wagon track to White Creek and survey the water level there.

Fortunately for the mules, their manger was still out of the water. Amos fed them a generous portion of hay and corn before untying the dugout. He had left the knee boots back at the cabin as they would be useless in deep water.

The track was easy enough to find though it gave Amos an odd feeling to paddle his way down a road on which he had walked and ridden so many times. The rain had slacked but had not stopped. Everything seemed so very wet and dreary with the leaves soaked to the point that refuge could not even be found under a tree as the excess water worked its way on down. Amos wondered about all the game, but on thinking about it figured everything small was in some den tree. The deer though would have to find safety on the ridges scattered throughout the bottoms.

Amos found that the dugout would travel faster than the mules could walk as he could cut across through the woods to shorten the distance. Once at the White Creek Crossing, he was disappointed to find that it offered little hope as the location of the creek bed was hardly discernible with the high water. The water was faster here and when Amos tested it with a long pole, it appeared to be about five feet deep.

Paddling back to the cabin, Amos anxiously went over their options. Certainly, the barn loft could offer a safe refuge for Speckle and himself as the loft floor was a good eight feet above the ground. But there was absolutely no possibility of getting Little Red and Big Ned into the barn loft. And if left to stand in the stable or lot below, they could only swim until they drowned when the water rose above their legs. The thought horrified Amos. Somehow he had to find a way out to high ground until the storm spent itself and the high water receded.

He considered returning to Hickory Ford, but under such conditions the trip would be exhausting. It normally took about four hours for the animals to walk those twelve miles to Red Gum Ridge, but that same walk through mud and high water could take an entire day. Without rest or feed along the way, it would most assuredly take a heavy toll upon the two mules. Besides, by the time he returned to the cabin and made preparations, there would certainly not be enough daylight left for the trip. The darkness would bring additional risks of an accident. And, if they waited until tomorrow morning, the water here in the bottoms would likely be too deep for them to get out alive. That realization increased his fear. Amos knew that no matter what happened, he would not leave either mule to the fate of the storm.

Paddling into the house-place, he knew that they must leave here soon. For the rest of the morning, Amos attended to the slow process of putting away his household goods in as secure a manner as possible. All the cooking utensils, the food, and his extra clothing were taken to the barn loft. He guided his canoe into the barn and tied it in one of the stalls. He chose the barn as the more secure place due to its much greater weight. Things of small value were hung in the rafters of the cabin. Amos wasn't sure what would happen to the cabin if the water continued to rise and a current swept through the bottoms.

Finally, they were ready to ride away from what they all considered their home. Amos chose to ride Big Ned as he stood higher out of the water than Little Red. And there might be places where the current could be too strong for the little mule. Speckle was stuffed into a tow sack with only his head out, an arrangement which he did not like but consented to out of trust in Amos. A sack of foodstuffs was hung on the opposite side of the saddle to counteract the weight of the hound. A bundle of blankets and extra clothes was tied behind the saddle along with one kerosene lantern. When he thought that these preparations would have to do, Amos hung his .22 rifle over his shoulders and stepped into the saddle above the big mule.

The mules seemed to sense the gravity of the situation and stepped out eagerly. At the edge of the clearing, Amos pulled them up as he had so many times before. Here he sat and surveyed what had become their home place. The river had no definition as the water had risen out of its banks and spread out as far as Amos could see in either direction. The only ground visible was at the far end of the field where he had planted the peas for hay. The corn which had looked so promising only a few days before was gone, as well as the hay and vegetables. How strange the clearing looked inundated with water until it resembled a sea more than a farm. Amos recalled that on his last trip inside his cabin, the water was even up in the stoves.

It was a sobering moment there for Amos, soaked to the skin with the wind driving the rain into his face. All of it seemed overwhelming, considering the sweat and sometimes blood they had all given to turn this rough clearing into a productive farm. But something within Amos brought a resolve forth that he set in his mind that he would be back to this place, as it was his home.

A half hour later the four of them arrived at the crossing on White Creek. Amos sat anxiously in a downpour of rain, awed by the risk of crossing the swift current choked with who knows how much brush. Here where the mules stood, the water was up to his knees as he sat astride Ned. Both Speckle and Little Red were very nervous with the high water, though the big mule appeared calm. Amos knew that the mules would have to swim, something which he had done with Little Red on several occasions. The worrisome part was the current and the possibility of trees or brush beneath the surface.

Knowing that to delay would not better their situation, Amos loosened Speckle from his sack and allowed the hound to swim free. As soon as Speckle got clear of the mules, Amos cast Little Red's lead rope over his back and squeezed Ned into stepping forward. Then at Ned's lead, all of them moved into the strong current of White Creek. Amos had intentionally guided Ned into the current at the head of the crossing, allowing for the mule to be swept downstream some before reaching solid footing on the other side. Amos aided Ned all he could by slipping back out of the saddle to hang onto the mule's tail, thus removing the burden of his weight. The distance wasn't far, only about fifty feet, but it took all the mules' swimming strength to break free of the pull of the main current without being swept into the thick timber downstream.

But the hound was not nearly as strong, and his light body was whipped away by the speed of the current. Amos' last glimpse of Speckle was as he was swept into the timber below. Tears for his hound came to Amos' eyes, but they were washed away by the surging waters of the creek.

Once out of the depths of the creek, the mules stopped to

catch their breath. Amos began to call down into the timber for Speckle. With fear in his heart, he ran through the thigh deep water to search for his beloved hound. But before he had gone far, a brown speckled head came swimming through the undergrowth.

Tears again filled Amos' eyes as he knelt to cradle up his dog. "I should have known you'd outswim thet ol' creek," croaked Amos.

In response, Speckle yipped joyfully.

As Amos caught up his mules, he knew that all four of them were relieved to have gotten across White Creek safely. He remounted Ned and with Speckle nestled in his lap, turned the mules on down their road of water. Amos was disappointed though not surprised that the Potter place looked deserted. Thinking back, Amos remembered that Mrs. Potter's people were at Willow Point and figured that the whole family had moved into town to wait out the flood.

Upon coming to the fork in the road which gave Amos the opportunity to either ride on east to Hickory Ford or turn west for Willow Point. He sat there, knowing that any decision he made would affect his three animals as well. Amos weighed the alternatives. Hickory Ford would mean probably ten hours of travel through almost continuous water and mud, not to mention having to cross the Fourche River. They'd all be fortunate to make Red Gum Ridge by midnight, and if they did the mules would be exhausted, possibly permanently injured from the stress. He could not ask them to make that effort. His mind turned to Willow Point and its possibilities. It was certainly closer, only about five miles. But then they'd have to cross The Little Sandy as the bridge on the south side of town would likely be well under water, if not washed away altogether. Swimming the Little Sandy downstream would be harder than White Creek as it would have much more volume and current. Besides, if they did get across to Willow Point, what would they find there? The people there were probably in quite a fix right about now, and Amos wanted to better his situation.

Sitting there in that expanse of water as the rain continued to come down upon him, he tried to remember what Mr. Potter had told him about this country during their few visits. Then the words came to him almost out loud, "Post Oak Hills." Aloud Amos asked, "Now Little Red, where did Mr. Potter say them hills were?" Hearing his name, the little mule perked his ears and looked up to Amos who was gazing off to the south. "Seems to me thet he said they were out yonder, 'bout four mile or so," spoke Amos.

Without further thought, Amos kneed Ned into motion and headed the party southwest. He didn't actually know where they were headed, but they could not stay there in belly-deep water and watch it rain. Frequently as the two mules walked forward, Amos watched the water level on Little Red's body for indications of their moving into deeper or shallower water.

After about an hour's travel, Amos noticed that the water was not quite as high on the little mule. Overjoyed he pushed Ned on at a faster pace, anxious to get to solid ground. The water continued to get shallower for the next half hour until unexpectedly high ground appeared before them. Anxious themselves to get away from the ever-present water, both mules broke into a trot until they stepped out of the water.

Ecstatic himself, Amos wearily stepped from the saddle and let Speckle down to run on his own at last. While the mules blew and stamped around, Amos dropped himself to earth, however wet. Little Red shook himself like a dog, showering all the rest of them with water which they felt they didn't need.

Amos remembered that for a time he had wondered if they would ever get away from what had seemed like a prison of water. Sitting there wet to the skin and muddy from his new position on the ground, he lifted his head to the rain dripping clouds above and thanked his God for deliverance. In a bit of reverent humor, Amos stated, "No more, Lord, will I ever thank of Noah as jest another Bible feller in a story."

Tired though they all were, Amos knew that they had to move on to find a place to camp as night would come early with the heavy cloud cover. On up into the small hills they traveled, seeking higher and higher ground, relishing in its security. Soon they realized that these hills were security for many others as ground animals seemed to be in abundance. These low hills were serving as a sanctuary for wildlife in the surrounding area which had no safe home.

An hour's searching revealed what Amos knew would make a good shelter for them. It was a pocket in the side of one of the hills, below the crest and away from the west wind but high up from the rising water. He had already noted that there were no large trees in these hills as he would find in the river bottoms. Down there a lost hunter could often find a large hollow cypress in which to get refuge from rain and wind as well as build a warming fire. Amos recalled Mr. Potter saying these hills were made of a poor white soil, capable of only making trees large enough for fence posts, thus the name of Post Oak Hills.

Stepping down from Ned Amos quickly unloaded him of bags and saddle before turning the big mule loose to graze on the sparse grass nearby. Little Red though was tied to a tree, as a loose mule would never leave his teammate. The tether then on Ned was an emotional one stronger than any rope.

Taking the axe from the bundle of clothes, Amos cut a few saplings and secured them into a framework over which he stretched a wagon sheet. Some dry bark was located underneath a tree which had fallen sometime in the past. With this and the small amount of kindling which he had placed in a waterproof can, Amos started a fire just under the shelter.

His supper that night wasn't much as he had been able to bring only limited provisions. He fried a few strips of ham in a steel skillet and ate that with some leftover biscuits. He'd had the foresight to bring some drinking water from the pump in a hollow gourd, so he also had a little coffee to help warm him up on the insides. Speckle, of course, shared in the ham and biscuits but declined the coffee. The mules would have to get by on the sparse grass which grew under the small trees in these hills. Amos had no way of carrying any feed for them without it getting soaked during their day's travel.

It was truly a wet camp, lying there on the wet ground in wet clothes. But the wagon sheet kept off most of the rain and after a time his little-sheltered area began to dry from the heat of the fire.

It was good light the next morning before Amos woke and rose from his damp bed of earth. He felt stiff and sore all over from the past day's experience. His mood was not improved by the fact that rain was still falling. Reluctantly, he stepped away from his shelter to untie one of the mules to graze, a rotation which he would follow again and again in the days ahead.

Stooping back inside his shelter, he paused to consider his situation. First, he determined that there was no hurry in anything he did as they were out of danger, and with no place to go. They would just stay in these hills and wait out the flood which would recede in its own good time. His only concerns were food and firewood.

Motivating himself to get some breakfast, Amos looked to the fire possibilities. He was disheartened to discover that all the dry kindling had been used last night with the wet wood. His fatigue had been so heavy last evening that he had not thought to split and dry any wood for his morning's fire. He gathered the driest and smallest pieces of wood from the small cache off to one side of the shelter and arranged it into an airy stack before pouring some of his extra coal oil over it. Amos told himself that he would have to be careful about doing this anymore as there was only so much for the lantern and they may be here for quite a spell. With a sparse breakfast of small amounts of ham and potatoes, Amos began to gather firewood from the surrounding woods. Using just the ax, he dragged in and split up the dead wood as he found it. Green wood would be too hard to dry out over his small fire.

The wood gathering continued for the rest of the day as a good amount would be needed over several days. As it was brought into the camp, some of the pieces were arranged in a circle around the fire to dry out. As the day progressed, Amos foraged farther and farther from camp, more out of curiosity than the need for more wood.

It was late in the afternoon when good fortune came his way as he saw a gray squirrel moving in one of the small oaks out to his front. Amos was able to sneak up close, but at the last minute the squirrel became startled and began jumping from tree to tree to get away. Astounding even himself, a single shot from the .22 brought the squirrel down while running up a long limb. Amos didn't know if it were an accident or not, as he'd never hit one running before. Anyway, it would make a good supper that night.

The following morning brought an end to the rain which had lasted for four days. Thinking that game would be out today to find feed, Amos skipped his breakfast and slipped through the post oaks in search of more fresh meat to fill in for his dwindling food supply. He was walking through some head high brush when a sound startled him so that his heart seemed to stop in mid beat. It seemed like a snort, but not just one, there must have been at least three. And whatever it was, he was in the middle of them. He stood there as stiff as one of the trees and listened as hard as he could for what seemed like an hour but was probably less than a minute. Amos thought that if he could just hear it again, he might know what kind of animal was out here. He also wondered as to the whereabouts of Speckle, as the hound would not have let Amos walk into the middle of trouble. As the long seconds passed by, Amos began to look about for the nearest tree should he need it in a hurry.

Then it came again, behind him in the brush, a loud snort so clear and close that Amos didn't even have to look behind him to know its origin. As his feet peddled him toward the nearest tree, the thought of wild hogs brought motion to him that he didn't think possible. A few long leaps and a fling upward placed Amos onto a stout limb about six feet off the ground.

Looking below he saw that the brush in all directions was shaking as if a whole herd of hogs was in motion. Realizing that no hog had come after him and that he was indeed safe, Amos began to catch his breath and allow the shaking to stop. Apparently, this time the hogs were as afraid of him as he was of them. But he well knew that this was not always the case as he had known of hunters who had been charged and ripped open by wild hogs. To be sure of his safety, he waited several minutes before easing out of the tree to resume his hunt.

Much more watchful now, he kept both eyes and both ears open as he slowly worked his way through the more open timber. Some time later he caught sight of a coon searching for food in the leaves under a persimmon tree. With a careful aim for a clean head shot, not injuring the hide or meat, the crack of the .22 dropped the coon. Pleased with himself, Amos returned to camp where he placed the dressed coon on a rack over the fire. There it would slowly roast and be a fine supper for himself and the hound. While the coon was cooking, he fried just a few pieces of the little remaining ham to hold him over until later in the day when the coon was done.

That evening Amos lay under his shelter and watched the bright stars overhead. Both he and Speckle had gorged themselves on the coon as there was no way to keep the meat for long. Amos realized that in the days ahead, he would have to bring in fresh meat daily to feed the two of them until they could get back to their cabin on the Little Sandy. He felt much better tonight as the day had been dry and restful. His sleep that night was deep and long, the first such since the beginning of the heavy rains. Breakfast the next morning was the leftover coon reheated, with no bread or potatoes. Amos knew it wasn't much of a meal, but this was not the time or place to be picky. He knew that he was fortunate just to have plenty to eat.

Amos spent most of the day riding around the north edge of these low-lying hills. He was curious as to how much area they covered. First, he rode back down to the place where they had come up out of the water and was surprised to see that the water level was even higher than it was three days ago. He dismounted and cut a sapling off at the ground, stripped it of all limbs and sharpened the large end to a point. This stake was then pushed into the ground at the water level so Amos could mark the rise and fall of the water from day to day.

While riding west along the water's edge, Amos saw tracks of the wild hogs but was not afraid with the mules along. Further along, a branch was draining water out of the hills into the low land covered by the flood. From this he chose a fairly clear pool and filled his gourd with drinking water, mentally reminding himself that this water would need to be boiled before drinking as it likely had wiggletails. Branch water often did in the summer time, and Amos certainly had enough problems without a belly full of wiggletails.

Speckle treed two squirrels which had been out feeding on acorns. Amos took both of them with the .22, and while he was picking them up from the ground, he thought he might find some acorns for himself to eat. Searching through the leaves, he was able to fill his pockets with last year's crop. Acorns were not normal human fare, but Amos needed every food source he could find to give variety to his diet.

The days which followed held to much the same pattern. Amos was relieved to find that the water level began to drop the next day and he marked the recession daily. Fresh meat was killed each day, with a variety of coon, possum, squirrel and even a pig was taken one day. One of his trips revealed an old slough which had been cut out many years before by another river channel or flood. Amos called it Hook Slough for its shape and went there daily to fish. He found that the fish brought a welcome relief to the straight meat diet. The acorns were a welcome treat. He not only ate them as nuts, but after being roasted and ground they were boiled for a form of coffee. Altogether, his food sources were plentiful for the few days he stayed in the hills.

Each day he had followed the retreat of the flood waters until the 14th day since the rains first began. It was on this day that he figured he could make it all the way to the Potters at least, and possibly get to his own cabin. He wanted to strike out for home, but with some of his gear back in the hills, he didn't want to have to retrieve it later. So he decided to give the water one more day to go down, and tomorrow he would attempt to return to his home on the Little Sandy. Because Amos wanted to know more about the Post Oak Hills, he spent the day riding a large circle to learn as much about them as possible before leaving the area. He was thankful to the Lord for placing them here, as these hills had in a way been his ark to protect him from his own flood.

Early the next morning he rode out of the hills with all his gear, hoping not to have to return here in the near future. This time it only required an hour's riding to reach the Potter's as the water had receded back except for isolated holes. Again, he was discouraged that the Potters were not at home and figured that they were still in Willow Point with her people.

White Creek was not nearly so fearsome this time as the water was well within the banks of the creek and neither mule had to swim in the crossing. Speckle swam across with ease now. Already, Amos had a foreboding about what he might find in his clearing. All around him the high water mark was higher than the backs of the mules with brush and small trees hanging in piles against the larger trees.

A half hour later he rode into his own clearing only to have his breath taken away. The mules instinctively stopped as Amos sat frozen at what he saw. The field which he had labored so hard over had been covered in silt and brush, not to mention several trees which lay here and there where the flood had deposited them. Not a single stalk of corn showed through the brown slimy mass that he had known as his field.

And there out on the ridge at the far end of the clearing among the dead trees sat his cabin, as if it were supposed to be there. Amos had to look to the house place to make himself believe that it was actually true. To be sure, there was no cabin across from the barn, only a bare spot of ground where it had been.

Looking on to the barn, he was relieved to see it where it was supposed to be and still standing, though it had been covered in mud most of the way up its sides. Brush and trees lay everywhere, and if he had not looked twice at a larger pile, he would not have known that it was really his Studebaker wagon, covered in mud and topped with a bushy tree. In silent awe, he rode on toward the barn. There he dropped to the silt and mud mixture below him and began to check on the condition of the barn. It had not been damaged, just muddied inside and out. Amos then climbed up into the loft to check on the items which he had stored there. He was relieved to find that all the contents of the loft were as he had left them. A quick check confirmed that his canoe was still in the stall where he had tied it almost two weeks ago.

Before he lowered himself from the loft to check the cabin, Amos dropped hay and corn down to the mules. It was the first such feed they had had in eleven days, and they both ate eagerly. With his gum boots on, Amos began the long muddy walk out to the cabin. Several times on the way up the length of the field, he stopped to turn with a look of awe at the scene around him.

Walking to where the cabin now sat, he saw that the reason

for its present location was two dead standing trees which had been in just the right place to catch the drifting cabin and hold it for Amos' return. As the flood waters lowered, the cabin had just set down upon the ground as if it had been here all along.

Pushing on the half-open door, Amos stepped in and stood dumbstruck. Everything appeared to be here, though in different places than he remembered them. What struck him was all the silt and mud, from about a height of about six feet down. The stoves, eating table, bed, and seemingly everything that had been left here was covered in a thick layer of mud. Not knowing what to do about it, Amos stepped back out into the field where the bright sun gave everything a shiny appearance.

He walked back toward the barn in something of a daze, finding himself climbing upon the lot fence, possibly to remove himself even a little bit from the reality of this place. The pile of firewood had largely floated away, as had much of the split rail fence forming the small pasture.

A question formed on Amos' lips, "How can I ever put this back together?" The minutes ticked by and the answer came to him. "The same way I did it the first time, by jest doin' it, one thang at a time."

CHAPTER ELEVEN

Moonshine Slough

ONCE AMOS HAD REGAINED HIS COMPOSURE after seeing the flood damage to his farm, he decided to stay there for an extra day. The high water in the Fourche River bottoms would make the trip back to Hickory Ford difficult. The barn loft was dry and contained feed for the mules as well as his own stores of food. He could just stay in the barn loft. Certainly, he had more resources here than back in the Post Oak Hills.

To brighten the scene, Amos pulled the dugout back to the river and washed it clean of mud and sticks. His mind was set somewhat at ease with just this one chore completed. Somehow now the cleanup and replanting did not seem as overwhelming. With his dugout cleaned, He decided to set out a few lines for fresh fish. He and Speckle had settled down on the river bank to watch the lines when the hound began a low growl in his throat. Amos saw the hair on the back of Speckle's neck stand straight up. Glad that he had by chance picked up the .22 rifle when he had left the barn, Amos stood there now, gripping it for security. He sensed that whatever was upsetting the dog was no little varmint.

Presently, he heard a slight sound, not loud enough at first to be distinguishable. Continuing to listen, he recognized it as the strokes of a paddle. As the sound approached, Amos knew that someone was coming downriver in a boat. He wondered who would have been upriver during the flood, or would have any business up there now.

As the boat rounded the near curve in the little river, he made out two men. They were dressed in rough garb, rougher even than most farmers wore. The man in the front was the older of the two. Amos judged that he was older than his Poppa, but not as old as his grandpa. The man wore the haggard look of hard living, like an old mule who had been rode hard and put away wet too many times. Beyond the haggard look on his face, his countenance was dispirited, as if some great calamity had happened to him. He worked at the paddle, but without any serious effort.

The man in the back of the boat seemed tall, even while sitting down. His face was serious, though not downcast. Somehow Amos perceived a darkness about this man, if not meanness, then mystery. There was such a fellow back at Hickory Ford who did odd jobs to get by but mostly lived up in the hills by himself, seldom socializing with anyone.

As the boat came downstream, the older man in the front suddenly became aware of Amos' presence. He pulled the boat in Amos' direction, to the displeasure of the tall man in the back. At their approach, Speckle began to bark ferociously, showing intentions of defending their place.

"Howdy there, boy," hailed the old man. "Might we have some fresh water from ye' pump yonder?"

"Hesh, Speckle, quiet now, hound," called Amos to settle the dog. "Shore, mister, ye kin hev' all ye want, there's always been plenty," responded Amos.

Though still cautious, Amos was trying to be hospitable. Showing respect for the older man who appeared weak, Amos stepped into the river to take the tie rope off the front of the boat. With it he pulled their boat up on the river bank where they could step out. The older man eased his way out over the boat's front and slowly straightened his stiff joints, all the while looking carefully over Amos' place.

Relieved now, the old man began to talk. "Terrible flood, ruinous to all a body sets out to do. How'd ya make it wi'out warshing away, boy, surely ya didn't hide out in the barn loft, did ya?"

Somehow this old man's manner put Amos on his guard. In his life at Hickory Ford, he'd never met any really bad men, but something about this man gave that impression. Still, Amos wondered where they had been and quickly decided not to ask. About this moment Amos noticed that the tall man stepped from the boat by just stepping into the shallow water alongside. The part which alerted Amos was his bare feet, feet that were long and showed a roughness which only comes from long use without shoes. Suddenly, Amos recalled the image of that footprint in his yard last summer. Then he recalled the memory of the two men in the boat last winter.

"Wal, boy, did ya' stay out the storm here or go somers else?" insisted the old man.

"Uh, I left out fer high ground, an' jes got back this mawnin'," answered Amos, not wanting to give these men any more information than they already knew. Somehow he thought that they knew a sight more about him than he did about them.

Still scared, but remembering the request for water, Amos offered, "Com' on up to the cabin, uh, I mean whur the cabin was afore the flood. I'll pump you fellers up some clean water."

They all walked to the pump, Speckle staying at Amos' side,

but keeping a close watch on these men of the river. Amos pumped a bucket full of water from the well and set out a dipper. The water wasn't as clear as before the flood, but still much clearer than the river water. The two men drank at leisure, all the while the old man mumbled to himself about the "turr'ble flood," "ruined fer good this time," "Jack Barret will take over the trade fer shore ... ruined fer shore."

The tall man had said nothing, only drank and looked about. It was apparent he noticed Amos that had not laid down the .22 since their arrival. Amos supposed that it did appear unneighborly, but decided it was a wise choice. Anyway, Amos felt better with it, though he'd never even thought of shooting a man on purpose before today.

After their drink, the old man turned back toward the river, the tall man following. Standing there, Amos didn't know what to do, for he had never seen visitors act in such a manner. He decided to follow them to the river bank for nothing else than to say goodbye.

The two men re-entered the boat in the manner of their exit and Amos pushed it off as he had pulled it in before. As their boat caught the current and began to move downriver, the old man raised his left hand in a small gesture of farewell. Amos watched them paddle downriver with the current, the old man mumbling with the tall man silent, just as they had come.

With the passing of these two men, the mystery of the night people had unraveled. Or had it? Amos still didn't know who they were or what they had been about. From the tone of the old man's conversation, Amos determined that they would not return up the Little Sandy again. Their leaving during daylight further confirmed this, as their travel before this had always been under cover of darkness.

Amos' curiosity over this year-long mystery reached a fever pitch. He decided that he would try this very afternoon to discover what these men had been doing, and why they had such a secretive manner. From the loft, he threw the mules enough hay to last them until the next day and then packed enough food for the same amount of time. He filled the water trough for the mules and then filled the gourd with water to take with him.

Supplied for several hours of searching, Amos paddled the dugout upriver as fast as he could. Speckle sat anxiously in the front as if he knew the nature of their trip. About a mile up the river, Speckle began to bark at a drift caught on the inside curve of the river. Paddling up to it, Amos saw a wooden barrel hung up in the brush. He pulled out the bung and was greeted with a sour smell. Moving on upriver, they saw other things, clothing, bottles, and other such man-made articles, obviously left by the flood. In one drift, he discovered a ceramic jug, tightly corked and unbroken. As Amos picked up the jug to examine it, he could tell that it contained a small amount of liquid. Removing the cork, he was greeted with a strong, unmistakable odor. Amos was repelled by the stench, but all the same knew what it was. It was "shine," or "white lightning" as some folks called it. This was home-brewed liquor, made in a still hid out here in the bottoms so the maker wouldn't have to pay taxes on it. Amos' family didn't drink liquor, but he'd smelled it many times when the older boys would bring some to a fishing camp.

Now Amos knew that those men had had a still hidden up the river and likely it had been lost to the flood. This could be the end of the story, but Amos paddled on upriver to see if he could find it. Amos knew that looking for someone's still could be very dangerous. Stills were usually well guarded against snoopers, particularly competitors. But he didn't think there was any danger now as the men had left the bottoms, probably for good.

Amos reasoned that the still would have been close to the river, allowing for easy transport. The river would make it easy to take the grain necessary for production in, and the finished liquor out. But, he told himself, it wouldn't be obvious. He began to think of how such a place could be hidden and yet be still close to the river. Certainly, if it were too close, anyone traveling on the river would see the wood smoke or catch wind of the strong odor of the sour mash.

It was probably three miles up river from his place where he came to what appeared to be a fork in the river. Letting his canoe drift in mid-stream, Amos studied each channel. He then realized that the left fork was the main channel while the one to the right was a former channel that was mostly grown up in trees. It was flowing strong now as it still carried the overflow of the flood.

Amos dug his paddle deep into the river, pushing the dugout into this older channel. He suspected that this old river channel would lead him right to the still. It was a perfect setup for such secret activity. There would be enough water for easy transportation of the still materials, with the main river traffic kept at a safe distance. Speckle was now alert as he sensed that they were close to what they sought. Slowly, the dugout plied its way through the cypress and tupelo gum, keeping in the middle of the channel as much as possible. The flood had left this old channel full of drifts and logs, making it hard to navigate.

A quarter of a mile up this channel, Amos came upon what remained of a large boiler wedged between two large cypresses and crushed from the force of water and debris. This must have been what was used to heat the liquor. For sure now, Amos knew that he and Sparkle were in the right direction.

A short distance farther, as the channel turned sharply to the left, the remains of a treehouse hung from four fifty-foot hickories, scraps of cloth blowing in the breeze. Amos put the dugout into the bank and got out to walk around. Several large rocks formed a fireplace on which the boiler must have sat while in operation. He knew that these rocks had to have been brought in from the hills at great effort. It seemed that the rocks were about the only thing which didn't get swept away with the flood. Amos guessed from the mental state of the old man that a sizeable amount of equipment and supplies had been lost, putting him out of business.

Standing there in the midst of the wreckage, Amos felt sorry for the old man's loss, but yet he had never known anything good to come from liquor or its making. It made men do stupid things, which they often regretted. John and his Poppa both spoke no good of drinking or of the people who did. And this old man had an air of menace about him that brought caution to mind. Danger oozed from him. And, speaking of danger, that tall barefooted man who never spoke scared Amos all the way down to his toes. Paddling back downriver for his place, Amos reasoned that he'd feel a lot better about living in the bottoms without those two men nearby.

It was almost dark when he returned to his own place, so Amos set about building a fire to cook his supper. It would be nice when he was once again able to use the cabin and the cookstove, but for now, living in the barn loft and cooking over an open fire sure beat the accommodations of the Post Oak Hills. After supper, he spread a blanket in the hay and slept soundly for the first time in days.

After a quick breakfast the next morning, Amos surveyed the situation. He knew that the only way to get things back in order was to start with one task. He chose to start with the wagon. His first chore was to remove the tree the flood had deposited on top it. After cutting the tree away, he was thankful that there was no damage to the wagon itself. Next, he shoveled the mud and silt out of the wagon box. With the heavier cleaning done, Amos hauled the harness down from the loft and hitched up the mules. He moved the wagon to the edge of the river, and with a bucket sloshed away the rest of the mud. When the wagon was finally clean to Amos' satisfaction, he pulled it into the clearing where the sun would dry it. With this chore done Amos felt better, but also knew that other things were just too wet yet for clean up. It would take at least a week of dry weather before serious work could be done here, and then it would be work unending for weeks and weeks. It was now near noon, and he had figured that he would wait until morning to take the wagon and leave for Hickory Ford. He knew it could be a long trip, as the Fourche River bottoms could take a long time to pass through with the mud and possibly still high water.

It was then that he noticed them. His poppa and grandpa were riding out of the wagon track and across toward the barn. Relief and joy flooded over him, just as the rain had flooded the place two weeks before. Trying to cover his emotion, Amos called out, "Are you two fellers lost, way off down here on them mules?"

"Son, we were a thinkin' thet we'd never find ya' after sech a flood," replied his Poppa.

"I told you, Poppa, thet there were no need fer worryin' 'bout ya, Amos. I know'd ya'd take ker of ya'self," stated John in a voice that was not convincing.

"Wal, I'm here, all right. Ya could tell thet I guess by my tracks on yore way in, but I wondered my own self fer quite a spell. An' iffen ya'd waited another day, I'd a been back at Hickory Ford," said Amos.

Getting down from their mules, the older men were awed by the effects of the flood. Both agreed that it was curious that anything was left. Amos learned that the bottoms was not the only area affected. His Poppa told how the heavy rains had destroyed crops around Hickory Ford as well. John added that they had been waiting for the Fourche River to go down so that they could cross to check on him.

Amos fed their mules while John laid out some fried meat and biscuits on the tailgate of the wagon as there was no other place clear or dry to take a meal. Soon after they had eaten their dinner, Amos' team was hitched to the Studebaker and the other two mules tied on behind. Then the three men rode the wagon back toward their home at Hickory Ford.

CHAPTER TWELVE

Digging Out
and Starting Over

IT WAS A LONG RIDE TO HICKORY FORD, through what seemed like
endless mud and water. Amos told his story about the flood and
how he had escaped its deadly force. His Poppa and Grandpa John
were moved by the peril Amos had faced and his work to save
himself and his animals. The were silently thankful to God for
caring for Amos through such an ordeal.

As they approached Red Gum Ridge, Amos was shocked
at what he saw. Most crops were ruined, damaged by the deluge
of water. What the days of falling rain hadn't washed out, the
floods had buried in silt. Only the crops on the higher fields had
any chance of making a harvest. The other fields would have to
be disked up and replanted. Many of the houses and barns had
high water marks on their walls. That was a sure sign that water
had been inside them, damaging furnishings and equipment, then
leaving behind a slimy silt.

His mother was tearful as she hugged him upon their
arrival. She had not cried from her fears that Amos had not
survived the flood, but now that she knew he was safe, she could
not hold back the tears. When Amos and James had left John at
the store on Red Gum Ridge, Grandma Janey had responded the

same way. For a full day after Amos had gotten home, his mother made several comments towards his not returning to the bottoms. During these times Amos spoke at length of his commitment to return and rebuild his place, not to allow the flood to defeat him. His momma did seem to understand this. After all, her entire life had been spent on a farm. She knew that a good farmer cannot quit, certainly not after a severe blow of nature.

For ten days Amos remained in Hickory Ford. It would take that much time for the bottoms to dry out from the flood, maybe more. For the first time, though, Amos felt like a visitor in Hickory Ford. His place on the Little Sandy was in a chaotic state and was too wet to work, but for the first time, he knew that it was home. Fortunately, he didn't have much time to worry about this. There was a great deal to do in Hickory Ford. All his family's crops had been ruined, and Amos resolved to do his part in the recovery. The whole countryside had been cut up by the raging water which had raced out of the hollows to run out over the flat farmland, wiping out crops, bridges, and even some roads.

During his stay, he alternated his time between his grandparents' place and those of his father and brother. Amos used his own team to help ready the soil for the replanting, which must be done soon if there would be a crop to pick come fall. The ground didn't need to be broken up again, only disked and harrowed before replanting. All of this went quickly, with Amos' team working alongside the others.

In the long days of replanting, Amos thought of little else than his own place on the Little Sandy. Working a good team required little attention during repetitive field work like disking or harrowing. As the dirt turned beneath his feet, his mind replayed the long days of the flood, seeing again and again the rising water level. He saw Speckle being swept helplessly down White Creek. He saw his small camp in the Post Oak Hills. And always, these images were climaxed by the devastation he saw when he returned to his home after the waters had receded.

This scene replayed itself over and over again. Amos saw it when he rode the harrow disk. He saw it while he was walking behind the wider harrow through the loose dirt. Day by day he helped replant his family's fields at Hickory Ford, and yet he never really felt fatigue at night. Amos recognized that there was a nervousness about himself, something akin to anticipation. As the days progressed, he decided that he couldn't relax until he was once again back at his own place on the Little Sandy.

As the replanting neared completion at Hickory Ford, Amos began to think more constructively about his place. The long days of field work had proven to be good therapy for him. Mentally, he made plans to clean up the clearing and get his own field replanted. This vision played over and over again in his mind. This vision was so strong that sometimes he felt like the work should be done already.

As great as this flood had been, it did not get the better of the farmers at Hickory Ford. They had seen floods before, and this was not the first crop which they had planted over. It did not break their spirit. As a matter of fact, spirits were elevated as people saw the progress they were making in the recovery. There was a mood of thankfulness for deliverance from the flood, and of celebration of their progress. For both of these reasons, on the Sunday following Amos's return, all the churches came together for a picnic. It was held in Charlie Branson's pasture, just below Hickory Ford on Bates Creek.

The ancestors of these farm families had arrived along Bates

Creek over three-quarters of a century earlier. From that time their descendants had forged a common spirit which transcended both individual family and church. Here they were one family under one God, united in hardship and celebration.

Today was a day of celebration, in spite of the flood and all it cost everyone in the community. They were thankful that it had come so early in the summer as there was still plenty of time to raise a good crop. And, they were rejoicing over the fact that no lives were lost, particularly Amos', as by now everyone in the community knew of his story.

Flatbed wagons were lined up under the shade of giant hickory trees near the creek. The women and older girls began to arrange the food, spreading it out on the wagons so everyone could have easy access to it. This was to be a great feast since each family had brought several dishes to this community meal. While the food was being arranged, the young men and older boys began a baseball game out in the flat of the pasture. The younger children played some game of their own under the trees along the creek, and the older menfolk sat on their haunches in the shade of one of the hickories. They talked of the floods they had seen and crops they had planted. Some of them adding to the scene by either whittling on a stick with their pocketknife or spitting at passing bugs, or both.

Over the course of the afternoon, the community came together. They talked, and ate, and played, and talked some more, all the while mixing together as one large family. Truly, family was real, as families had intermarried over the generations so that many people in the community were related to one another in some distant fashion. With the lowering of the sun, wagons began to fill, and teams began to pull out for their home. At this time of day, every mule would automatically go home. They knew where their feedbox was and would hurry to it.

It was a Friday morning when Amos drove his team away from Hickory Ford back to the Little Sandy. His mother had tried to convince him to wait until Monday so that he could be with them for church services again on Sunday. But Amos' anxiety to get back home to his own place was driving him. Even though he was afraid that the bottoms would still be too wet to plow, he could not wait any longer.

Although Amos kept the mules to a quick walking pace, the hours and the miles passed slowly this morning. He had needed to get away from the bottoms while they dried out. Emotionally, he needed a rest after the flood and the events that had followed. He thought back to the days since the flood and was comforted that Hickory Ford seemed to have restored itself. And, though the flood had caused much destruction and brought with it sorrow, there had been news of a lighter sort also.

Henry and Eula Walker had their first baby the week before the flood. Both Henry and Eula had been in school with Amos in the one room school on Thompson's Branch. Amos had ridden over to their place in Scott's Hollow to pay his respects and congratulate them on their new baby. Henry and Eula made quite a fuss over Amos' visit as they weren't used to company. Eula insisted on fixing Amos something to eat while Henry pressed him with all sorts of questions about what it was like to farm down in the bottoms.

Amos had cut his visit short after tasting Eula's effort at blackberry cobbler. The cobbler tasted as if it hadn't a bit of sugar and it was very heavy on dumplings and light on berry juice. He had tried to wash it down with her coffee, but it was wretchedly strong and bitter. Typically, people just added grounds to their pot over the course of a week, then dumping it to start fresh. Eula's coffee was so strong and bitter that she surely hadn't emptied the pot in quite a spell.

Amos tried to smile a lot and act as if he were enjoying their company, but in truth, the food had soured him on the whole experience. And, if that wasn't enough, they had given him a chair right next to the cook stove where they had hung up the baby's wet diapers to dry. The smell of ammonia hung in the air so thick Amos thought he could have cut it with a knife. Apparently, the shower of rain earlier in the morning had prompted Eula to hang the diapers inside instead of outside on the fence.

About the time nausea began to set in on Amos, Eula asked him if he'd care to stay for supper. Startled into movement, he excused himself by saying that he had to get on home to help his Poppa with the feeding. Also, in case this reason didn't dissuade Eula, he added that his mother was fixing a special supper for him that very night. Keeping his feet moving at least in a shuffle, Amos worked his way to the door, all the while telling them how good it was to have visited with his friends again, and how pretty their baby was, saying it all several times before making it to the freedom of the door. Once there he almost ran to where Little Red was tied to a catalpa tree. Taking the reins, Amos leaped into the saddle and waved a quick goodbye as he put the little mule into a lope straight for home.

Thinking back over the experience now Amos regretted having lied like he had, though he had always helped his Poppa with feeding the stock. And, every night he had been home his momma had fixed some of his favorite food. For just a moment Amos wondered if all marriages started out like Henry and Eula's.

They seemed euphoric together though, so Amos decided that perhaps it didn't matter what he thought.

Another happy occasion had occurred during Amos's last stay in the bottoms. Myrtle Johnson had gotten married to Lester Jones. Amos figured that she had finally given up on him and looked to someone else for a husband. Amos didn't know much about women but did understand that Myrtle was one of those girls who was driven to get married. Her sights were set on a man, any man. Myrtle seemed to be a nice person, and Amos thought no less of her for having been so preoccupied with marriage. It was just that Amos wasn't ready for that part of his life yet. Still, he couldn't help but smile at having gotten loose from Myrtle so easily and was thankful to Lester Jones for unknowingly being his rescuer.

It was toward noon when he pulled into the Potter place. Mr. Potter was trying to plow the still damp soil of their garden spot while Mrs. Potter was boiling wash water. The children were scattered throughout the yard, excited by Amos' arrival.

"Boy, we've been wonderin' what happened to you. We thought maybe ya'd got warshed off downriver somewhere. Why, Essie sent me down t' the Little Sandy to look fer ye after we got back here on the place. See'd them wagon tracks leadin' out and figured yore people had come fer ye," called an excited Mr. Potter.

"Wal, I'd wondered 'bout you folks too, as ever' time I'd come by durin' the flood, there'd be no one t' home here 'bouts." called back Amos, pleased to have been noticed, or at least his absence.

They gathered about Amos' wagon and related their stories, Amos allowing the older Potters go first. It seemed from their tale that things had gotten scary in Willow Point before the river

finally subsided back into its banks. Many families had been
nestled on their rooftops with boats tied handy in case even that
lofty perch was endangered. The Potters had been back on their
home place about a week and had their log house cleaned up
enough to be livable again.

After they had talked for quite a spell, Mrs. Potter broke
in to invite Amos to dinner. "Here we all are a standin' out here
talkin' up a storm as if we were ready fer another one. Lands
sakes, iffen I don't never go through no more floods like that las'
un, I'll be shore glad. Now, Amos, git down offen thet wagon and
take dinner with us. All I've got is beans and cornbread, but yer're
welcome."

"Don't mind iffen I do," replied Amos. "Thank you, Miz
Potter."

They continued their conversation about the flood all
through a lengthy dinner. Amos was anxious to hear all about
what had happened to Willow Point during the high water, and
Mr. Potter seemed equally interested in the situation at Hickory
Ford. It seemed that this past flood had been one to keep folks
talking for years to come.

Mrs. Potter was right about having nothing but beans and
cornbread. The flood had washed away young vegetables that had
been growing in the garden. Their little remaining salt pork that
had been forgotten in their hurry to get to safety at Willow Point
was ruined, too. But even in that simple meal, Mrs. Potter showed
herself to be a worthy cook. Amos couldn't help but think that
Eula Walker would do well to take some lessons from an older
woman like Mrs. Potter.

With their meal and conversation over, Amos drove on down
toward his place. After visiting the Potters, he already felt good

about being back near his own home. Mrs. Potter had admonished him "Don't be a stranger ... just come on t' see 'us anytime."

Though he had seen this stretch of bottoms immediately after the waters had receded, he was still amazed at how high the water had been on the trees. As he forded White Creek, the high water mark on the timber was above his head as he sat atop the wagon seat.

As Amos drove the team into his clearing, he forced himself not to draw up the team in a reaction of awe at the appearance of devastation. Amos reminded himself that he had seen this scene before and that stopping to look again would not change it in the least, only make him dread all the more the work before him.

Stopping before the barn, Amos stepped down to the firm but still damp soil. Focusing his attention on unhitching the team and unloading the wagon, Amos avoided for now noticing all that had to be done in the coming weeks. He made something of a camp under the large hickory where he figured to cook his meals over an open fire and sleep on the ground. This arrangement would have to work until the cabin was moved back to its original position. Late in the afternoon Amos rehitched the team to the wagon to go downriver in search of dry wood for the fire. By dark he had enough dry wood cut and split for several days, and the rest of his camp was set up sufficient to get by for the time being.

It was just good light the next morning when Amos backed the team of mules up to a heavy harrow with iron teeth. His Poppa had loaned it to him since the planting in Hickory Ford was done for the summer. James knew using the heavier harrow would help Amos get his clearing ready for replanting, especially since he now had the use of a team instead of just Little Red. So they had loaded it into Amos' wagon before he left Hickory Ford.

The mules dragged the harrow to the edge of the field where Amos paused and looked about him before starting his day. This had become a habit of his over the last year. The sun was just beginning to show color through the upper branches of the tall timber on the east side of the clearing. Fog was drifting from the river across the field. Small animals could be heard scurrying about in the woods surrounding the clearing and the slap of a beaver's tail sounded from upriver. A peckerwood could be heard working a bug out of a dead tree.

Looking to the field before him he saw brush and puddles of standing water scattered about as from a sower's hand. The soil in the high spots was beginning to dry, but much of it was still very damp. There were three good sized trees which had been uprooted from somewhere upriver and washed down to settle in his field. And, of course, out on the highest ground in the newer part of the clearing, sat his cabin, still wet and filthy from the flood.

Finished with his "morning look," Amos clucked to the team and out they stepped across the clearing, dragging the heavy harrow behind them. The harrow scraped and gouged its way across the damp field, leaving it loosened and exposed to the sun and the wind to dry. Amos spent most of the morning harrowing back and forth across the field so that it would dry out as quickly as possible. The sooner he could get his corn planted, the longer it would have to grow and mature before the fall frosts.

Though heavy, the harrow was not a burden on the well-conditioned mules, particularly since the soil was smooth. But still, Amos gave them several chances to catch their breath, taking the opportunity to do some small chore himself. On one of these breaks, he took a shovel and a hoe out to the cabin to begin removing the silt on the inside. This would be a job for Amos over the next several days, as he fit it in with larger chores.

With the surface of the field worked loose to speed its drying, Amos began the task of picking up the brush left by the flood. This was piled throughout the field, where it would later be burned. The job seemed to go on forever. At first, he thought he could finish in three days. Saturday was the third day, but by then Amos could see that it would take at least two more days. Two days seemed like two weeks to an anxious farmer wanting to get his crops planted.

Sunday brought a halt to his hurry, as there would be no work on this day. He rode out to Willow Point earlier than usual so that he might see some of the effects of the flood. Also, he knew that some of the sloughs were still full and a direct route was impractical today.

For a full two hours, he rode a circuitous course through the bottoms toward Willow Point. As much as he had been in the bottoms, Amos was still amazed at the power of high water. New channels had been cut into the soil from the powerful action of the moving currents. Trees, large and small alike, had been lifted from their anchor of roots to be relocated by the force of the water. On more than one occasion, he saw brush left to rest in the tops of small trees. From the tracks in the bare earth, it was apparent that small animals had returned to begin their life over again. He reasoned that raccoons would be having a feast catching fish from the many shallow pockets of water.

Riding into Willow Point, Amos sat on Little Red in open-eyed amazement. All along he had noticed that the water line in the timber was getting higher, but he could not have imagined, even from what the Potters had told him, what he would see in Willow Point. The water line on some of the lower-lying buildings was just under the roof line, with many smaller structures having been completely under. It was common to see buildings which had floated off their blocks to settle down in a different location, just like his cabin back home. The church folks were as amazed at Amos' arrival as he had been in the appearance of Willow Point. They, like the Potters, had feared that he had been drowned. The men wanted to hear of how he had survived the flood on his own. With the telling of the tale, Amos sensed a greater respect from them than before. Two of the older men called Amos forward to sit with them during the preaching, ending Amos' hideout on the back pew. After preaching, Mrs. Barrow insisted on his coming home with her family to Sunday dinner. "I just cain't wait to hear all about how ya got through that awful flood all by ya' self."

Arriving home about mid-afternoon, Amos took advantage of the day of rest to do some fishing of a different kind. On the way home, he had thought about all those shallow pockets of water where the coons were feasting on a steady supply of fish. Thinking that he might do some easy fishing himself, he set about fixing a gig. Taking his ax, he walked into the woods where he chose a slender hickory about an inch and a half thick. With this cut to a length of eight feet and cleaned of limbs, he returned to the barn for some stiff wire. Amos cut two six inch lengths which he forced into the heavy end of the pole, wrapping the end tight with some flexible wire. The points of the wire were filed sharp.

With his homemade gig, Amos walked out through the bottoms with high hopes of a fish supper. Several holes were investigated before finding a suitable one. The slough needed to be shallow enough so that the surface would move with the movements of the fish and have enough clarity for a fish's shape to be discernible.

It didn't take Amos long to figure out that he was more visible to the fish than they were to him. This procedure was proving to require great stealth. His first thrust only impaled the gig in the muddy bottom, bending the wires. Trying again with more care he almost connected with a carp. He didn't want the carp, but thought that as long as it was swimming by, it would be good practice. Wading slowly in water half knee deep, Amos made his way along the length of the slough. Coming to where three logs had been washed together, he could see several fish moving. Standing quite still, he poised his gig and waited. Soon a large V-shaped wave moved off to the right. Amos quickly struck the gig into the head of the wave, resulting in a wild thrashing under the water and a jerking of the gig. Keeping the gig held against the bottom, he eased forward and moved his hand down the pole's length to grasp the fish. Holding it now aloft, he became instantly hungry at the sight of the catfish.

Turning around to wade out of the slough, Amos was struck by the sight of five water moccasins which had moved up behind him. Taking an avenue of safety, he ran from the water with his catch. With mixed feelings of relief over his safety and frustration over his not bringing along the .22, Amos silently told himself to be more careful as the snakes would also be getting much of their feed from these shallow sloughs.

Monday morning brought a return of the field's cleanup. Amos piled brush all day, except for the early afternoon when he harrowed over the clearing once again, further speeding the drying process. With the close of the day, he wondered if he might spend the rest of his life picking up and piling brush as it had surely been his major work over the last year.

Tuesday's supper was something of a celebration. The entire

clearing was now free of brush, roots, and logs from the flood. To celebrate he fried up a large drum that he had caught on a set line the night before. He thought as he ate his supper that however hard life might be here in the bottoms, there was usually plenty of fish.

After his supper was eaten and the dishes washed, Amos stepped out to the clearing to look over all the scattered piles of brush, both large and small. Suddenly an urge came to him to not wait on the morning to burn the piles. The thought came to him that he would sleep better tonight if he knew that the piles would be burned by daylight. He took some matches from over the cook stove and the small can of coal oil from which he filled his lamps. Thus armed Amos walked out to the nearest pile and poured some oil on its base, then struck a match and touched the oil. Within a few seconds, a small fire was burning up through the pile. Amos stood back for a moment to watch the flames destroy his old adversaries, the roots, and brush which prevented him from planting and harvesting his crop of corn and hay.

When some of the larger roots in this first pile had caught fire, Amos carried one to the next pile, using the first fire to start the second. In this manner, he worked his way across the field until all the brush was burning brightly, like so many campfires. By this time the daylight had faded to darkness broken by the light of his fires. It was eerie to Amos, standing there alone in the middle of the great bottom country, surrounded by many fires, each casting off light creating flitting shadows upon the dead trees on the edge of the field. These trees stood bare of any leaves, like sentinels standing guard around the camp fires of a large army.

Amos and Speckle sat on their bed and watched the fires until the larger ones had settled down to glowing embers. Now satisfied that he would be able to work the soil tomorrow, Amos laid back on his pallet to sleep before the first morning light.

Amos slept later than usual the next morning but was still up before the sun crested the top of the timber. Sitting up he looked out at the smoldering fires scattered throughout the field. Rising, he walked barefoot to the barn for a pitchfork before searching the fires, pitching any unburned wood into the center of the remaining heat. This would make sure that no unburned branches or roots would be left to get in the way.

After a quick breakfast, Amos hitched the team to the harrow. Wanting to drag off the field one more time to speed its drying, Amos skirted around the few fires that were still burning and soon finished harrowing the field. He then plowed and harrowed the garden. The garden was dry enough to plant, so that was how Amos spent most of the afternoon. When he finished the garden, there were still a few hours of sunlight left, so he ran the harrow over the field once more.

The day was almost over and Amos was almost finished with the harrowing, when he heard the sound of trace chains out on the wagon track. Looking up, he saw Gray Jack and Buster pulling a wagon into his clearing. Amos was surprised to see James on the wagon seat beside John since his father had never been down to the bottoms except after the flood.

As they pulled up near the barn, Amos called out his greeting, "Howdy, you fellers lookin' fer work, are ya'?"

"Wal, we thought we oughta give ya' a hand gettin' yore crop replanted, Amos, like ya' hep'd us," replied his Poppa.

Like always, it was good to have company as a break from the loneliness in the bottoms. The older men had brought the fixings for a grand supper, particularly as they knew that Amos was probably still camping out. There was fried chicken, stewed potatoes, pickles, corn bread, fresh onions, and a large peach cobbler. Amos hadn't had any food of this nature since he left Hickory Ford and expressed his appreciation by taking seconds and even thirds.

"Whoa, there, Amos, iffen ya' eat yourself sick, who'll hep yore Poppa and me replant that field of corn?" John asked cheerfully. To this Amos only grinned as he took another large spoonful of the cobbler. That same grin was on his face later as they each found their pallet for a night's sleep. Getting up time always came early to farmers.

Early light found Amos cooking their breakfast with fresh eggs and some of last year's ham. There was no oven for baking bread, but Grandma Janey had filled a large can with some of her own. Amos figured that she must have made several batches to turn out that many biscuits.

With their breakfast prepared, he rose and called toward the barn, "Grandpaw, Poppa, breakfast's ready."

"Comin', Amos," called back John from where he and James had been unloading a corn drill and disk by using Gray Jack to pull them down an incline of planks from the wagon.

Before they had finished their breakfast, Mr. Potter drove in the wagon track with his team and wagon. As he pulled up near their fire, James called out, "Clem, have ya' et? Thar's still some breakfast left here, that is, iffen Amos don't go and eat as much as he did las' night."

"No, thank ye, James," replied Mr. Potter as he stepped to the ground, Essie fed me before she let me git off."

Their familiarity told Amos that John and James had stopped in at the Potter's on their way down yesterday. James then explained to Amos that Mr. Potter had offered to help them move the cabin back into place this morning. It came to him at that moment that he had been so preoccupied with cleaning up the brush that he had forgotten all about moving the cabin. Of course, it had to be moved before the field was planted.

Within the next half hour, the four of them were assembled in front of the cabin. Mr. Potter's wagon, containing many tools that might be needed to accomplish the move, was positioned near the cabin. Little Red and Big Ned were hitched to Amos' wagon, which was loaded with all the loose items from the cabin. This reduced the risk of their being damaged and lowered the weight to be pulled. The bed and two stoves took up quite a bit of space, but everything else could be packed in around them. This wagon load was driven back to the house spot, where it would wait until the cabin was in place and clean enough to once again be lived in.

All three of the older men walked around the cabin, stepped in and tested its floor, shook its walls and otherwise checked it for its strength and weight. Finally, a chain was wrapped around each of the two logs on which the cabin was built. The two chains were then hooked to the clevis on a doubletree. After some discussion of the pulling strength of the mules, it was decided that Gray Jack would be hitched with Big Ned. They were the two largest mules present. Each had demonstrated his pulling power on prior occasions.

Hitched together with the single trees connected to their trace chains, the two mules sensed the expectancy of the men and stood nervously. John took the lines and clucked to the team to step out. Full of nervous energy, the pair stepped into their collars briskly, causing the chains connected to the logs to snap tight with a pop. The force of the big team pushing against their collars jerked the cabin free of its hold to the ground. It lurched forward and spun to follow the team on the slight downward grade toward its original location.

It was an enormous weight even for the two big mules, but John kept driving them forward. It was easier on the mules to keep going than to have to restart the cabin if it stopped. On across the field, the two big mules pulled their load as the men cheered them on. John expertly directed them forward with the lines until they were at the right spot to turn and spin the cabin back into its original position. Everyone was elated when the cabin did come to a halt. It had been quite a feat for any team, and the men expressed appreciation of their strength.

"Amos, I'm almost sorry thet I give that big ol' Ned mule t' ya, he's quite a puller, he is. The trouble I keep havin' with my Gray Jack is that he wears down ever' mule I put with him," expressed John. As the men worked, they talked of crops, weather, mules, and taxes. During this conversation Amos was mostly silent, yielding to the older men. It felt good being there as a man with these men. Having his own place and having made a crop on his own made Amos feel that he was treated as something of an equal, a man rather than a boy. Amos liked the experience.

After Mr. Potter had driven back out the wagon track, Amos' wagon was backed into the river where each item, in turn, was washed thoroughly and placed upon the bank to dry. During one of their afternoon breaks for the teams, the three men moved the cabin furnishings near Amos' temporary camp, setting stoves back inside the cabin as Amos would not be able to do that by himself. This would make for a better camp for Amos until the cabin was ready to reoccupy. Amos appreciated the help, as the stoves would be quite a chore for one man to move by himself.

The remainder of the day was spent working up the field for

planting. John used Gray Jack and Buster to pull the disk while Amos drove Little Red and Big Ned with the harrow. The disk loosened the soft soil down about three inches and the harrow smoothed it over so that it would be easier to plant and not lose its moisture so quickly. All the while James cleaned up the remaining fires.

By supper time the field was ready for the planter. Since John and James would need to leave by noon tomorrow to get back to Hickory Ford by supper, they started their planting with what daylight they had left. Planting that evening and the next morning, the pea hay and corn were planted by the end of the morning.

It was hard for Amos to see them head out the wagon track. They had broken the loneliness which often pervaded his life here in the bottoms, and he appreciated their time to help plant his crop. Otherwise, he would have been Thursday of next week getting it planted by himself.

The rest of Amos' Saturday was spent scrubbing out the cabin. The hoe and broom had pried most of the dirt and mud out, and then the washing began. Bucket after bucket of water was carried from the pump to slosh against the walls and floor to remove the remaining residue of flood grime. Then came the toilsome chore of scrubbing with hot lye water and a hand-twisted corn shuck brush. But when it was done, the cabin was ready to be his home again, and that would feel good after sleeping and cooking outside day after day.

Sunday was again a welcome day off from the persistent work in the clearing, but Monday found Amos with more work to do. With the crop replanted and the cabin reoccupied, he set himself to the dirty job of cleaning the silt from the walls and floors of the barn so that it too could be used again. By mid-afternoon, he was satisfied with its condition but aghast at the filth all over him. A long swim in the river was called for! The river also provided the opportunity to wash his overalls and shirt, which had caught most of the silt from the barn. Relieved of both dirt and clothes, he walked peaceably back to the cabin for a pair of dry overalls before seeing to his supper.

Early Tuesday morning he drove the team and wagon out of the clearing to the east, generally in a downriver direction. His purpose was to retrieve any of his firewood and split rails which might have settled between his clearing and the juncture of White Creek and the Little Sandy River. Speckle, of course, accompanied them as this would be of infinitely more interest to the hound than common field work.

For two days they searched in this manner, even crossing White Creek and continuing on southeast for several more miles. In all, three wagon loads were returned to the clearing for the rebuilding process. It was not as much as was lost, but it would help a great deal.

Week after week, Amos toiled in the mid-summer heat. Few breezes could reach his small clearing in the bottoms and bring any relief. There was always something to do. Firewood was sawn and split. More fence rails were split for the rebuilding and enlarging of the pasture. The corn came up quickly, but so did thousands of other plants. The weeds in the middles between the rows could be plowed out with the single stock. But, the weeds that came up between the corn plants in the row could only be removed with the hoe. Hour after hour, day after day, Amos worked steadily. His only relief came from his daily swims and Sunday afternoon scouting trips upriver in the dugout. More than one night in those weeks he had dreams of the sweaty hindquarters of a mule with a tail constantly swishing at flies and mosquitoes. He felt sorry for the mules but knew that they, like himself, were tough enough to handle what was asked of them.

Chapter Thirteen

Barn Raising

AMOS' SUMMER WAS A LONG SEASON of seemingly endless hard work. Over the previous winter, he and John had cut several hardwood trees out on the high ridge, beyond the clearing. This timber would be used for building projects around the place. Trees with straight trunks had been chosen. In addition, several cypress trees were cut near the river, both for saw logs and for shingle or shake blocks. All this timber had been cut while the sap was down and left to dry. Amos now was glad that the logs had not been cut out of the trees as the flood would have floated them down the river. As it was, all the trees had only shifted from their original position, settling down against standing trees after the flood waters receded.

Whenever Amos wasn't plowing or hoeing, he worked in this timber. On one of John's trips down to the bottoms, the two of them worked at the timber with a 6' crosscut saw. Because of the pattern and large number of teeth, some people referred to this saw as the "thousand-legger." This saw, definitely a two man operation, was used to cut logs to the appropriate lengths. Some were cut into saw logs for the sawmill at Willow Point, where they would be sawn into dimensional lumber. Others were intended for posts, rails, or blocks for shakes or shingles. It was striking to

Amos that for all his youthful strength, he could not easily keep up with his grandpa.

By himself now, Amos worked at turning this timber into building material which he could use to expand his structures. One of his first efforts was to haul the saw logs to the mill in Willow Point. As was common practice in those days, the transaction between Amos and the mill did not involve cash. Amos took more logs than he needed, and the mill returned part of the lumber as payment for the logs. With Mr. Potter's help, Amos removed the wagon box and used just the frame to haul the logs to the mill. Mr. Potter also showed him how to load the logs by himself. This made it possible for Amos to continue working even when his neighbor or grandfather was not there to help.

This method involved leaning small logs from the ground to the wagon frame. The saw logs could then be rolled up onto the wagon frame by pulling from the opposite side with the mules. Amos used the team to first pull each log to a spot in the clearing where the wagon could easily be loaded. Then he used a cant hook to adjust the position of the heavy logs before they were pulled up onto the wagon. On the first few trips to the sawmill, Amos returned empty. From then on, each trip home carried the lumber that would be used for the construction projects he and John had planned.

Of all the work needed to turn this bottom land into a real farm, splitting posts and rails was hardest for Amos. The two tasks were similar, differing in that posts were shorter and thicker, making them somewhat easier to make. Rails were cut to a length of ten feet and split to a thickness of about four inches. It took a practiced eye and hand to turn out good rails each time. They had a tendency to split crooked and sometimes break in the middle.

Amos became angry more than once when this happened, as he disliked to put that much effort into something to see it break right away. The splintered wood could be used for firewood, but generally firewood did not take such effort.

It was their plan to add onto the barn before winter came. Long cypress logs had been cut for this purpose. Cypress would make longer beams than could be gotten from many of the hardwoods. It was also much lighter to lift into place and lasted longer in the damp climate of the bottoms. Two sides of each log had to be flattened. Amos first scored one side with a double bitted chopping ax, then chiseled away the side with the massive broad ax. This was much the same method used to make railroad ties. The logs were much longer than a railroad tie, but only two sides were flattened. It always looked easy when John did it, but for Amos it was toilsome work, often with less than a smooth result.

John had chosen to make shingles rather than shakes so they would match the shingles on the existing roofs. Loads of blocks were hauled to the sawmill to be sawn into shingles. Amos could have rived out the thicker shakes with a froe, but he had enough work to more than keep him busy over the summer. As with the saw logs, extra blocks were hauled to the mill in exchange for the sawing. The mill, in turn, would sell the extra lumber and shingles to individuals not having the timber to exchange.

The first building project was begun in mid summer. Amos added a porch to the front of the cabin. It was eight feet wide and ran the entire length of the cabin. The construction was simple enough that Amos could complete it himself. Cypress blocks, which would not rot even when they were set on the ground, were used as a foundation. Hewn beams were placed on the cypress blocks and leveled with the cabin floor. Rough sawn boards were used for floor planking, and a roof was built above it. This was built much like the floor but of lighter material. Four white oak poles served for posts to support the roof and frame the cabin doorway. Now the front of the cabin would be protected from sun and rain.

An addition to the barn was the next construction project, but that was too large a task for Amos to undertake on his own. Waiting for the time when he could get some help to complete the barn, he started rebuilding the pasture fence, this time enclosing over twice as much area as before the flood. John and Amos had considered putting up a wire fence. However, the abundance of the right size trees for rails, trees that had to be cut anyway to clear the land, decided the issue. Load after load of rails were hauled from the ridge. Rail fences require a great deal of material but go up fairly quickly. There are no posts to set, only the process of laying the rails alternately one upon another in an offset angle fashion. This may seem fragile, but the split rail fence was strong. The fence required no nails, could be built quite high, if necessary, and would restrict small animals because of its tight pattern.

Liking the looks of the pasture fence, Amos decided to fence the corn field, as he intended to bring his own hogs down to the bottoms before fall. That gave him two choices. He could keep his hogs in a pen and feed them year-round, or he could let them run free range and forage in the bottoms. All he had to do was notch the ears of his hogs to establish ownership, and feed them some corn occasionally to keep them in the habit of coming back to his place. This, of course, would require fencing the corn or they would not wait until it was harvested and in the barn to eat it. He knew this would be a big task, but believed that it would be worth the effort. Amos was about half way through the building of the cornfield fence when his help arrived for the barn raising. This was a project too big for just Amos and John, so James, Tom, and Uncle Zeke had come along to help.

Amos had already skidded the logs into a deck near the barn. What remained to be done was to move the logs individually to their respective sides, notch them and lift them into position, forming the walls of the new barn stall. Their first day went slowly as a routine had to be set for the work. Over the second and succeeding days, the walls went up quickly, as Mr. Potter had joined the crew and proved to be an able axe man.

The new stall was sixteen by sixteen feet, exactly the same size as the existing one. It was set in line with the present structure, twelve feet away. The two stalls now formed an alleyway. Extending the roof and ceiling of the first stall across the alleyway and over the new stall to form a loft forty-four feet in length.

With the walls set up, smaller logs were set across at the height of seven feet. Heavy two inch planks were then laid over these poles for a loft floor, making it easier to set up the long poles for the roof rafters. These were then overlaid with lathing and a covering of shingles. The whole process took only four days for this crew of six work hardened men. Basic barns of this type were easy to assemble if all the material was at hand. Here Amos' hard work of the summer paid off. With the barn completed, there was enough of the rough sawn lumber left for another project. The men quickly erected one more building. This structure was a commitment to the future, as Amos did not yet need a smokehouse. A real farm would need a place to cure and smoke meat. The smokehouse was of simple box construction, even needing no floor. A dirt floor would allow the building of a small fire for smoke without the risk of burning the building down.

Though their work had been hard, the men had all enjoyed

themselves. They would work from early light until the sun was almost straight up, then take an hour and a half dinner break. This provided enough rest for them to work on until almost dark. Tom and Amos used this time for a quick swim in the river, refreshing themselves for the afternoon's work. The older men usually took a short nap under the shade of the big hickory.

Uncle Zeke had volunteered himself to be camp cook. This was an important job, because it took a great deal of food to keep a crew this large going for twelve hours a day. Besides, it was understood that he could not keep up with the younger men any longer. Several sacks and boxes of foodstuffs had been brought from Hickory Ford. In addition, John had caught several young chickens the morning of their departure. He had simply clipped their wings and tied their feet together before setting them into the rear of the wagon. Upon their arrival, he had released the pullets into the yard just as they had been back at his place on Red Gum Ridge.

Seeing this, Tom had asked, "Grandpaw, don't ya think that them chickens will run off from here, seein' they ain't penned up or nuthin'?"

Grinning with a glint in his eye, John replied, "Tom, ya' jest see iffen ya' kin run them chickens away from here."

"Wal, Grandpaw, I don't want 'em to git lost," said Tom. Laughing still, John explained, "Tom, have ya ever heard of a chicken runnin' off from someone's place? A chicken will always stay where people are, ya couldn't run these chickens away from her' if ya tried. They'll stay right here, thet is, until we have need of 'em."

The chickens had indeed stayed around, scratching and pecking as was their nature. To Amos, they made his place seem more like a farm. A farm really needed a variety of livestock, whereas he only had two mules. They sure came handy at meal time, those chickens. Each day, Uncle Zeke would fix one, either for dinner or supper. The chicken was, of course, in addition to the fresh fish. His poles and lines were always baited and set out. Uncle Zeke never went anywhere with water that he didn't fish.

With the major projects done, the day came when the men from Hickory Ford pulled out just after dinner. Amos found himself still in a building mood, itching to use the new skills he had learned over the previous days. The jingle of harness was not quite out of earshot when he began gathering some planks and tools for a new structure. He carried a collection of heavy planks and tools to the river bank, near where he kept the dugout. He then selected several poles from the wood pile. He chose only cypress poles for this job, and cut them into lengths from three to six feet. He then sharpened one end of these poles with the ax. Amos carried all these back to the river bank and shucked his overalls before wading into the river. The sharpened poles were driven into the soft river bottom in pairs, from shortest to longest. The last ones were set in water almost three feet deep, leaving about two feet above the river's surface. Next Amos nailed heavy cross pieces between the pairs and overlaid these with longer planking. This platform was crude, but it would serve him to get into and out of his dugout, as well as to do his clothes washing. Of course, he would set out lines here for his steady supply of fish.

The following morning Amos began what he figured to be his last building of the summer, and yet, in some ways, the most important. Though the new building was not large, it did take Amos all morning to complete. Standing back, Amos thought that this was the first outhouse he had ever built, and he was quite proud of it. Now he would not have to use the barn like the stock but would have a place of his very own. The thought gave him a feeling of progress realized.

It was late Saturday when Amos finished cleaning up after the past week's building projects. Unused lumber had to be restacked so that it would shed rain water and not rot prematurely. All the tools were carefully put away in the barn. As John had set the example, Amos took the time to sharpen the axe and any other tool with a cutting edge before putting them away.

After supper, he and Speckle sat on their new porch and took in the enormity of the changes. Amos sat there with a look of wonder on his deeply tanned face. It seemed that the whole place looked somehow larger. The new barn was huge compared to its previous size, though not large at all compared to many of the barns back in Hickory Ford. The larger pasture fence gave the appearance of the house place reaching much farther toward the river than before. The new smokehouse seemed to call for the meat which would one day fill it. The platform at the river bank complemented this picture. But, for Amos, what set the place off the most was the new outhouse. Some folks back at Hickory Ford didn't have one, but here in the bottoms, he had his own. "Why," he thought to himself, "I'm in tall cotton now!" Amos sat there for more than an hour, letting dusk fade into darkness while the whippoorwills serenaded him with their music.

Sunday afternoon Amos was returning from church at Willow Point when Little Red stopped suddenly, pointing his head and ears off to their left. For several minutes Amos sat the saddle silently, waiting for the mule to make the next move. Amos trusted him to know when something wasn't right. Directly, Amos saw movement in the farther brush along one of the sloughs. In another moment, four hogs walked out into a small clearing. They didn't notice Little Red or Amos as they were intent upon their feeding. The flood earlier in the summer had washed away most acorns, so the hogs were having to search for their food. Feeling more comfortable now, Amos eased Little Red slowly toward the hogs. The soft damp earth allowed them to get within about one hundred feet before the hogs noticed them. From this distance, Amos could tell that the hogs had no ear notches for identification and were rangier in appearance than most farm hogs. So this meant that these were wild hogs, probably lost from a farm sometime in the distant past. They lived in a herd here in the bottoms to breed and raise their young without the care or harvest of any farmer.

Suddenly, one of the hogs looked up and discovered the mule and rider. Instantly, he gave a deep grunt and wheeled off into the thick brush with the other three quickly following. The hogs created a loud racket as they plowed through the brush, but soon were out of sight and slowed their pace.

Riding on toward his place on the Little Sandy, Amos wondered what this meant for him. He had never seen wild hogs this close to his clearing before and realized that they could pose a threat to the crops, especially with the shortage of feed throughout the river bottoms. It stood to reason that the hogs would now be ranging far and wide in search of food. Amos became nervous at the thought that his hay and corn crop could become the feed for wild hogs even before he could gather it into the barn. Kneeing Little Red into a lope, he hurried home to check his fields.

Arriving at the south edge of the clearing, Amos slowly walked Little Red around the entire clearing checking for hog tracks. It was a great relief to find none, though he resolved to get back to the fence around the crops at first light tomorrow.

Amos worked all of Monday at a pace which would have set back some grown men. With the wild hogs as close as they were already, it would only be a matter of time before they found his corn and hay. He knew that in one feeding they could destroy much of his precious second crop. So, he worked throughout the day, stopping for nothing except for a quick dinner and a few drinks from the pump. It was near dusk before he quit for the day, exhausted with seemingly every muscle in his body hurting. After a forced supper, Amos collapsed onto his straw tick to sleep a dead man's sleep until the next morning. He knew that the work would continue at this pace until the corn was safe. But a full night's sleep was not to be his that night, no matter how tired he was. Sometime after midnight, his mind slowly became alerted to a loud noise outside the cabin. As his mind cleared, he could tell that it was coming from the field. Rising as quickly as he could, he held his head steady, sorting out the noise. Finally, it came to him. Speckle was in a fight with something out there, making a noise like Amos had never heard before. Jumping into a pair of overalls and snatching his .22 from the cabin wall, Amos ran out and leaped from the porch, barefooted, with only one galush of his overalls hooked. Without a light, he raced at his top speed toward the sound of the fight which seemed to be coming from the pea patch beyond the corn.

Amos ran through the shoulder high corn until he reached the far end where the pea hay grew. There Amos saw the source of the commotion. Wild hogs had found their way into the corn through the broad area yet to be fenced. Speckle had tried to run them out of the corn and in the process become entangled with a huge boar. Instantly, Amos wondered how the hound had stayed alive this long as the boar probably outweighed him ten fold. He could see the long right tusk spear its way forward as the boar lunged at the dog. Though the boar was large and could move very quickly for its size, the hound had been broken in on fighting coons which were as quick as a cat.

Through the din of grunts, snarls, and barks, Amos lifted the .22 to his shoulder and sighted with only moonlight. In an instant that the boar stood still, Amos squeezed the trigger. At the sharp report, the boar roared and spun to run out of the field after the other hogs.

But the hound wasn't finished as he chased the fleeing boar, biting at his hocks at every chance. After a distance, the boar turned to stand and fight again. "Oh, no," moaned Amos, "ya' should've let him go." Running to the new fight, Amos realized that he had not thought to bring more shells for the rifle. Almost in a panic now he ran to catch up to the fight. Coming close, Amos let out a shrill scream with tremendous volume to announce his entry into the fight. The sudden unknown scream startled the boar, and once again he turned to run from the field.

Again, Speckle persisted in chasing the boar. The two ran from the clearing and into the darkness of the woods. Amos ran behind, calling until he was hoarse, fearing what would happen to the hound if the fight got away from him. At the clearing's edge, Amos was met by the hound. Speckle seemed utterly happy with himself. Amos sank to the ground and clasped the dog in his arms, crying from the exhilaration and fear of the incident. "Speckle, don't ya' know any better than to go off chasing an old' boar hog, 'specially by yourself, an' in the dark too," cried Amos.

Afraid now that the hogs might return, Amos pulled the hound after him back toward their cabin. With the lamp lit, Amos examined the hound thoroughly for wounds, yet found none. "Boy, Speckle, how did ya' keep away from that ol' boar like ya' did. An', did ya' know, that was Ol' One Ear hisself. I got a good look at 'im when he turned after I shot. Thet boar had no ear on the left side. I hear that he's the boss hog down here in these bottoms. An' thet he raids farms whenever he gets the chance, eatin' an' killin' whatever he kin." With a slow voice now, Amos tells his hound, "An' I hear thet he's kill'd many a good dog in his day, so's I want ya' to stay away from 'im." But in his mind, Amos wondered how that could be. Ol' One Ear and the pack of hogs he led would surely return to the corn and peas. Amos knew at that moment that he and Speckle would have to deal with Ol' One Ear again.

Though wide awake now, Amos was still tired, for he had slept only a few hours. Afraid that the pack of hogs might return again that night, Amos took up a quilt for a pallet, a lantern, and a dozen .22 shells and walked back to the far edge of the corn patch. Here he bedded down for the night, taking the precaution of tying Speckle to one of his legs before lying back for more sleep. In the moments before sleep came again, he thought that now they would be ready for the hogs, though the light from the lantern would likely keep them away if they did decide to return tonight.

It was a good hour after daylight before Amos awoke. Seeing no hogs, he doused the lantern and turned the hound loose. Then he picked up his pallet and headed for the cabin. The memory of the previous night filled his mind all day. There was now even greater urgency as he continued to split and haul rails for the fence. He had recurring thoughts of going after the old boar to kill him and end the problem but had serious misgivings that he and the hound could accomplish that on their own. It was common knowledge that wild hogs were very dangerous, and that with a pack, the danger multiplied. So with no other plan at hand, Amos continued on the fence day after day and slept with the hound in the field night after night.

Amos worked feverishly over the next four days before encircling both the corn and the pea hay. The garden had been fenced at the same time as the pasture, so that was not a concern now. The rail fences were only built about thirty inches high, and Amos hoped that this barrier would be sufficient for the wild hogs as he knew that they would be persistent to get at the sweet-smelling corn and hay. Of course, he could add onto the fence's height later. But right now he was tired of splitting and carrying rails. And, the roughness of the rails wore on even Amos' heavily calloused hands.

After the rail fence had gone up, he daily checked for tracks in the newer part of the clearing beyond the fence. On several mornings, he had found fresh hog tracks, and always after a night when Speckle had raised a ruckus from where he was tied on the porch. Amos knew he couldn't take another chance of letting the hound take on the pack of wild hogs. Whenever Speckle sounded the alarm, Amos would quickly rise from his tick, light the lantern, get extra shells for the .22 and with lantern and rifle, walk the inside of the fence all the way around the field before returning to his bed. He figured that between Speckle's barking and the approaching lantern, the hogs decided to leave the clearing.

Sometime during late August, Amos determined that the wild hogs had stopped trying to get into the field and had moved on to another part of the bottoms. At this point, he could have relaxed his night vigil, but for the raccoons. He and Speckle continued to spend many nights on a pallet in the corn field, now to scare off the coons which were after the sweet forming ears of corn. He was up so much at night that it became common for him to take naps after his dinner every day, something he'd only known old men to do.

It was early September before Amos felt comfortable making a trip back to Hickory Ford to visit his family and friends. Certainly, he had never known a summer when he had worked as hard or as long as this one. First, there was the first workup of the fields and planting, then the tiresome cleanup and replanting after the great flood, then the major building projects which began with working up the timber, then the seemingly endless task of protecting the corn first from the wild hogs, and then from the raccoons.

Somehow during all of this, he had enlarged the clearing by four acres. At least, he had removed the timber from along the high ridge which he and John had cut the previous winter and girdled the remaining large trees which John had determined unusable. The smaller ones had been cut down with the axe and pulled to the woodlot beside the cabin to be cut into firewood.

It was a different Amos who sat on the wagon seat before driving off for Hickory Ford. This Amos had suffered great hardship and had fought back to regain his niche here in the bottoms. He had had to work harder than many grown men over the past four months. He sat for several minutes, taking a long look out over his place, with all its improvements and its tall crop of corn which was now beginning to turn yellow as it matured. Amos was still small in size, maybe more so since his summer's experience. But every ounce of his flesh was muscle, as tough and as wiry as a hickory sapling. And, there was a strength to his gaze as he took in the view of his own place. It was his time and sweat which had built it up over the last months, and he felt very good about it all.

As Amos' wagon rolled along Red Gum Ridge, he thought of

what good times might be had during the few days he had allotted himself away from his own place. He wondered what Homer Smith's reaction would be at Amos' story of his summer. Amos doubted that Homer would want to exchange places with him now. "Yes," said Amos aloud to himself, "There's more to building up a farm in the bottoms than fishin' and swimmin' ever' day."

CHAPTER FOURTEEN

Ol' One Ear

AMOS ALLOWED HIMSELF THREE DAYS AT HICKORY FORD. He would have stayed longer, but he was still worried about the wild hogs getting into his corn patch. His stay wasn't nearly long enough for his mother, who hadn't seen him all summer. Amos assured her that he would return in a few weeks when it was time to pick cotton. That was long and hard work which always required extra help.

During his trip, Amos had visited family and friends and attend church at Hickory Ford on Sunday. Except for the early flood, the summer here had been much the same as all the others Amos remembered. His own summer in the bottoms stood out in stark contrast. In reflection, it seemed that everything about his summer on the Little Sandy had been extraordinary. It had taken him much more time and effort to recover from the flood than it had the folks in Hickory Ford. Then had come all the heavy building work, from the barn to the fences and other things in between. The struggle with the wild hogs and the raccoons over the corn crop was also unique to his own farming venture.

Amos thought about all this at length as he drove the team of mules back to the Little Sandy on that Monday morning. In comparison, life was much easier and simpler in a more developed community like Hickory Ford. For some time Amos had thoughts of how it might be for him to return to Hickory Ford and farm there. Farms would come available from time to time, not to mention the uncleared land on the outskirts of the community. He reminded himself that boys his own age were beginning to marry and set up places of their own.

It amused Amos for a moment when he remembered that Homer Smith had been sparking Lucy Davis over the summer. Amos figured that most of his friends would be married and have children before he took that step. It struck him that Lucy Davis' Poppa had a big farm, too big for him ever to develop by himself. And, as Lucy was the oldest, her husband would likely find himself with a ready-made farm. Homer would be fortunate if that came to him. Amos wondered what that would be like, starting out with a farm mostly cleared and with plenty of outbuildings, not to mention being close to Hickory Ford with its stores, smithy, mill, and churches.

In comparison, Amos lived way off down in the bottoms. He was an hour's ride from the nearest neighbor, an hour and a half in another direction from the nearest community for stores or church. And, he had to build or clear almost everything it took to make a thriving farm. The differences were startling, but Amos felt no pangs of regret. Without a doubt, he knew within himself that he would not trade places with Homer Smith. The bottoms, even with its isolation and hardships, held a strong attraction for Amos. He didn't fully understand it, but knew that building up a farm on the Little Sandy was the life for him.

Having stopped briefly at the Potters, Amos now encouraged the mules to hurry their way home. He held them to a brisk walk, even through White Creek as they neared their clearing.

On several occasions, Speckle barked from his spot on the wagon seat at squirrels that he could see or smell among the overhanging trees. Amos held a hand tightly to the hound's loose hide as a hunt was not uppermost on his mind.

Finally, they drove through the wagon track to see their own place laid out along the river. Amos looked over the enlarged clearing with the patch of tall green corn dominating its center. "We've shore got us a purty patch of corn, as purty as ever I've seen," spoke Amos to the dog and the team, "Yep, we worked up the ground, not onct but twice, plowed it, hoed it, and guarded it. Yep, it's a fine patch of corn," said Amos with great pride.

Rounding the near corner of the corn patch, Amos looked with even more pride at the structures which marked his home place. The newer structures still held the look of fresh wood, giving the place a look of change. As Amos pulled the team up in front of the barn, he fairly swelled with pride over "his place."

Leaving the mules hitched, Amos and Speckle jumped from the wagon and walked quickly around the split rail fence which encircled the corn. In places, there were tracks from the wild hogs, but the fence had held them back and kept the corn safe. This brought great relief to Amos as he knew full well that a hog could go through about anything he set his mind to. Satisfied now that the corn was indeed safe from marauding hogs, he made his way back to the barn where he unhitched the team and set about unloading the wagon.

After unloading the groceries and tools which he had just brought from Hickory Ford, Amos sat at his table and slowly made his dinner from pieces of a cold fried chicken and corn fritters his momma and grandma had packed for him. *No use to hurry through this,* thought Amos, *I might as well make it last as long as I can.* In the afternoon Amos settled himself back into a routine of his own place. He thought that he'd like to get a better idea of what was happening beyond his clearing. His summer had been so busy that he'd had no time to pay attention to anything but work.

Having saddled Little Red, who was his favorite riding mule, Amos rode down the river, making his way through the tall timber which lined its banks. Here Amos was attentive of the river's edge, giving notice to any and all animal tracks. His thoughts were on the hunting and trapping prospects for the fall and winter ahead.

Amos rode on to the deserted logging camp at the juncture of the Little Sandy and White Creek before circling to the east. He now followed White Creek upstream as he had just followed the Little Sandy downstream. Walking through a woods could reveal a certain amount of information about its game potential. By observing fresh nests and the feed being consumed, a hunter gained knowledge for the fall hunt. But waterways gave a clearer picture. The bare soil along the water's edge was like a paper showing the travels of the game which came here to cross, feed, or drink. This edge strip could tell not only how much game was in the woods, but its routes of travel as well.

Proceeding in this manner, Amos slowly circled the entire area in the vicinity of the cabin, an area of about six square miles. It was a treat for Speckle who checked out every hole, log, and tree within fifty yards of Amos and Little Red for the entire trip.

Arriving back at the cabin from the north, Amos thought it had been a profitable trip. He had learned that the game seemed to be plentiful, in spite of the flood. And, due to the changes in the life of the woods, several new den trees and logs were in used now. These were mentally noted for the months of coon hunting to come. The mast crop of nuts would be good this year as the trees were loaded far beyond what the squirrels and deer could eat in a single winter. What had struck Amos with relief was the absence of wild hog tracks. This pleased him immensely, but he knew it would not last for long. He wondered where Ol' One Ear had taken his pack, and when they would return.

Amos made supper for himself and Speckle out of the two squirrels he had taken that afternoon. Speckle had treed the two of them in the same white oak. Now they were fired up to add fresh meat to the eggs and biscuits that he fixed for his supper. Coffee, fresh pickles, and some of last year's sorghum rounded out their meal.

After the supper dishes had been done, Amos took up a pallet and lantern and walked out to the river bank. Of course, Speckle went along. Here in the approaching dusk, he set out two fishing poles, one from the platform and one out from the large white oak which grew at the water's edge.

Sitting there and watching darkness come, Amos reveled in his place on the river. As he casually watched his two floaters, Amos listened more intently to the night sounds. There off on the other side of the river, two owls called to one another in their lonesome hooting way. Up and down the river frogs croaked; some low and weak, others loud and challenging. Sound after sound came to Amos' ear, forming an orchestra of music. The evenings were Amos' favorite time of the day. In these moments he relished the coolness of the air and the ever-changing music of the wildlife. And, from time to time, he caught a fish which would serve for his dinner and supper the next day. Here he stayed until sleepiness drove him to his pallet for the night.

As pleasant as Amos' evening had been, his night brought

a different experience. A dream came to him in the night which caused him to sleep fitfully. There were wild hogs in the corn with Speckle getting into a terrible fight with Ol' One Ear. The dream was so real with snarls and grunts and squeals that Amos woke up in a sweat. Seeing the hound asleep near his feet, Amos realized that it had been only a dream. The hound and the corn were safe, at least for this night. He rose from his pallet and washed his face in the river before lying back to regain his sleep. He lay there those few minutes, looking up through the tree tops to the stars high above. His last thought before sleeping once again was that they would all have to deal with the old boar in the future.

For the next three weeks, Amos set himself about any and all small tasks that needed doing before time to help gather the crop at Hickory Ford. Whenever these ran short, he worked at cutting his winter's firewood from the tree tops left from the summer's building projects. It was slow work sawing short lengths from the hardwood, but Amos knew that, together, his cook stove and heating stove would consume quite a stack of wood throughout the cold winter months.

It was a chance mention of this during one of his Sunday visits to Willow Point that opened up an opportunity for some cash money, a scarce item among farm people. Mr. Blaine, one of the local store owners, overheard Amos mention that he had been splitting firewood. He asked if Amos had any that he wanted to sell. Amos was a bit caught off guard at first, as he had not thought of selling firewood. The grocer went on to say that he always bought his wood one winter ahead and allowed it to dry in a large woodshed at the rear of his store. And at this time, he only had enough to get through to spring.

Seeing this a good chance to earn some much-needed cash,

Amos agreed to cut, split, and haul the wood to Willow Point. The wood would be measured by the rick, a stack two feet wide, four feet high, and eight feet long--one wagon-load. Amos would receive one dollar a rick as the wood was delivered.

As Mr. Blaine wasn't in any hurry for his wood, Amos worked on it as he had time, or when he had the right wood at hand. Mr. Blaine only wanted red oak or white oak. When the time came in late September for Amos to help his folks with their cotton picking, he had hauled three loads of wood to Willow Point.

Amos noticed changes as he drove his team up Red Gum Ridge. The fields which had lain empty since mid summer were now occupied by farm hands. In every cotton field, myriad puffs of white appeared. The cotton bolls were opening up, exposing the dry fluffy cotton. Cotton pickers were labored throughout the fields, dragging their partially-full sacks while bending their backs over the cotton stalks.

A dinner stop was in order at his grandparent's place. This gave Amos and John another opportunity to talk over his progress in the bottoms. Amos always found an excuse to linger at his Grandma Janey's at meal time. She was one of the best cooks in the community. Today proved to be no exception, as she put out a spread that made Amos' mouth water. When he began to brag on all the steaming dishes, Janey responded with, "Just cat all ya want, Amos, they's plenty."

After the noon meal had been finished, John and Amos sat out in the porch swing to talk of crops and such. Amos relished this time with his grandpa, when there was just the two of them together. Amos perceived that John was giving more credence to his opinions. Amos could not have put his pleasure into words at his Grandpa showing respect for him. They agreed that it had been a good year for crops, in spite of the flood. John recounted past crops which had not been so good, like a crop which had been washed away in mid summer, just as the ears of corn were beginning to form and the cotton was in full bloom. "Not much picked that year, an' there were many a hungry belly thet winter too," said John.

Riding away that day, Amos thought about his grandpa and grandma. He realized that, though his grandparents lived pretty much like everyone else in the community, they were better off financially. Both of them were hard workers and good managers. When they had married, their parents had helped them to a start, but everything else they got in life came through hard work and good choices. Amos believed his grandpa to be smarter than most men, though he hadn't had much schooling. He had had the wisdom to put in the store on Red Gum Ridge when all they could afford was a wagon load of groceries. Their small start had grown into a thriving business, though small compared to the big mercantile in Hickory Ford. The store provided a steady source of cash money, allowing them a modest cushion during hard times. Grandpa still farmed himself, though mostly crops for his live-stock. He didn't plant any cotton. It required too much labor, and they had no more children at home to work it.

The harshness of farm life and often inadequate medical care resulted in short life spans. However, serious illness was something that John and Janey had somehow eluded so far. John had a reputation for being the hardest worker in the Hickory Ford community, even at his age. It was said that there was no one stronger for his size, and certainly there was no better tie maker.

By mid-afternoon, Amos reached his parent's place, and soon fit right in with the age-old routine of harvest time. For six weeks he helped his parents pick their cotton crop and get started on their corn. Each week he took a day to ride back to the bottoms to check on his own place, mainly his corn. Each trip showed no sign of the wild hogs. With no hogs about and the river people gone, little remained to worry Amos.

Time passed swiftly as work filled their hours from daylight to dark. It was an anxious Amos who drove back to the Little Sandy in early November. But this trip home was different from all the rest. This time he carried a different load; his own sow and shoats. Also, his cow and her calf were tied behind the wagon. Adding to his livestock, Amos' mother had caught up three hens and a rooster so that Amos could have his own fresh eggs. Amos saw this as his own farm coming together. The stock had been at his Poppa's place and under his care and feeding. True, Amos still contributed to his Poppa's farm, but he felt very strongly that he should be husbanding his own stock.

This step meant other things also. Amos would no longer be able to stay as long at Hickory Ford. These animals would require regular care. Also, it meant that enough feed would have to be raised on his farm to sustain them. Amos realized that bringing them down to the Little Sandy would make life different for him.

For the first week, the hogs were kept in the small pasture along with the cow and her calf. This gave them time to orient themselves to this new home before being turned out to live off the freshly fallen acorns which were abundant throughout the bottoms.

A killing frost had hit the week before Amos came back, causing the foliage to assume the beautiful reds, oranges, and yellows of fall. The same freeze allowed the ears of corn to be snapped off from the stalk, signaling that the corn was ready to be picked. For two weeks Amos picked his corn. It was a slow process working by himself. First, there was the picking, then shoveling the ears from the wagon into the crib. In the end, his cribs were overflowing with corn. Amos remembered that someone had said that "corn in the crib was like money in the bank," meaning that corn would feed hogs which could be sold for cash.

With the corn crop gathered, Amos turned his attention once again to the firewood requested by Mr. Blaine in Willow Point. Between a few other chores, it took two days to saw, split, and haul a rick to Willow Point. It was on a return trip from there that he first saw hog tracks near the deserted sawmill. Pulling up the mules, Amos stepped from the wagon to examine the tracks, hoping that they had been his sow and pigs wandering too far from the cabin.

But his hopes fell quickly as there were several grown hogs in this group, meaning that it had to be the wild hogs. Amos remounted the wagon and drove on to his clearing, thinking soberly all the way about what this would mean to him and his own hogs.

For the next week, Amos managed to keep his own hogs somewhat close to the cabin by using Little Red to catch up to them when they strayed too far. Each night, he fed them a few ears of corn for their feed. Despite his concern over the wild hogs, Amos was pleased that his shoats were growing as they ate the surplus acorns.

One evening in late November his hogs failed to return by full dark, something they had not done before. At first light the next morning, Amos rode out on Little Red to find them. It was mid-morning before he located the sign that told the tale. The tracks of his own hogs had merged with those of the wild hogs north of the White Creek crossing. It seemed to Amos from the sign that though there had been some jousting about, the two groups had merged, being of the same kind. But, of course, the larger group of wild hogs had determined their direction of travel when they left.

From this area near White Creek, Amos followed the tracks north through the bottoms for about a mile before coming upon a large canebrake. Here the hog sign was plentiful, with both old and new tracks. It appeared that this area had been used by the wild hogs for several months. The cane would prove a secure place to find shelter from a winter storm. Skirting the canebrake, Amos determined that the cane covered an area about ten acres in size, with several openings throughout it. Pausing at the edge of the cane, he tried to think the situation through. Going in after his own hogs could be very risky to himself and Little Red. Speckle certainly would be in danger. The cane was so thick in most places that a hog could not be seen more than a few feet away.

Amos knew that if he left his own hogs here with the others, they too would go wild in a short time. Thinking back to the circle he had just made of the canebrake, Amos remembered a heavily traveled trail which the hogs apparently used to go to water at a nearby slough. Amos saw this trail as a weak link in the wild hogs' defenses, as here in the open woods they would not find the concealment afforded by the canebrake. With these thoughts in mind, he rode on back toward his own clearing.

Instead of riding directly to his own clearing, Amos reined Little Red in the direction of the Potter place. He had an idea of what could be done to retrieve the stolen hogs, but he thought it only wise to get an older man's opinion. Mr. Potter was skinning out some squirrels as he rode up.

"Howdy, Little Man," called out Mr. Potter, "What are ye up to this'evenin'?"

"Not too much," responded Amos. Already Amos felt easier about the situation as he was confident in Potter's wisdom. "I'd be up to more iffen I knew whut to do 'bout them wild hogs that stole my sow and shoats," volunteered Amos.

"Wild hogs, ye say. Would that be Ol' One Ear himself," asked Mr. Potter, who had momentarily stopped the skinning process.

"Yore right there. It's him. An' I shore wish it weren't," said Amos with despair. "I figure he took 'em sometime las' night. They're all hid out in that big canebrake between White Creek and the Little Sandy."

"Shore sorry to hear that," said Mr. Potter who returned to cleaning the squirrels. Speaking again, he asked, "Whut ya' figure t' do, Amos?'

"I aim t' ketch 'em up an' bring 'em home, iffen I can," said Amos. "They'll take to being wild right off with that Ol' One Ear bunch. I do have somethin' of a plan, though. But, I wanted to see iffen ya had any ideas first. I'm a little nervous 'bout tangling with Ol' One Ear again. Speckle came close to gittin' himself killed the last time."

"Wal, all right. Whut's yore plan so far?" asked Mr. Potter."It's purty thick in that brake, an' be mighty hard to slip in on 'em, 'sides I don't like the ideer of gittin' thet close to them wild hogs without seein' 'em. So I figure to bait 'em out 'er the brake with corn an' build sorta a pen to ketch 'em."

"Wal, that's good thinking, especially the part 'bout not gittin' too close to them hogs. Boy, they could jest eat you alive right out 'er yore shoes, an' while you's on a dead run too," replied

Mr. Potter. "An' I like yore trap idea, but what ya' goin ' to do once ya' ketch 'em? Ya' could cut the tusks out 'er the young ones, but them sows and 'Ol One Ear, why, ther' ain't enough men in all of Willow Point to hold thet 'ol boar down to cut out his tusks."

Amos sat on a stump in silence while Mr. Potter filled his pipe. The two of them sat in silence for several minutes, Amos barely hearing a nearby peckerwood through his despair.

Mr. Potter finally broke the silence by saying, "Just shoot him, Amos."

Startled, Amos said, "Ya mean, shoot "Ol One Ear, then what?"

"Drag 'im out in the woods, the wild critters will eat 'im," answered Mr. Potter. "Look at it this way, Amos, that old wild boar has raided 'bout every farm throughout the bottoms. He's killed pigs, chickens, and dogs, not to mention all the corn and garden stuff that he's et up. He needs killin', that's fer shore."

Amos thought on it for a moment, then agreed that it was the only way. The old wild boar would never be tame again, if he ever was at all. He didn't like killing without using the meat, but the old boar's meat would certainly be tough and have a strong taste. But the prospect would in no way be as easy as it sounded. The hog in question was clever, having proven himself a fighter over many years.

Riding back toward his own clearing, Amos thought over the lay of the canebrake and the conversation with Mr. Potter. The older man had given Amos several good ideas as to how to build the catch pen, expressing his regret at having to work the mill as they were shorthanded. What stuck in Amos' mind most of all were the admonitions regarding the danger of the effort. Wild hogs were both fierce and aggressive, in addition to being agile and unyielding. Mr. Potter had even said that he'd rather face a bucket of cottonmouths as to face down one wild hog. The man had gone so far as to loan Amos an old double barrel shotgun along with several loads of buckshot. He said that using a .22 at close range against a mad hog was like spitting into a high wind.

Upon his return to the cabin, Amos filled a tow sack half full of ear corn, collected his ax, shovel, and all the wire that he could gather, along with nails, a hammer and saw. It was too late to get started that day, so Amos had to spend an anxious night. He sat out at first light the next morning.

This morning Amos did not use the saddle but sat astride Little Red's harness as he would need it to drag up poles for the catch pen he planned to build. When he arrived in the area of the canebrake, there were no hogs in sight, but a check of the trail to the slough revealed fresh tracks. Still astride Little Red, Amos scanned the area for a place suitable for the pen. The best place seemed to be just outside the brake, in an area thick with young trees.

Unloading the mule of its burden of corn and tools, Amos used the axe to chop down every tree in an area about thirty feet across. He was careful to leave individual trees which formed an irregular circle. These would serve as posts to strengthen the pen.

Amos worked hard throughout the day, stopping only for a short dinner break of cold biscuits, bacon, and hard boiled eggs, all leftovers from his breakfast that morning. At the end of the day, he had the sides raised about two feet high for two-thirds of the circle. A few posts had been set, but mostly the small trees sufficed. The poles which formed the sides were laid interlocking as with a rail fence, though here secured to the posts and young trees by large nails. Amos felt bad about nailing a fence into trees.

He had been taught that this was a "lazy man's fence." These trees would likely be damaged forever and possibly hide nails that might do great damage to axes and saws someday. But Amos' two major issues were speed and strength. The hogs had to be caught quickly before they wandered out of the area. And, once caught, Amos needed to feel confident that they could not escape.

Riding home that night, Amos figured that the hogs had laid up in the brake all day and slept since wild hogs fed mostly at night. Also, the sounds of his axe and hammer might have kept them from coming out. He was satisfied that when they came out in the evening to water at the slough, they would find the ears of corn he had left on the trail. Even wild hogs that fed mostly on acorns would be drawn to the smell of corn. Amos had scattered a trail of ears from the trail to the center of the pen where he had dumped the rest of the sack. Hopefully, their fear of the pen would be lessened by the daily rations of corn which Amos would leave until he was ready to catch them on the inside.

Three days of baiting were required before Amos was satisfied that the catch pen would work. Each evening after Amos left, the wild hogs came out of the brake and ate all the corn which he had left for them. By the third day, he had no need to leave any on the trail or nearby, only leave all the ears in the center of the pen. As he had hoped, his absence and the attraction of the corn had drawn the wild hogs as well as his own into the pen. Day by day, he built the pen walls higher and completed the circle, until the walls were three feet high. The circle was completed, except for a six-foot gate. This gate was hung so that the bottom could be suspended higher than the top and tied to the limb of a nearby white oak. With the gate set in this position, Amos left the area with the decision not to return until the next afternoon, wanting the hogs to get comfortable with the overhanging gate.

As he attended to small chores about the place the next day, Amos' thoughts rarely left the catch pen. He wondered if the corn he had left the night before had been enough to hold the hogs in the area of the brake another day. And he wondered if the gate suspended over the opening had scared any of them off. Though it was hung four feet above the ground, Amos had attempted to disguise it with bushy limbs.

Finally, at mid-afternoon Amos could wait no longer. He took up two sacks of corn, one hanging off each shoulder. In addition, he carried enough food to get himself by for the next twenty-four hours. Together with the .22 and the shotgun, it all made a heavy load for the mile walk, but he didn't want to risk Little Red's presence scaring off the wild hogs. Speckle also had been left at the cabin. Amos wasn't sure what might happen in the next hours as he tried to spring the trap on the wild hogs. When he arrived at the catch pen, Amos found all of last night's corn to have been eaten, and everything about the pen appeared to be ready for the catch. He dumped all the corn out of the sacks into the back end of the pen to get the wild hogs as far into the pen as possible. He then tied his axe and food sack up in a nearby tree in case he needed them later.

Well before dusk, Amos was in position above the catch pen. Here he would sit in a fork next to the tree's trunk and wait until the hogs were penned. At which time he would release the rope holding up the gate. He hoped that his position fifteen feet above the ground would eliminate any of his fresh scent which might make Ol' One Ear too wary to enter the pen.

The hour he waited before the first of the hogs walked down the trail seemed like an eternity. He watched them come, first only a few of the young shoats, then the sows with their young pigs. The first pigs had already turned off the trail for the pen when Ol' One Ear finally came into view. Amos was beginning to worry that the old boar would not show up with the others. All in all, including his own hogs, there were thirty-four head. Amos wasn't sure that all of them could get into the pen at once, but did not have to wait long to find out. He determined to catch what he could and worry about any others later. He was hopeful that the old boar and his sows would be in the pen. It was most important to catch them, or his own hogs would never be safe to feed in the bottoms.

As the hogs approached and entered the pen, Amos looked down to check their condition. They were a rangy bunch of hogs, with no signs of farm raised grain or markings. Directly, his own sow with her young pigs came underneath him. To his shock, several of them, including the sow, were cut up from fighting. It saddened him to think of how his sow must have been bullied about in the last few days. Hopefully, that would all be over soon.

The minutes slowly passed before Ol' One Ear approached the gate. Even from high in the tree, the hog looked gigantic. There were scars from one end of him to the other, telling of battles with all manner of other animals. One scar, in particular, caught Amos' attention. It was a long straight line across the boar's forehead, and just above the eyes. Then it came to Amos that the line had been drawn by his .22 bullet that night the boar and Speckle had fought in the hay patch. Well, Amos figured now to get a second and better chance to end this old boar's rampaging.

Ol' One Ear approached the gate with something of a saunter, as if he were coming to steal this corn. It almost appeared to Amos that the old boar displayed an arrogance in the act. Holding his breath, he watched as the wild hog followed the rest of his pack through the pen gate. As his hindquarters cleared the inside of the trip gate, Amos almost released the rope, but decided to hold off to allow the hog to get some distance inside the pen.

As Ol' One Ear jousted his way through the pack to get to the corn, Amos released the gate which swung down with a crashing thud. The old boar roared and spun around in a flashing motion, sending the other hogs tumbling in all directions. The boar stood motionless for three or four seconds before leaping forward. He charged the gate like a living battering ram. Amos held his breath as the boar drove himself into the gate, attempting to force it out of his path. Though the gate creaked and groaned, it held against this onslaught.

As the boar regained his footing, the other hogs reacted with a melee of squeals and grunts. Wild hogs were running in all directions in their attempt to get away. Ol' One Ear didn't hesitate long before jumping into a hard run for the opposite side of the pen, launching himself into the air as he approached the rails. Only his front feet cleared the top rail, but his weight caused the rail to snap, allowing his momentum to push his front end over the top, with his hind feet flailing at the air behind him as he slipped down to freedom. Ole One Ear was free.

Following his lead, one of his rangy sows made a run at the damaged rail. It was a little easier for her, as the pen wall was some shorter now. When the other hogs attempted to follow at this weakened rail, they fell short. None made it out, since too many arrived there at once and the congestion prevented any from getting the lift needed to clear the top. As this drama was unfolding, Amos sat open-mouthed, fearful that he would lose the whole pack, including his own. As the hogs below receded from the wall and began to mill around aimlessly, Amos looked out across the bottoms to see Ol' One Ear and the rangy sow running into the canebrake.

Climbing down his secreted rope, Amos was both jubilant and despondent. He had been successful at catching all the pack but two. But the two he had lost were the two most capable of rebuilding the pack. Not knowing what to do now about the escapees, he retrieved his axe and cut another pole to replace the rail which had been broken. Also, he wired the bottom of the gate shut to prevent any of the caged hogs from working their way out. By now the hogs had calmed down. They had stopped running crazily about, frantic to find an opening for escape. Some of them had gone back to feeding on the corn. His own hogs had been the first to do so.

Thinking over his present situation, Amos was uncertain how to proceed. The lost hogs would never be baited back into such a trap. And, until they were captured in some manner, the hogs in the pen would not be safe. It was certain that the old boar would return to rip open the pen at one place or another. Darkness would settle in soon, allowing little or no time to pursue them before nightfall. Amos stood there in the dusk, working out a plan which he hoped would work. If it didn't, he might never see his beloved clearing again.

From some dead trees laying about the area, he cut a large supply of firewood which should keep the cold from him the entire night. With a few branches, Amos built a cookfire, boiled himself some coffee, and ate corn fritters and a piece of apple pie which he had brought along from the cabin. His lantern hung from an overhanging limb as he settled down between two quilts. His intention was to remain here and guard the hogs in the pen all night, before setting out after Ol' One Ear and the sow at first light.

It was a fitful sleep. Every sound seemed to warn Amos of the boar's approach. Each time that he rose from his pallet to look out through the lantern light, nothing seemed out of place. Between the usual woods noises and the snoring coming from the hogs across the fence, Amos had difficulty in returning to sleep. Finally, he awoke to see the woods lightening up from the rising sun. Stretching himself to wakefulness, he looked over into the pen to find all the hogs still asleep. It occurred to Amos that at this moment, none of them looked wild, but just like all the hogs penned back in Hickory Ford.

Amos waited for full light before walking into the canebrake after the old boar and his rangy sow. He had intentionally left all his extra food and water back near the pen as he didn't want any encumbrances if he had to move fast. He carried the double-barreled .12 gauge, loaded with buckshot, while the .22 was slung over his back with a small rope. The decision had been made before now that the two hogs had to be killed.

After a couple hours of searching, Amos couldn't help but question the wisdom of his plan. Here he was off down in the bottoms alone, without even his hound, hunting two notorious wild and hogs. In most areas of the brake, he couldn't see more than fifteen feet, and sometimes less. He knew that this was without a doubt the most dangerous thing he had ever attempted, but he had to find and kill them, or else he would be fighting them away from his clearing forever.

Amos used not only his eyes, but also his ears. Once he was sure that he had heard one of the hogs, but it turned out to be nothing more than the wind rustling some leaves. After that experience, it took several minutes for his heart to stop racing and his breath to even out again. On two occasions, he had climbed one of the isolated trees for a further view, but still saw neither of the hogs.

He was slowly moving down one of the many trails when some sense caused him to stop suddenly. Then a shift in the wind brought an odor to him, something strong with sweat and animal waste. Spinning quickly, Amos looked frantically for the source of the smell. But before he could locate it, a brown blur with a series of blood-curdling grunts attached to it leaped from the cane to propel itself across the fifteen feet separating them.

Amos, who had been hunting with both hammers cocked on the shotgun, pointed the long gun at the fast-approaching hog, jerked one trigger to the effect of a heavy recoil and a thundering boom. The hog let out a high squeal and turned sharply to its left, where it staggered about. Amos saw that it was the sow. He had shot her in the side of the head. The sow was bleeding badly and would surely die, but to ensure that she would do no harm to him, Amos put the second load of buckshot into the sow's brain, just behind her right ear. With a final grunt, she heaved and fell slowly onto her right side, dead to rise no more.

Breathing heavily, Amos tried to collect his senses after this sudden attack. But for his split-second reaction, it might have been Amos lying dead, instead of the sow. Before he regained himself, Amos detected motion out of the corner of his right eye. Turning quickly, he saw the boar not more than fifty feet away. The boar looked enraged and about to charge. Suddenly Amos realized that in the emotion of the previous moment, he had not reloaded the shotgun. Now his attempts to break the action failed. The borrowed gun was stuck closed. At that instant the boar charged like something shot from a gun. In an instant, Amos knew what he must do. He dropped the shotgun and turned to sprint through the cane. He had always been agile and quick. Now he raced like never before. As a boy, he had raced his friends and almost always won. Now he raced for his very life.

With a fifty-foot lead, he had a head start. But the big boar's speed and power would quickly catch Amos if he didn't find a place of safety soon. As he bounded through a patch of cane, Amos caught sight of a small hickory about thirty feet distant. This tree now became his target as he heard the boar closing the few feet between them. With maybe seven feet remaining, Amos leaped through the air to wrap himself around the tree about five feet above the ground.

Not content with his safety, he struggled to pull himself up the limbless shaft. It was then that something very heavy latched itself onto his left shoe. With panic in his heart, Amos knew instantly that the boar had his left foot and shoe in the strong grasp of its mouth. The leg stretched itself down away from him, and the boar's teeth began to pierce through the shoe's leather to press against the skin of Amos' foot.

The weight of the boar tugging on his foot began to pull Amos from his low perch. To resist, he desperately jerked his leg to pull free of the boar. This succeeded, as the shoe tore off his foot, relieving him of the boar's weight. Now Amos wasted no time in pulling himself into the upper reaches of the little tree. Angry at losing the foot, the boar began lashing at the tree with his huge head. Each time the boar struck, Amos shook in the small tree's upper branches.

Not wanting to remain there and have the sapling torn down from beneath him, Amos sought out a stronger refuge. A few feet away stood a tupelo gum which, though not large, was substantially thicker than the hickory sapling where he was now perched above the raging boar. Since the outer limbs of the gum were a few feet beyond Amos' grasp, he began a swaying motion which took him in an ever-widening arc. Amos continued the arc until he was afraid that the slender hickory would snap under the strain. If it did so, he would fall to the ground under the feet of Ol' One Ear. But he still could not reach the heavier limbs of the gum.

Knowing he could not stay in the hickory but a little while before the boar brought him down, Amos made a desperate move. Like so many squirrels he had seen, Amos vaulted from the sapling just as the arc brought him the closest to the gum. The momentum of the arc shot him through the intervening space and into the limbs of the gum. Grasping wildly for fear he would fall to the ground, Amos finally caught hold of a solid limb with his left hand. With this grip he swiveled himself to grasp with his right and pull himself toward the tupelo gum's heavier inner limbs. Amos gasped for air as he hung tightly to his new refuge. The boar saw the change of trees but did not relent in his attempts to dislodge the man who had captured his pack and killed his sow. Within its small and limited brain, the boar also knew that this was the same man who had hurt his head that night while he had fought the dog in the clearing.

Now with his front feet on the broad lower trunk of the tupelo gum, Ol' One Ear sent up his threatening grunts. Looking down from his safe haven, Amos couldn't but be intimidated by this fierce beast of the bottoms. The long, curving tusks jutted out so menacingly that Amos seemed to feel them ripping the flesh of his legs flesh. Standing there upon the flared base of the tree, the boar stood all of seven feet tall, with a gnarled head, set off by the four-inch tusks bathed in a white froth. Somehow Amos noticed the missing ear more than the one still in place. With such a close look, Amos could see that the ear had been ripped off, probably in battle with another boar.

Alternately, Ol' One Ear would charge his way up the trunk of the tupelo gum and then race around the tree, tearing at all the vegetation, as if to scare Amos from his perch some fifteen feet above. After several minutes passed, Amos began to calm, knowing now that there was no way the boar, no matter how huge and menacing he was, could dislodge him from his safe position in the gum.

It was only now that he remembered the .22 hanging off his back. He was surprised that it had hung on during all his climbing and jumping. He realized though that it weighed too little to have been noticed during the panic of his escape.

In a flash, Amos decided that this was the moment to end it all. There would likely be no better time to kill the mad boar, who would surely continue to steal and kill if not stopped here today. Knowing that animals could be smart enough to know the meaning of a gun being pointed at them, Amos discreetly brought the little rifle around to his front. Now he thought about the best time for a shot, as there would likely only be one chance. If he missed, the boar would probably break from his rage and dash off into the cane, requiring Amos to have to hunt him again. Amos knew that he didn't have it in himself to go after the boar again today. Also, Amos knew that if he climbed from the tree while the boar was still alive, he would be the hunted. To have faced the sow with two loads of buckshot had been risky enough, but to face Ol' One Ear with only a single shot .22 held far greater danger.

For the moment the boar had retreated to a patch of cane to cool himself. Amos had no clear shot, he would have to wait.

After a few minutes of no return by the boar, he began to worry that the boar might retreat through the cane, depriving Amos of another opportunity to shoot him. Amos knew what would bring the boar on again, so he made some movements to fake his climb down from the gum.

Unable to contain his hate long enough to ensure the man was on the ground and within his reach, the wild boar charged from his shade to once again attack the trunk of the tupelo gum. Amos' retreat was not enough to cancel the boar's raging attack. He grunted and snarled while ripping the bark with his tusks, stretching himself the full seven feet of his length up the tree's side. Try as he might, Amos could not get a clear shot while the boar lashed from side to side. Patiently, he waited until the boar spent himself enough to drop from the trunk and whip about the tree, tearing at every piece of vegetation in its path.

Amos knew the moment he wanted, and he waited for it to come. Just as he had planned, the boar finally vented enough rage and energy to slow down, coming to a stop to breathe heavily. At a distance of thirty feet and the rifle barrel tracking the boar up until the instant he stopped, Amos focused through the sights on the spot right between and just above Ol' One Ear's eyes. With a slow deliberateness, his finger squeezed the trigger. The crack of the .22 was sharp in the morning air. The boar only grunted softly, and fell straight down to its belly, without another sound or movement. Amos knew then that the small piece of lead had found its mark, but he remained in the tree for several minutes longer, coming to terms with the strain on his emotions. Finally, after the sounds of small animals came once again to his ear, Amos lowered himself to the ground. Here he stood close to the tree's wide trunk, still a refuge should life return to the boar. After several minutes, he slowly walked forward to make absolutely sure that the wild boar was indeed dead. Standing close, Amos knew that this hog would raid and kill no more. Amos turned and made his way out of the brake and back to the catch pen.

It was after midday when Amos stepped into his clearing on the little Sandy. The sight made him proud that it was his. The past 24 hours had been the most dangerous of his life, even more so than the flood. The experience had left him shaken. More than once during his return walk, he had stopped to look through the canopy of limbs above to thank God for saving him during the narrow escapes of the morning. As he walked to the mule lot, Little Red let out his snuffling bugle to show his pleasure at Amos' return. The little mule's call was echoed by Ned and Speckle. Between the three of them, the yard was a din of noise loud enough to wake the dead. Anyway, it pleased Amos to have been missed by these his friends. Calling out to them over their bawling and barking, Amos said, "it shore is good for a fellar to have such good friends who miss 'im."

CHAPTER FIFTEEN

Christmas

TWO DAYS BEFORE CHRISTMAS, Amos headed his team toward Hickory Ford. The iron rims of the wagon wheels grated and crunched their way across the ground, frozen hard as stone by mid-December. The wagon rocked and bounced on the uneven road, and every sway and jar impressed the cold into Amos' bones. Once underway, Christmas with his family was a close reality. His mind wandered back over the weeks since his encounter with Ol' One Ear and his pack of wild hogs.

For about two weeks following the capture of the hogs, Amos had fed them morning and night, hauling corn from the barn. The water trough, hewn from a cypress log and dragged into place by the team, also had to be filled morning and night. Water had to be carried by bucket from the slough. This was hard work, particularly lugging the water up from the slough. But he had a plan for making that hard work pay off. On the day after the capture, he had released his own sow and shoats, who gladly followed him back to their clearing. His plan would call for them to eventually rejoin that herd, but right now they were at a real disadvantage in the pen with the wild hogs. The day after capturing the wild herd, he took the first step of that plan. It took money, but he earned enough from selling firewood to Mr. Blaine.

With some of his cash, Amos bought 20 pounds of salt, and three pounds each of sage and pepper from Mr. Blaine's store. These spices Amos used to cure and season some of the wild hog meat. In the days following, he killed and processed first one of the sows, then another.

Butchering hogs had never been a one man job back in Hickory Ford. Here in the bottoms, though, Amos had to forget some of the methods which might be used where there were more tools and plenty of help. First, Amos had built a small holding pen on one side of the main enclosure. He had trapped the hog he wanted to butcher in the small pen. This separation was not always easy, and more often than not, other hogs also got into the small pen. After slaughtering, one of the mules drug the dead hog onto a pole rack near a kettle of boiling water. The boiling water was then doused over the carcass to loosen the hair so it could be scraped from the hide. Only then had the hog been gutted and washed out with more hot water. The carcass was then cut into six pieces; two hind quarters, two front quarters, and two rib sections divided at the backbone. Four people could lift the hog and dip it in the vat of boiling water, but Amos had to use a rack made of poles. Working alone, he couldn't get the carcass into the water without scalding himself, and he couldn't get it out quick enough that the meat didn't start to cook from the heat of the boiling water. It was three times the work, but Amos' pole frame worked.

As a hog was butchered, the meat was hauled by wagon back to the clearing where it was hung up in the new smokehouse. It was laid on a table of poles and covered with salt. It would remain like this for four weeks before finally being suspended from a pole over a slow hickory wood fire. The salt did the curing while the hickory smoke both flavored and continued to dry the meat. For the meat to keep through the next summer without being frozen all the time, it had to lose most of its water content.

It had taken Amos a day to butcher each hog, but even more time was needed to process the sausage. Here he elicited the help of the Potters, who were more than willing to help in return for a share of the meat. The meat used for the sausage, both lean and fat cuts, were ground in a hand grinder, seasoned with the sage, pepper, and salt, and then fried before being stuffed into glass jars. These jars were then capped with grease before being covered with a lid. Preserved in this fashion, the sausage could be stored until hot weather the following summer.

As planned, Amos butchered four of the wild hogs. After the first of the year, with the meat cured and seasoned, he hoped to peddle it in Willow Point for more cash money. There was more to his plan than just butchering four sows. Amos cut the tusks from all the smaller wild hogs, making them safer to handle at a future time. He castrated all but two of the young boars to take some of the strong taste from their meat before he butchered them next year. Besides, he didn't need that many boars running around his part of the bottoms. Each pig was ear notched to identify it as his. He chose to cut out a "V" from the very end of the right ear. He accomplished all this by setting out a snare rope and catching a hind foot. The captured pig was then pulled up the side of the pen and tied tightly to one of the trees serving as posts. While standing on his side of the fence, Amos could lean over and do his work safely.

Only after all the butchering and cutting had been done did Amos open up the pen, allowing the hogs to once again run loose. By this time they had depended upon Amos for all their food and water for a solid month. Released to roam the bottoms at will, they would be able to take care of themselves, but Amos knew they would continue to consider the area of the canebrake and the pen as their home. To ensure this, Amos planned to bring a small load of corn to the pen every few days.

As he drove to Hickory Ford, Amos also thought of all the wood splitting and hauling he had done for Mr. Blaine in Willow Point. The money Amos had earned would allow him to buy some things he needed, like cartridges for his .22 rifle, a new pair of gum boots, and other necessities which he could not produce on his own.

After the sausage-making project, Mr. Potter and Amos had continued to work together. Felling and sawing timber was definitely a two man job. A six foot crosscut saw required two strong men to operate it. And, as Amos was alone on his place and the oldest Potter boy was still too small to handle one end of the saw, the two men swapped work in order to make progress on each place. Trees were cut for ties, as well as some for more rails and posts. For Amos, this hard work was nothing new, but a continuation of the efforts of the summer.

This fall had been a busy time. Because of the hogs and his timbering, this trip home for Christmas would be his first since helping with the harvest in October. Since he planned to stay at Hickory Ford for several days, Amos left his cow and calf as well as the chickens with the Potters. He had taken the Potters enough corn and hay to feed the animals for a week. His hogs could forage for themselves in the bottoms as there was still an abundant supply of acorns and other wild foods.

In the three-hour drive from the Potters to Hickory Ford, Amos experienced no relief from the biting cold. The mules seemed to handle it without trouble, as they were working hard enough to stay warm, but not hard enough to tire them. Speckle lay curled up on a pile of sacks in the wagon. Amos had the worst of it. Twice, he got so cold he stopped the team and built a small fire. These warming fires made the ride bearable, though not enjoyable.

Christmas at home seemed to make up for all the hard work and loneliness of the past summer and fall. It was a festive time with decorations, treats, large holiday meals, and joyous visits with friends. All the churches around Hickory Ford joined together for a Christmas pageant, providing a time for the entire community to come together. Almost everyone attended one church or another, on occasion if not regularly. At this combined pageant, the spirit of the community came through the Spirit of God. It was at the pageant that Amos took the opportunity to visit with Henry and Eula so that he would not have to go back to their house.

Amos spent his last night in Hickory Ford with his grandparents on Red Gum Ridge. Grandma Janey had cooked a big supper; a young raccoon and sweet potatoes. Amos was already quite full when she brought in dessert, a hot apple pie.

"But Grandmaw, I've eaten so much now I'm sick," stated Amos.

"Now, Amos, shorely ya kin eat some of this here apple pie. It'll be the last you'll have fer some time, least ways until ya git back this way," teased his Grandma.

John grinned at their exchange as he helped himself to a large piece of the pie. With a groan, Amos did likewise. As he ate it, he reminded himself that down in the bottoms on the Little Sandy, there would be none of Grandma's pie, and his own attempts at pie-making never turned out anything like hers.

Later, as Janey washed up their supper dishes, Amos and John took a walk out to check on the chickens. Seems another mink had been making raids on some of the other local chicken houses. The walk in the cold night air helped to settle Amos' stomach. Tonight Amos thought he noticed something different in his Grandpa's manner. Their relationship had grown significantly closer since that spring morning when they left for the Little Sandy the first time. Now tonight Amos could sense that he was being given a new respect, one beyond that automatically accorded a grandson. He knew that John didn't give that level of respect to just everyone. It was apparent that John gave more credibility to Amos' opinion than he did to most grown men with families. Also, John seemed more relaxed and happier whenever Amos was around.

The two of them stood for a long time at the lot gate, talking about the events of the past year. John particularly liked to hear Amos talk about the flood and the wild hogs. Over the past days, it seemed that everyone in Hickory Ford had asked Amos about those two episodes. Most folks said that John had told them all about them. They also told Amos how John bragged on the way he had built the place on the Little Sandy into the beginnings of a good farm. Amos was touched that John would say such things about him. He wasn't able to put these feelings into words but tried to show even more respect for his grandpa, who had been the one to give him the chance to prove he could make it on his own.

Finally, they froze out and headed for the house and its warm fire. There they found Janey sitting in the front room in her rocker, knitting at some piece of clothing. Amos settled into a straight back chair nearby while John went back to their bedroom. At first, Amos thought that his Grandpa had gone to bed, though nothing had been said about it.

A few minutes later John walked into the front room carrying something like a long straight sock. "Here, Amos, thought ya' could use this."

Taking hold of the object, Amos knew instantly what he had in his hands. He could feel the hard steel of what could only be a double-barreled shotgun. Sheer joy overwhelmed him as he gripped tightly it with both hands, afraid if he loosened his grip the shotgun would somehow disappear.

"Bought thet from a feller over in Hampton," said John as Amos untied the leather lacing which held a flap over the butt end. "Ye Grandmaw made ye that case, figured thet would keep it dry and clean of scratches," he continued. Janey looked on from her rocker, smiling warmly.

Reaching inside the case and pulling the shotgun from its covering, Amos' eyes widened as he gasped a breath of air. "It's a, ah, uh, why it's a Remington. Gosh, Grandpaw, this is a rich man's gun. It must have cost a fortune!""Wal, not so much, Amos, it's a used gun, though it looks brand new. I got a good deal on it. It's time ya had yore own shotgun, and this 'un will last ya' yore whole life. A man needs a good shotgun iffen he intends to feed himself reg'lar,"

With the heavy emotion of the moment now gone, Amos stepped nearer to the lamp to inspect this new shotgun. It did appear to be new, like John had said. Looking close, Amos could read "Remington Arms Company." It was a 12 gauge with large recurved hammers on either side of the barrels. Amos thought to himself that this gun would outlast his lifetime. Maybe, some Christmas far in the future, he would find himself gifting it to a grandson. For now, he would certainly take good care of it.

Later Amos lay awake in the bed in the front room, thinking about this new gun. In the dim light cast by the holes in the front of the stove, Amos could barely make out the outline of the barrels where it stood in the corner. In these moments Amos was not sure what excited him most, the future hunts he would have with this new gun, or how he felt about Grandpa giving him such a wonderful and expensive gift. Heading out the next morning, the return trip to the Little Sandy proved to be no warmer than the trip to Hickory Ford had been. The temperature was well below freezing, bone-chilling cold. But this trip went by much quicker, as thoughts of all the hunts he would take with the new Remington kept him warm. Since he had not had the opportunity to show it to any of his family or his friends, Amos was bursting to tell somebody about the new shotgun. The Potters gave him the first (and last, of course) opportunity before he reached his own place on the Little Sandy.

It was near dinner time, and Mrs. Potter set out another plate while Mr. Potter admired the Remington 12 gauge. He spoke highly of the gun, making Amos all that much the prouder of having it. The talk over the new gun led to swapping hunting stories past and future as they waited for Mrs. Potter's call to the table.

Driving the remaining hour to his own place, Amos thought back over the past year's happenings. It had been a very hard year, one he hoped would not repeat itself ever again. Amos reminded himself that farm life was more often hard than not, with few cash rewards. And then there were the risks of accidents or illness. Doctors were few and far in between. Not to mention that there were so many illnesses they could do nothing about. Nevertheless, Amos enjoyed the life and looked forward to the future.

CHAPTER SIXTEEN

'Numonee

IN THE FIRST WEEKS AFTER AMOS' RETURN TO THE BOTTOMS, he worked mostly in the woods, either hewing ties or splitting firewood for Mr. Blaine. As loads of either were ready, Amos hauled them to Willow Point where he collected his payment amount in cash. At seventy-five cents a tie, Cutting ties paid better, but the railroad was not always buying them.

Each trip Amos hauled some of the wild hog meat, as by now it was well cured. Cured with salt, and flavored with smoke and seasoning, the meat had a rich flavor. Mr. Blaine bought some to resell through the store, but most of the meat was bought up by folks from the church. As cash money was hard to come by, most of the meat was traded for other foodstuffs which Amos did not have himself, or maybe small tools or handcrafted items. One man traded Amos a new cane bottom chair for a pork shoulder and a slab of bacon. Amos was delighted to received anything of value from the wild hog meat, which—except for the risking of his life— had cost him nothing.

Each day he hunted the timbered bottoms and fished the Little Sandy, keeping fresh meat or fish on his table every day to give variety to the salted hog meat. He couldn't afford to shoot very many squirrels with the new Remington as the shells were expensive, but the shotgun proved to be an asset for ducks. Amos loved to eat ducks, and the down from their breasts was prized for pillows and mattresses.

Whenever he tired of working at the ties or firewood, Amos hauled corn out to the pen by the canebrake. The wild hogs had stayed in the area and had little hesitation at re-entering the pen for the ears of corn which Amos brought them. Amos thought that these hogs could be the start of a large hog operation for him. Here in the cane brake, they bred and raised themselves, foraging for their own feed from the nuts and other vegetation which were usually plentiful. Of course, there would be more losses as there was no regular care for the sows at farrowing time or when one got sick. But then Amos had only to bring them a little feed from time to time to keep them somewhat tame and pen them up a few times a year to cut the young boars and notch an ear on each one. He would be able to catch and kill them throughout the winter, peddling the meat whenever he could find someone with whom he could sell or trade.

Whenever the weather wasn't too bad, Amos and Speckle spent much of the night hunting coon up and down the Little Sandy. This winter wasn't as good for coons as the flood seemed to have dispersed many of them out of the area. He was still able to collect several good hides which he sold on his trips to Willow Point. Besides the sale of the hides, the carcasses brought in a little cash as there were quite a few folks who didn't hunt but liked the taste of roasted coon.

In this manner, Amos occupied himself all through January and into early February. It was a life that he thoroughly enjoyed, except that he still disliked the isolation. Often he thought that he would much prefer someone to share the time with regularly, as well as the chores.

The weather was cold with a drizzling fog the day that a lone rider came out of the wagon track. Speckle's bark alerted Amos who was at the wood pile splitting firewood. At first, he didn't recognize the rider as the fog gave everything an obscure appearance. But as the rider came across toward the cabin, Amos realized that he was Homer Smith. Elated at first, Amos thought that it would be good to have the company of his friend for a few days. But then it came to Amos that this was an odd time of the year for Homer to visit, as it wasn't the best season for hunting or fishing. Amos wondered what else could have brought Homer all this way. Then Amos saw the cast of Homer's face as well as the slump in his shoulders. Homer was known to be somewhat emotional, and whatever was going on inside his head was reflected in his demeanor.

Worried now, Amos waited until his friend came near before calling out in a flat voice, "Wal, Homer, what is it?"

Not speaking, Homer rode close before sliding off his mule. Standing now before Amos, Homer looked sadly at Amos while saying, "It's yore Grandpaw John, Amos, he's ailin' bad. Yore Poppa sent me to fetch ya' home."

Shocked beyond belief that his Grandpa who was the picture of strength could have anything seriously wrong with him, Amos stood rooted in place. Finally, he asked, "Whut's he ailin' with, Homer, he's never been sickly."

With some hesitation, Homer replied haltingly, "it's uh, he's uh, got the numonee."

Now shocked more than before, Amos realized the gravity of the situation. Seldom did anyone ever get over a case of pneumonia. At the time, there was no cure for it. Once it set into a person's lungs, it was mostly only a matter of time before death took them.

With the wind taken from him, Amos dropped his head and turned as tears came to his eyes. Homer stepped alongside and placed a tender hand upon his shoulder while saying, "Sorry, Amos, sorry I had to tell ye'."

An hour later the two young men were driving the wagon into the Potters' to relocate the cow, heifer and the few chickens while Amos was in Hickory Ford. Mr. Potter stepped from the house at the sight of them, having the look of understanding that something was wrong. Pulling up near the barn, Amos stepped down to face the man who had become more than just a neighbor.

Looking now to the older man, Amos struggled with the words, "Its my Grandpaw, Mr. Potter, my friend Homer here says thet he's got t' numonee." Amos paused a moment to regain himself before continuing, "Says he's got it real bad. My Poppa sent fer me. I'd be obliged iffen ya' could look after my stock 'til I git back. There's a plenty of feed in the wagon. I'll jest ride Little Red. Reckon we kin git back quite a bit quicker that way." Finished now, Amos looked bedraggled under his burden of grief.

With a softness, Mr. Potter placed a hand on Amos' shoulder and said, "Shore, Little Man, ya' just stay home as long as ye' think ye' should. I'll take kere of ya' stock."

Amos nodded his head in thanks before turning to unhitch the team. Little Red was then saddled up for the long ride to Hickory Ford. The two young men rode side-by-side out of the Potter place, eyes forward.

As Mr. Potter stood there watching them ride away, his heart was heavy for Amos. He knew how much store Amos set in his Grandpa. Mr. Potter thought highly of John Sawyer as well.

In his opinion, there weren't many men who had worked harder or done better for himself. And not many men would have given such a big responsibility to a boy of fifteen. Apparently, the elder Sawyer had seen himself in young Amos, knowing that he could get along by himself while doing a man's work. Looking up into the low gray sky, Mr. Potter spoke a prayer, "Lord, I know I don't talk to ye' much, but I'd 'appreciate it iffen ya'd look out fer this young feller right about now. This road home's likely to be the hardest one he's ever ridden. Amen" With this closure, Mr. Potter stepped toward his house as Homer and Amos rode out of sight into the gray afternoon.

After they had ridden the first few miles, Amos turned to Homer, asking, "How'd he catch the numonee, Homer, did anyone say?" Up until this point, Amos had responded very mechanically to the bad news, making whatever preparations necessary to allow him to leave the bottoms for several days.

"Yore Poppa sed thet he'd had a bad cold before goin' to cut ties a few days back. The weather warmed up thet day an' yore Grandpa got himself hot, sweatin' an' all from the tie cutting. Then on the way home a cold wind com' up and he took a bad chill. From thet he must've taken the numonee. I think he's been to his bed fer several days now," responded Homer.

Now with a heightened sense of fear, Amos called Little Red into a lope, a gait the mule could maintain for a long distance before letting up. Alternating between a lope and a fast walk, Amos and Homer reached Red Gum Ridge within three hours, far short of the normal four.

Riding into the store yard just after dark, the pair were greeted by several men folk, some neighbors, and some family. Tom, Amos' oldest brother, and Uncle Zeke were among the family members. As Amos and Homer got off their mules, Uncle Zeke came up to Amos.

"Amos, he's gone." Amos' great uncle, Zeke, continued, "I Hate to have' to tell ye', boy, as I know ya' thought the world of 'im. I did too, we'd hunted and fished together fer the last sixty-odd years. But he's with the Lord now, we kin rest easy on that. I know it, an' you should too."

Amos had prepared himself for this, and yet he at this moment felt totally blindsided. His stomach began to cramp, and his knees became rubbery. It helped when Uncle Zeke clasped one of his long arms around Amos' shoulders and walked him to the house. Here Amos found more small crowds of people, clustered about the door. Uncle Zeke spoke a few words which opened a path for them, and they walked on into the house. The house was packed with close friends and family. Amos' momma came and took him from Uncle Zeke, clutching her youngest son to her as she cried and spoke of being glad Homer was able to find Amos and bring him back so quickly. Amos tried to be strong for his mother but wasn't quite sure how. Somehow he held back his own tears. It was harder not to cry when his Poppa came to him. The two had been very close.

It was his Poppa who took Amos into the bedroom where John Sawyer still lay. Amos looked at the body, never having thought that he would see his Grandpa this way. The bed covers were pulled up to his chest, leaving his arms exposed. A penny rested on each eyelid to hold them down until they would stay of their own accord. Amos was shocked at how pale his Grandpa looked, and thinner than he remembered him. His Poppa explained that first a cold and then pneumonia had caused him to lose weight and his normal color.

The two of them stepped forward together, seeking to be close yet needing the support of the other. Standing close now, James reached down to take his own father's hand, showing Amos that it was all right to touch his grandpa. James talked to his father as if the dead body could hear, telling of his love and how much he would miss him. Amos had trouble finding any words at all. It was all too new to him, as he had not been present during any of the illness, arriving only after the death.

After several minutes, James came to a pause in his tears and sorrow. Reaching forward, he touched his hand gently across his father's cheeks, then lifted the two copper cents from the eyes. As the lids stayed down, Amos' poppa did not replace them, but placed one in Amos' hand and the other he clutched in his own. Haltingly, he spoke, "Amos, ya' hang onto that. We'll each have one t' remember him by."

The two returned to the front room, rejoining the mourners there. Here they would stay throughout the night, keeping their practice of "sittin' up with the dead." They would talk, step outside to relieve themselves in the cool night air, drink lots of coffee, even talk of crops and hunts that they remembered, especially those the deceased had joined in. It was their way of sending John Sawyer off and supporting his family.

At first light, those who had stayed the night left for their own homes and morning chores. Many of the men would gather at the graveyard above Hickory Ford in a couple of hours to dig John Sawyer's grave. Some of the women had already come by early last evening to wash and dress the body before it was placed in a coffin. It was just past mid-morning when James pulled out of the store yard on Red Gum Ridge. On the seat beside him sat his mother and in the wagon box behind lay John Sawyer, in a coffin he had made himself some weeks before. Amos rode behind on Little Red. Those two miles seemed like an eternity to Amos as he sat astride the mule and looked ahead to that long box in the wagon.

The Methodist church house was packed as John Sawyer had been well known and respected throughout the entire community. From time to time, Amos broke from his grief to understand something the minister said, but for the most part focused upon his own sorrow. Amos had been to many funerals in his short life, but never before had the deceased meant this much to him. For him, this seemed like the end of the world, for he had no idea of life without his Grandpa John. He hurt all over and through, and his crying turned to sobs which he could not control or stop. Gradually, he felt relief, though embarrassed for his crying.

He thought back to the time he'd been in the bottoms and knew that he owed it all to a grandpa who believed in him and would entrust the building of a farm to a boy. But somehow Amos knew that he had not been any ordinary boy, but a Sawyer, one of a family who worked hard, carefully chose their decisions and above all, valued God and family.

Later at the graveyard, Amos walked with the family to encircle the coffin resting over the deep hole. That hole seemed like it would swallow up Amos and the rest of his life. But it was during the preacher's last talk there at the graveside that Amos had a change of mood. Somehow it made sense to him beyond his grief that Uncle Zeke had been right. Here in the coffin was only Grandpa John's body. His spirit had gone on to be with God Himself. It came to Amos that God was mighty lucky to have John to help Him out up there in heaven. As the preacher called everyone to bow their heads for that last prayer before the body was lowered into the grave, Amos looked skyward. It surprised him that the gray had been burned away by the heat of the sun and the bright blue sky showed all above. Amos spoke his own prayer, silently saying, "Thank ye' Lord, fer givin' 'im to me fer this time. Now I'm willin' to give 'im to Ya'. One day, I'll be along to join Grandpaw. Ya keep 'im safe til' then. I ask ya', Lord, to guide me like ya did him ." With these words, the preacher finished his own prayer, and the family embraced one another tightly through their last tears before turning to thank their friends and neighbors for their support.

This time at the graveyard lasted longer than usual as it took some time for the family to interact with the large funeral crowd. No one seemed to be in any hurry while they waited for their opportunity to offer sympathy and support. Some passed the time by visiting the graves of their own family, taking this opportunity to tell their young about their departed family. As the time at the graveyard came to a close, several close friends and family members were invited back to the Sawyer house on Red Gum Ridge to share a meal. So much food had been brought in by the neighbors that Janey could never eat it all before it spoiled. Besides, she still needed support to get through this day.

It took several days after the funeral for Janey to establish any sense of normalcy for her life alone. The routine of the farm and the store helped her, as did the continued visits from close family and friends. James spent a great deal of time with his mother and Amos spent almost all of his time there, sleeping on the bed in the front room so she wouldn't be alone. Amos did most of the chores and even minded the store on a few occasions, something that he knew little about. With this support, Janey set up a routine which would allow her to get on with her life.

Decisions had to be made about those things which Grandpa John had always done, yet were beyond her means. The heavier farm work was something she could not do, and even the lighter chores like the milking and tending to the chickens could be too much for her in energy and time as the store had always taken most of her time beyond the house work. With James' help, the land was rented out to Henry Russell, a young man with a family but not enough farmland of his own to feed them. Homer Smith's uncle Dave was hired to tend to the milk cows, hogs, and chickens. He and his wife lived on a small place about a half mile distant from the store. They were on up in years now and couldn't manage the heavier work of plowing and gathering. The cash money received from the chores would help them get by.

Janey's characteristically resilient spirit began to reappear with these decisions. Her comment to James and Amos was "See here, just look at how the good Lord has worked somethin' good out of my John's passin'. Here's two families who's being helped along now. You two always remember, the Lord don't forget his own, no sir'ee, he don't. Always trust the Lord, no matter what comes yore way. He'll take care of me and others too."

It was an early May morning that Amos sat the wagon seat on his return to the Little Sandy. Over the past three months, he had made the round trip from the Little Sandy to Red Gum Ridge more times than he could count. He told others that he needed to check on his grandma and help her with the heavier chores, but had recently come to realize that he had gone more for his own needs. Strong feelings drew him back to the home on the ridge, as there Amos could once again sense his Grandpa Sawyer's spirit.

And with each trip, Amos had brought some item of his Grandpa's back to the clearing on the Little Sandy. As Henry

Russell had his own farming equipment, the implements and mules were divided among the family men who were still farming: James, Tom, and Amos. James took the team as he held special feelings for Grey Jack, just as his father had during the many years he had worked him. Amos was given the disk, and Tom got the corn planter. The smaller tools were divided among the three of them.

Amos felt wonderful about getting any of Grandpa John's things but was struck speechless when Janey had handed him the deed to the place on the Little Sandy. When his voice returned, he protested, "Grandmaw, this is too much fer ya to give me."

"Now, Amos," she replied, "I've thought it out. Yore Grandpa thought a great deal of you. He was right proud of how ya had worked up that place on the Little Sandy, not to mention how he went on about ya comin' through that awful flood. An' then he had gone on and on 'bout thet time ya' had with them wild hogs. I've got more'n enough right here on this here place to take care of me, with the rent from the land and what I git from the store. 'Sides, I'm not ever gonna want to go off down to the Little Sandy to look after that land. Thet was somethin' John cared for. So I'm a giving it to ya' for yore very own. It'll be a good start fer ya', an' I reckon you've earned it."

Amos found himself hugging his Grandma to say with his embrace what he could not with words. As he had driven his team away from her place early that morning, they were both tearful. Each represented to the other a link to the past and to John Sawyer, someone that neither wanted to lose. Amos saw in his Grandma memories of a Grandpa who had been bigger than life. And Janey Sawyer saw in Amos a young John Sawyer setting out upon his life. On this trip home, Amos turned upriver at the Fourche River to see something that had become the talk of the whole country. The government had begun a dredging operation to open up the smaller rivers and streams which drained the bottoms ever so slowly. These cut ditches were to allow the bottoms to drain more quickly, making them profitable for farming.

About a mile above the crossing of the Fourche, Amos came to the dredge boat as it was called. As all the sounds frightened his team, Amos tied them up some distance away and walked through the overflow water to get a good view of this remarkable sight.

Setting in an open channel of water was a large flat-bottomed barge, equipped with a steam powered dredge which opened up the channel on the downriver side. The barge floated in the channel freshly opened up by the dredge's bucket. Directly behind the dredge, a house of sorts had been built on the rear of the barge to accommodate eating and sleeping quarters for the men who kept the dredge operational.

Amos climbed upon a tall stump to stare at the scene played out before him. Several crews sawed down the timber in the path of the dredge, using teams of mules to drag away the trees. The remaining stumps would be dug up by the dredge's powerful bucket. The dredge operator steadily worked the bucket to lift both stumps and soil from the river bottom, depositing both to either side of the channel. In this fashion, a straight channel was cut through the river bottom, with a bank of earth piled on both sides. At intervals, a hole would be left in the two banks, allowing water to flow into the channel. Other crews were cutting up dry trees for the steady supply of firewood required by the steam engine which powered the dredge. In this fashion the dredging barge worked its way downstream, floating in the water which poured into the newly cut channel.

For more than two hours, Amos watched. He had never seen such a thing. At noon, the dredge operator stopped his bucket and released a valve which sent a blast of compressed air through a whistle, signaling the crew's dinner break. Amos was invited to dinner with them, but declined, saying that he had a long ride yet before he got back home.

On the ride home, he thought mostly of the dredge and how it could impact the bottoms. Land that was under water so much of the year that it was worthless for farming now would be cleared for corn and cotton. But even with the dredging, Amos didn't think many people would ever live down in these bottoms. Most folks preferred to farm the higher ground in and near the hills. Settlements like Willow Point were unusual.

In that last hour's ride between the Potter place and his own, Amos' thoughts traveled back to Lilly Brown, a young lady he had met at his Grandma Janey's store. She had been buying some groceries for her family who lived on the north end of Red Gum Ridge. Amos had been struck by her manner. She had seemed very sympathetic to Grandpa John's death, yet not all mushy as some girls got over such things. And her eyes could not be forgotten. They were soft brown eyes, bright with their own light. Amos remembered that he had almost said to her that her eyes reminded him of a Jersey heifer, but thought that might hurt her feelings. Amos would have meant it as a compliment for he thought that the eyes of a Jersey heifer were beautiful.

On several occasions Amos found himself spending more time in the store than he had ever before found comfortable, hoping this girl might come again. And she had come back, so often and for such small items that Amos wondered as to her judgment in coming to the store so often. Unlike most other girls,

Lilly's company felt comfortable to Amos. It was a strange feeling, but a good one. He could talk to her easily, though he had little to talk about except mules, coon hunting, and farming. To Amos' surprise, these things seemed to interest Lilly.

It was with some resignation that Amos drove the team across White Creek. This had been the last of his frequent trips to Red Gum Ridge as now was the time to plow and plant. He knew that he would miss his little visits with Lilly and wondered if she would think of him in the coming weeks.

In the early morning light the following day, Amos drove his team of mules ahead of the plow to the edge of the corn field. Here he stopped as had become his way. He stood there taking in the scene around him. Ducks could be heard thrashing around out on the river, and two squirrels again played out on the shagbark hickory. Birds sang a variety of songs out in the timber. Out before him lay his clearing of made dirt, now enlarged from the original seven acres to over fifteen. Lush vegetation grew from the rich soil, proving the potential of another good crop.

A flood of thoughts raced through his head in these short moments. Memories of John and himself first driving into this clearing. The many days of back-breaking work and sweat required to clean up the clearing. The good hunting and fishing he had enjoyed. The struggles: first with the great flood, with the wild hogs, of the isolation here by himself. Then of John's death and how that had changed his life. He thought of Janey's words: how God would take what happened in our lives and bring something good out of it.

Lastly, he thought of Lilly Brown. His Grandma seemed to like her, said she was a girl that she enjoyed visiting with in the store. "Lilly Brown," Amos spoke the name out loud. Focusing back upon the field before him, Amos knew that it would take him a good three weeks before the seed was in the ground. After that, he would drive back to Red Gum Ridge. Maybe Lilly Brown had thought of him as he had thought of her.

ᔆ ᔆ ᔆᔆ ᔆ ᔆ ᔆ

Born in 1948, the youngest of four brothers, Norris Norman was raised on a farm in Northeast Arkansas where his ancestors had resided since 1824. After serving in the United States Marine Corps, he attended Arkansas State University, and the School of Science & Arts of Oklahoma University, earning a BA Political Science and History and a Masters Degree in Theology. After careers as a pastor in Washington state and teacher in Tennessee, he returned to his native NE Arkansas to write its history.